EMPRESS OF NEW BEGINNINGS

The Guardians of Light Saga
Book 3

by Mia Herald Hill

A Mightier Than the Sword UK Publication

©2023

Empress of New Beginnings
The Guardians of Light Saga

By Mia Herald Hill

A Mightier Than the Sword Publication

Paperback Edition

ISBN Paperback 978-1-7386037-7-0
ISBN Hardback 978-1-7386037-8-7
ISBN Kindle 978-1-7386037-6-3

Copyright ©Mia Herald Hill 2023

For
Nugget and Fizzle

and their continual efforts to prevent me from writing with their cuteness.

AUTHOR'S NOTE

What follows is the account of the fall of Her Royal Highness, Queen Kasnata, Anaguran & Queterian Queen and Queen of the united peoples of Celadmore. The language of the Order is highlighted by the use of a different font in the paperback copies and in bold in the electronic format. The other languages of Celadmore are also displayed in different fonts in the paperback and digital copies, but because of e-reader formatting, it may not display properly.

THE CHARACTERS

Queen Kasnata — *Queen of the Order & Nosfa kingdom. Wife of Mercia*

King Mercia Nosfa VI — *King of Nosfa kingdom. Husband of Kasnata*

General Lord Rathe Bird — *General of Nosfa*

Phoenix General Marissa — *General of Kasnata's Phoenix division*

Kestrel General Amalia — *General of Kasnata's Kestrel division*

Hawk General Kia — *General of Kasnata's Hawk division*

Eagle General Kia — *General of Kasnata's Eagle division, Daughter of Kasnata and Nosfa, Princess of the Order.*

Condor General Samara — *General of Kasnata's Condor division*

Vulture General Quisla — *General of Kasnata's Vulture division*

Raven General Misna — *General of Kasnata's Infiltration division*

General Avner — *General of Kasnata's Order of the Hound*

General Shamgar — *General of Kasnata's Order of the Bear*

General Yoav — *General of Kasnata's Order of the Wolf*

Abendigo — *Yoav's second-in-command*

Duke Kelmar DeLacey — *Regent of Delma, a nobleman*

Joab — *Shadow of Hermia. A bodyguard*

Layla — *Shadow of Hermia. A bodyguard*

Cassandra — *Warrior, mercenary, pirate and spy. Guardian of the Wilds*

The Abbott — *Warrior, mercenary, priest and spy. Guardian of the Spire*

Hermia Nosfa — *Former Queen of Nosfa*

Tola — *Hero of the war of the east, Rathe's second in*

	command
Lord Haston Bird	*Lord of Mercia Nosfa's court*
Shaul	*A Queterian, also known as Tam*
Methanlan	*A Queterian, also known as Sidney*
Rosla Nosfa	*Former King of Nosfa*
Lady Marcia Bird	*A lady, deceased*
Lady Mia Bird	*Forced consort to King Mercia Nosfa*
Jephthah	*Shield of Hermia. A bodyguard*
Haman	*Leader of the Gibborim*
Mathias	*Assassin*
Neesa	*Assassin, Bodyguard of Mercia. A Valian*
Helez	*Exile from the Gibborim*
Asahel	*Exile from the Gibborim*
Leinad	*Prince of Nosfa & the Order*
Kasna	*Princess of Nosfa & the Order*
Payne	*Healer of the Order*
Scattergood	*Leader of the Eight*
Merinda	*One of the Eight*
Lucinda	*One of the Eight*
Warner	*One of the Eight*
Resha	*One of the Eight*
Colm	*One of the Eight*
Vaike	*One of the Eight*
Adino	*One of the Eight*
Jericho	*Brother of Scattergood, presumed dead.*
The Baron of Fintry	*Mercia's steward and dogsbody*

Jack	*A soldier of Nosfa*
Harry	*A soldier of Nosfa*
King Baruch Delich	*King of Delma*
Queen Adina Delich	*Queen of Delma*
Horsemistress Cara	*Horse mistress of the Order*
Swordmistress Anna	*Sword mistress of the Order*
Bowmistress Serra	*Bow mistress of the Order*
Horsemaster Horace	*Horse master of the Order*
Swordmaster Oswin	*Sword master of the Order*
Bowmaster Wist	*Bow master of the Order*
Benaiah	*Master of the Forge*
Deshanna	*Daughter of Rathe & Kasnata*
Gildow	*Son of Rathe & Kasnata*
Lieutenant Thomas Regus	*Lieutenant in Mercia's Guard*
Madame Ella	*Madam of a Brothel*

PROLOGUE

There are many gods and goddesses to be found on the plains of Celadmore, for the worship of nature and life takes many forms. Yet, so does the worship of death and destruction.

The Order and many others across the realm of Celadmore worship the Goddess Arala, for they believe that She is the one true deity. However, there is one that stands in opposition to the Goddess Arala - those that worship the Seven Stars.

The religion was once thought to be dead, relegated to nothing more than an exclamation of surprise with no power in the realm of light. But the faithful endured. A small sect worshipped the Seven Stars, the light of waning stars growing brighter as more fell to the darkness of the seducer, Hyse.

The dead Goddess Hyse, enemy of the light and named seducer by all those of wisdom, will destroy all life save for those that worship her if she is ever resurrected. Her words poison the minds of men and twist sanity to madness.

Hyse once ruled over all the realms, but was cast down by Arala, slain and defeated, but not vanquished. To resurrect her, those of the Seven Stars need the blood of Arala to be shed on an altar where power is held above all things.

No ruler ever did more for our people, Queen Kasnata fought for her people like no other. She brought balance in an impossible time, using her wits as well as her sword. There will never be another like her amongst our lineage, and our people will diminish for it. Her legacy is greater than that of a tragic demise or those of her children that have survived; she gave our people an empire that reaches across the whole of Celadmore. She gave us back our mantle to protect and watch over the people, not be chained dogs of war, kept away from the mainland, only to be unleashed when our own existence is threatened.

Benaiah
Master of the Forge

CHAPTER 1

2432GL 95th Sagma/Sumar

"The battlefield; a place where heroes are made, legends thrive, myths enthral and lives are broken."

A sword plunged into the frozen ground. The white powder of snow mixed with the mud of the battlefield and freshly split blood splattering against the blade as it pierced the permafrost. Dark eyes scanned the remnants of the camp that had been attacked and crippled by the enemy.

All things were clear to Kasnata, only daughter of Tsmara and Jadow, Queen of fire and destruction, bringer of death, dark angel, scourge of the wicked, wife of King Mercia Nosfa VI and Sovereign of the people of the Order. The siege of Delma had gone on long enough and the pride of her husband had caused the deaths of many.

Kasnata stood and watched as the men of Nosfa attempted to bury their fallen comrades, hacking at the frozen ground with whatever they could find. The warriors of the Order helped to salvage what they could from the camp.

Princess Kia, youngest child of the king and queen of Nosfa, worked tirelessly, comforting those that had lost and directing the warriors to collect good wood from around the camp. Shaul was beside her, every move she made, the Queterian spy was by the princess' side.

"He's a true asset, your highness," General Kia said as she approached Kasnata. The princess was named after the general and facing the retaliation of Delma against the camp of Nosfa had been the first time that they had ridden

into battle together.

The attack on the camp had been led by the Duke Kelmar DeLacey, the Regent of Delma. He had once been a friend and ally to the Order, but the war of the nine kingdoms had changed old alliances; broken ancient treaties.

Kelmar had attacked the fortress that Kasnata's daughters were being held in by their father, chased the two girls across Celadmore, murdered General Renta of Kasnata's army when she tried to stop the duke, taken Kasnata's eldest daughter hostage, and finally, led the assault against the camp of the army of Nosfa to allow a small unit to break the dam that was blocking the river that supplied water to the city of Delma.

War was a bloody business, especially when civilians were caught between armies and the stubborn pride of their leaders. Kasna was a prisoner, but she was still alive, and though Kelmar had every opportunity to kill Princess Kia, he had merely talked to her before riding away from the front lines.

There was something amiss in Delma, and the actions of the duke only served to muddy the waters further.

Shaul had fought at the side of the princess in the battle and ensured that she survived.

"He always has been," Kasnata replied. "Kia is gathering wood; does she plan to build a funeral pyre?"

"There is no way to dig down far enough with this accursed Wentrus. She is speaking to each of the men individually for her consent. Shaul has taken it upon himself to act as her bodyguard," the general replied.

"So I see," Kasnata smiled to herself.

"How are the wounded?" the Hawk General didn't sound hopeful.

"Most will die. Payne is doing what he can with the other healers aiding

him. The man who helped with General Seaton, Harry, he didn't make it," Kasnata's voice was laced with regret.

"His injuries were too severe. I am surprised he lived long enough for Methanlan to take him to Payne," Kia sighed.

"There are many who didn't," Kasnata shook her head, her attention returning to the salvaging of the camp.

"Delma will send an envoy soon to ask permission to recover their dead. It might be wiser if the men of Nosfa were not here when they arrived," the general advised.

"No, they won't be sending an envoy," Kasnata said narrowing her eyes.

"Do we leave their bodies for the crows?" Kia asked.

"No, have them loaded onto the broken carts in the camp. There is no moon tomorrow night, we'll wheel the bodies to the walls in the darkness and leave them at the gates," the queen said firmly.

"No moon? It will be a relief to be out from under its evil influence. Do you think there will be a thaw?" Kia remarked clapping her hands together to restore the circulation that the cold was restricting.

"Perhaps, but it will only last for a day or so at the most. Without destroying the power behind the blood moon, we have no way of returning the moon to normal or ending this forsaken Wentrus," Kasnata clicked her tongue against her teeth with frustration.

The two women watched the activity in the ruined camp in silence.

"Did Avner go to the gate today?" the queen asked.

"He did. He received no answer," the general replied.

"Very well. When Kia has built the pyre, have the dead brought to it from the infirmary. I must speak with Benaiah about rebuilding this mess and some better fortifications to help protect against further raids," Kasnata sighed to herself. General Kia saluted as the queen walked back to the camp to speak to the forge master.

Methanlan was sat with Jack. The man hadn't spoken to him in nearly four hours, but it didn't matter to Methanlan, he wasn't going to leave the grieving man on his own.

They were sat in the healing tent beside the lifeless body of Harry. He'd been killed when Kelmar's forces had attacked the camp of Nosfa.

Harry and Jack had survived the war of the east, they had fought beside one another against the Naladi people and Jack had always imagined that the two of the would live to see old age together; perhaps go into farming together and watch their grandchildren grow up safe and happy.

But that wasn't to be. One of the spears that the warriors of the Order had thrown at the enemy had been returned, piercing Harry in the chest. Methanlan had bought Harry to the healer, but there was nothing that could be done. Methanlan gave his own blood to extend Harry's life, but it had not been enough. Not even the skills of the Order's healer, Payne, could save Harry.

The misery that Jack was feeling was made all the worse by the betrayal he felt that Methanlan and Shaul had perpetrated against him. The two Queterians had infiltrated the camp of Nosfa to spy for the queen. Jack had known Methanlan from wars past and never imagined that he was a spy.

They had fought beside one another in two conflicts; Jack had even fought against his own countrymen to defend Methanlan. Jack had believed that Methanlan was a man from Nosfa, from one of the outlying farms, pressed into the service of the king.

He had never suspected Methanlan of being anything other than a sorry soul force to war and a friend. Discovering that he was of the Order and had been spying on the army of Nosfa for years hurt Jack deeply. Shaul was less of a betrayal; Jack had only met him when the queen had first arrived in the joint camps. But Jack had liked him, liked his sense of adventure and the contrast he provided to Methanlan.

Every time that he thought about Shaul and Methanlan, Jack felt anger boiling inside his veins and wanted to be as far away as possible from both of them.

Yet, Methanlan was the only one that was there, and though the idea of staying friends with the Queterian made him sick to his stomach, he didn't want to be alone.

Jack couldn't trust the man, wouldn't share confidences or secrets with him again, but Methanlan had tried to save Harry and Harry had still liked the Queterians, even after their betrayal had been revealed.

"When we've buried Harry, that's it," Jack mumbled.

"That's it?" Methanlan asked.

"Our acquaintance is over. You won't talk to me again and I won't see you. I've had enough of being lied to, of fighting in wars for kings that don't care about the lives of their men," Jack said stoutly.

"You're leaving the camp?" Methanlan frowned.

"We're just lost a lot of men fighting in that skirmish. Who's to say I didn't die on the battlefield?" Jack shrugged.

"Where will you go?" Methanlan asked.

"Somewhere to the north. Somewhere there isn't fighting. I'll send for my family and Harry's when I'm settled," Jack said in a resolute voice.

"If that's what you want," Methanlan said, standing up and glancing about the room. "Go to Benadrocca. Tell Epoch I sent you. He'll send his daughters to get your family and Harry's; they'll bring them safely to you. Less risk of Nosfa discovering you're alive and deserted. Less likely you'll finish up on the wrong end of a rope." Methanlan sighed and shook his head. "I'll go see what is happening to the bodies. Sooner we get Harry buried, the sooner you can go. The longer you delay, the more likely you'll be caught. You should depart before dark."

Duke Kelmar DeLacey lay awake in his quarters. Kasna was sleeping soundly beside him. The princess was a puzzle to the duke. When she had first offered herself to him, she had claimed she had been abused and Kelmar had dismissed it as impossible, but the princess' attitude had caused him to question whether or not she'd been telling the truth.

The idea of anyone hurting Kasna in that way made him feel sick to his stomach. He wasn't a squeamish man by nature. He had fought in battles since he was a boy; he was raised to lead the armies of Delma against its enemies and had tortured more than his fair share of prisoners. But he was a man of honour, and the abuse of children and civilians was something that left a bitter taste in his mouth.

One thing Kelmar knew, he didn't want to know the truth. Whatever had happened in Kasna's past was best left there. He watched as the princess stirred slightly in her sleep and rolled over. He smiled in spite of his thoughts.

Out in the corridor he could hear armoured soldiers marching, the clanging of the metal could be heard at every hour of the day and night. He'd become so used to hearing the sound that the rhythm of the sound was almost soothing.

Kelmar sighed and slipped quietly out of his bed. The stone floor was cold on his feet as he crept towards the windows. As the Regent of Delma, Kelmar had rooms in the palace and lands outside of the capital city. His rooms in the palace took up the tower to the east that rose high above the battlements. From the window in his bed chamber, Kelmar could see for miles, though the only thing he wanted to look at was the army encampment that the Order and the men of Nosfa had erected and used to blockade his city.

He could see how quickly the warriors and soldiers had cleared the debris from his attack. The bodies had been removed and a watch had been set around the edge of the camp. The water into the city had been blocked again, but enough had been collected and stored to last for a few months, and it had been enough to give the people of Delma some hope.

Kelmar had ordered the water that they had collected should be rationed and appointed Colonel Deena Mae to oversee the distribution of the valuable resource. She not only would make sure that the water was given out to the people fairly, but would monitor the levels and keep Kelmar informed. There were very few people that he knew he could trust, but Deena was one of them.

The other was an old wise woman in the city that was known only as the Mother of Dawn. There were rumours that the old woman was one of the founders of the city, that she was known as the Mother of Dawn because she had *been there since the dawn of time and some even believed that she had existed before time began.*

Kelmar didn't care for rumour, but the Mother of Dawn was a woman that had provided him with sage counsel since he was a small boy. He hadn't seen her since he had returned to the city; there had been military and civil concerns that had to be dealt with. He wanted Kasna to meet the Mother of Dawn and to see if she knew anything about why the king wanted her brought to the city, but he would have to bring the old woman to the palace to do that. It didn't seem a wise idea to bring the Mother of Dawn to the palace to question her about what she knew about the king, if anyone were to overhear what was said he was sure that it would be considered treason.

"You can't sleep?" Kasna asked as she stifled a yawn. Kelmar looked away from the window and smiled at the young woman as she pulled the blankets around her body and sauntered across the room towards him.

"There is a lot on my mind," Kelmar replied as he wrapped his arms around the princess.

"How is it looking?" Kansa said leaning her head against his chest.

"Your people work quickly," Kelmar smiled. "I didn't expect them to have cleared the devastation so quickly. When the water we have is gone, I don't know what we'll do. Your mother will be prepared for us trying to remove the dam. Unless we can find some other way of providing the city with water, people will start to die of dehydration." the duke shook his head.

"Will the king not surrender?" Kasna frowned.

"No. Whatever reason he has for me bringing you here, it isn't what I thought it was," Kelmar said thoughtfully.

"If it was, he would have had you march to mother's camp and tell her

what you want in exchange for my safety," Kasna looked up at Kelmar. The duke's face had a troubled expression fixed on his features.

"It would have been the logical thing to do. It worries me, especially after what happened with the Abbott at the Spire," Kelmar said as he took Kasna's hands and led her back to their bed. "There is nothing we can do about either of those things now, and even if I can't sleep, you should be getting your rest."

Asahel sat looking out over the city. The bell tower gave him an excellent vantage point to monitor the city of Grashindorph from. The normal morning patrols were passing by in the streets below, none of them thinking to look up to see the exile from the Gibborim sat on the ledge that ran around the top of the bell tower. Asahel had spent weeks watching the city, taking note of the numbers of soldiers, the patrols, the people who reported to the soldiers and the habits of the nobles.

In an ideal world he or Helez would have infiltrated the guard and gained intimate knowledge of their orders and personalities as well as their patrolling patterns. But this was not an ideal world. Paranoia was rife throughout the city and new additions to the guard were only being made from within the families of the existing guards. The people of Grashindorph were also reporting anything they found that seemed suspicious, so stealing some guard uniforms and exploring the city was also not an option.

Asahel had to content himself with watching from above. Helez had gone out to the market to see whether he could learn anything from the gossip between merchants. It was easy to merge with the large chaotic crowds of the markets, but as fear had increased in the city, the number of people in the market had fallen and some of the merchants had been dragged away by the guard for questioning or worse.

It was far from a prosperous or peaceful time in the city. In the belly of the bell tower, Mathias was sleeping. The assassin from Roenca had been asleep for several days and barely spoken two words since he had been rescued. His journey across the plains of Celadmore had not been easy, which had been compounded by the capture of the Lady Mia Bird and the death of Joab. Mathias and Joab had been escorting Mia to Grashindorph, she had come to save her brother from the king, but the king had been ready for them. Joab had been killed, Mia taken, and Mathias rescued by Helez, Asahel, and the General Rathe Bird. Asahel was sure that it was depression more than injury that had sunk Mathias into his current state, but as the assassin was unwilling to talk, there was nothing that he could do to help.

Rathe was still recovering from his time as a prisoner at the hands of the king. He had been held in an outdoor cell in this perpetual winter that had been unleashed on Celadmore without enough food or water to sustain him. He had injuries that had been inflicted on him by the king's men, had yet to fully heal. He was healing faster than either Asahel or Helez had expected, the training and conditioning he had been put through whilst serving in Kasnata's army had meant that the torture and lack of food had not had such a debilitating effect on his body.

The young general was a general no longer, but the lordling's military training meant that the two men of the Gibborim and Mathias still used his title. He had spent the first three days after Helez and Asahel had rescued him resting. But he had soon become restless and taken up a simple training routine.

The sound of Rathe training was a sound that Asahel was quickly becoming accustomed to. It made him think of life before he and Helez had been exiled, when they had lived underground as part of the Gibborim. The sound of training was not commonplace among the people of the Gibborim, but for as long as he could remember; Asahel had been trained every day. He had been forced to take part in sword drills, forced to learn to fight without weapons and learn how to defend himself and those that he was to protect. He had been trained by Jephthah, the Man Mountain and shield of the Lady Hermia.

Jephthah was like a father to the dark-skinned warrior. Asahel had been born into the Gibborim, his parents were outcast from Nosfa as they had openly opposed Mercia's ascension to the throne, and he had been raised for a single purpose – to serve as a shield when Jephthah was killed or removed from his position. Helez had been trained for the same thing, but now the two men were no longer welcome among the members of the Gibborim.

They had been exiled for murdering Bracha. Bracha was Jephthah's wife and a traitor to the Gibborim, she had been responsible for sending Helez's sister, Ilana, to the surface. Ilana had been arrested by Mercia's soldiers and executed. Asahel and Helez had been in the crowd at her execution. When Bracha had been sentenced by the Gibborim, Helez had been expecting her to be executed. When she wasn't, Helez and Asahel had taken the matter into their own hands.

Neither of the men regretted what they had done, but Asahel missed his parents and the attention of the women in the Gibborim.

"The general is training again?" Helez asked as he climbed out onto the ledge and sat beside Asahel.

"He is. I'm not sure how Mathias is managing to sleep through it. What did you find out in the marketplace?" Asahel replied.

"Another three merchants were taken last night. People are terrified, no one stops to talk in the street and even the taverns are quiet," Helez sighed and looked down at the patrol that was passing beneath their feet. "I always have to resist the urge to spit on them when they do that."

"If we don't do something soon, there won't be any people left in the city," Asahel shook his head and moved off the ledge. Helez followed his friend down the ladder to where Rathe was training.

"There is one thing I did find out though," Helez said, sitting on one of the many barrels that were stored in the tower.

"Oh?" Asahel asked.

"The king is due to make a proclamation to his people. I think it'll have something to do with Mia," Helez yawned. Rathe faltered mid-stroke at the mention of his sister's name.

"If he is making a proclamation, then we should all be there," Rathe insisted as he lay down his sword.

"No, you and Mathias are both wanted criminals - traitors to the crown," Asahel said flatly.

"You are both wanted and traitors to the crown," Rathe replied.

"Yes, but no one knows what we look like. There are notices with your faces drawn on them all over the city. Until we are ready to move against the king, you two aren't leaving this tower," Helez countered. "I'll go to the proclamation. There is no point in us both being there. People have seen me around the city in the last few days. As far as anyone knows, I have come from one of the outlying farms to the city for a few weeks to avoid being married off.

Seeing me at a proclamation won't arouse too much suspicion."

"You do realise that when most people talk about running away because they don't want to be married off, they are women," Asahel gave his friend a withering look.

"No reason a man wouldn't do the same thing. Yes, there are a lot of toads out there that no woman would want to have to sleep beside for the rest of her life, but there are also plenty of women out there that I wouldn't marry, even if my life depended on it," Helez retorted with a slight tone of indignance.

"I'm sure that the queen would agree with you," Rathe grunted.

"When Mathias wakes up, we'll tell him what is going on, and if you've finished training for the morning, it's your turn to make lunch, general," Asahel said with a boyish grin.

Chapter 2

The night was silent and still as three horses approached the camp of Kasnata.

"Halt, who passes this way?" The challenge was issued from the dark.

"Lavinia, Lacenta and Muse. We are here to see the queen," the reply was given.

"Are you expected?" a member of the nightwatch stepped into the weak ring of light that was cast by the torches that the riders held.

"No. If you wish us to wait whilst you send a messenger to the queen, we will stay on this side of your picket lines," the woman at the head of three spoke calmly with an edge of condescension to her voice.

"Very well," the warrior signalled for another member of the nightwatch to join him. The two spoke in hushed tones for a moment before the newcomer disappeared off into the dark. "If you will stay where you are until the messenger returns." the man said curtly and moved back to his post.

The three guardians had been riding for days to reach Kasnata's camp, but as they had not been invited and were not known to the men and women of the Order, they would only be allowed to enter the camp if Kasnata gave them permission.

Though they couldn't see the man of the nightwatch any longer, the three women could feel themselves being watched. Lavinia sighed to herself and slipped out of her saddle so that she could make her horse more comfortable whilst they waited.

She knew that the warrior that spoke to them was not the only one that would be watching them from the dark and there was little point in trying to slip past them.

There was nothing to do but wait.

Lieutenant Thomas Regus was a man that enjoyed his duty. In the service of the king, he was able to indulge his most base desires without fear of reprisals from senior officers. He was well-known amongst the men of the king's guard as a perverted cad, one that they would never leave alone in the company of their wives and daughters.

His particular appetites were something that the king used not only against his enemies but also as a way of keeping those closest to him close to heel. There wasn't a man amidst his personal bodyguard that would dream of disloyalty for fear of Regus being unleashed upon their families.

One man had spoken up against the king's plans to cancel a festival in the city. This man was unmarried, but his mother and sister paid for his insolence. His father had tried to stop Regus, only to end up on the execution block.

His sister had committed suicide and his mother had lost her mind after they had been exposed to Regus' depravity.

King Mercia Nosfa VI had ordered Regus to show the Lady Mia Bird a taste of what would await her if she chose to defy the king. Mercia had threatened Mia, but he knew there was a great difference between imagining what fate awaited her and experiencing the horror of it first-hand.

No matter what Mia had thought it would be like to be turned over to Mercia's men, the punishment that Regus inflicted upon her was far worse than she could have possibly imagined.

For three days, Regus was locked in her cell. He would torture her for two hours at a time, satisfying his baser nature, and then sit staring at Mia, for half an hour whilst he dreamed up new ways of enjoying himself at her expense.

Her screams were ignored by the guards and her pleas for mercy fell on deaf ears. On the third day, she didn't scream or beg; she knew there was no point. No help was coming to her. Kasnata couldn't save her, Joab and her father were both dead, Mathias and Rathe were prisoners, her brother sentenced to death for treason and Mia was sure that Mathias would be sentenced to death, just as Rathe had.

"I hope you turn the king down," Regus said as he gripped Mia by the chin. His face was inches from hers, but Mia couldn't bring herself to raise her eyes from the floor to look at him. "Having a woman that is so pliable is a pleasure that I am not quite ready to do without."

Mia shuddered and the door the cell opened.

"You are done here, Lieutenant," Mercia boomed as he stepped into the room. The king was in his early forties and had a thick beard growing in that was flecked with grey.

His eyes were a watery blue that constantly seemed to be staring off into the distance. Once, they had been a crisp blue, but age and pressures of being at war for so long had dulled their colour. He was an imposing figure in any room, his broad shoulders and chest still well-muscled coupled with his height gave him a royal bearing that was equalled by his wife.

The lieutenant released Mia's face and stepped back from her. He bowed low to the king,

"As you say, sire."

"You were careful not to leave any lasting damage?" the king asked as he stepped past Regus to inspect Mia's body. She was completely naked; her clothes had been reduced to rags that now littered the floor of the cell.

"I was, your majesty, the bruising on her arms will be gone by the morning, her torso and legs may take longer, but they can be easily hidden," Regus replied.

"Indeed, there are a few marks on her neck, but her hair can be placed over them," the king observed as he ran his hands over her body. Each movement of his hands caused Mia to tremble with fear.

"Her face isn't blemished though," the lieutenant assured the king.

"No, it is seemingly perfect. So, my lady, a choice lies before you. Are you to be my wife and queen of Nosfa or are you to spend what remains of your pitiful existence at the mercy of men like the lieutenant?" the king whispered in Mia's ear.

"I will do what the king commands," Mia replied in a defeated voice.

"Is there anything more you need from me, sire?" Regus asked. He was beginning to feel uncomfortable in the presence of the king, watching him caress the naked woman was causing his pulse to race.

"Not for the moment. I will send for you later," the king replied, his eyes were fixed on Mia's face and he didn't bother to look over at Regus as he slipped from the cell.

The lieutenant walked past the guards without acknowledging them, he wasn't a popular man amongst his peers, but he didn't care. He walked silently up the dungeon stairs that led to the barracks courtyard, across the courtyard and out into the city.

Three days of indulgence had not diminished his desires, breaking the *spirit of one so delicate and desirable as the Lady Mia had awakened his imagination. He had fantasies that he wanted to play out that included Mia, but with her acceptance of the king's proposal, she was out of reach, for now.*

However, there were plenty of brothels in the city, exclusive and expensive whore houses that allowed their patrons to do whatever they wanted to the inhabitants, as long as they paid enough. There were those who went to these brothels to enjoy a wide range of sexual pleasures, some even specialised in bacchanals, which Regus often enjoyed after he had been sent out on the king's business.

He walked through the streets of the city, not paying any attention to those that he passed by, he was lost in the memories of the last three days.

He turned down a narrow street and ducked into a conservative looking building. Inside there was a large man, he pulled aside a curtain and allowed Regus to pass. Behind the curtain were several staircases that led to different floors. A lecture was set in the middle of the landing for these staircases, upon which sat a series of twenty-seven different bells.

The bells were rung by patrons to summon what they desired. The tone of each bell was different and corresponded to the gratification that was wanted rather than to individuals. The patron could select and ring as many bells as they wanted in order to ensure their needs were met.

Regus picked up four of the bells, the smallest one, made from silver, a brass one that was the size of his fist, a steel bell that could be used to put out church candles and a meran bell that was as long as his middle finger and twice as wide.

He rang them in combination, first the silver bell, then the steel bell, followed by the brass bell, the meran bell, and the silver bell for a second time.

The sound of a door opening on the top corridor told Regus that his request had been accepted. The lieutenant looked up to watch a willowy woman descending to greet him. She was wearing a long sheer gown that floated as she moved.

"Lieutenant, what a pleasure to see you again," the woman said with a smile.

"I am not in the mood to talk," he said curtly. The woman nodded and led the way to her chamber. Regus followed behind her, studying the way her hips moved under the thin dress she wore. She opened the door and moved to the centre of the room as Regus shut the door behind them.

The room was richly furnished with cushions and throws, and a variety of different tables. A tea set was sat on a sideboard at the edge of the room alongside a platter that was piled high with fruit. A variety of restraints, weapons and scarves adorned the walls, candles burned on every surface and three pokers were being heated in the lit fireplace. A raised platform at the back of the room had curtains drawn around it, which hid the bed.

The woman stood in the centre of the room, waiting for Regus. The lieutenant walked slowly towards the woman and kissed her. He slipped the dress from her body and let his hands move to the scars that her skin bore from their previous encounters.

"The bed," he whispered as he moved his lips from hers and bit hard into her neck. The woman gasped and moaned as his teeth broke her skin. She felt the warm trickle of blood seep from her neck to her shoulder as she stepped back from the lieutenant and walked slowly to the platform. Regus waited until she had drawn back the curtains before he moved towards the dais.

He removed his own clothing as he approached so that he was naked by the time he reached the bed.

"The manacles," he ordered as he climbed onto the bed. He watched the woman retrieve the chains from the wall and carry them to him. He raised his arms over his head as the woman returned and felt the cold of the steel against his wrists as she chained him to the wall.

The woman smiled as she locked the chains around his wrists. She enjoyed her work and had many patrons that she found it a pleasure to serve, but Regus was different. Since he had first visited the brothel, she had felt a connection to him. Over time, this connection had grown into love on her part and the frequency of his visits to her bed convinced her that, on some level, he returned her love.

"How long are you staying for?" she asked as she knelt beside him.

"A week," he replied. The woman smiled broadly,

"A week? Then we have no need to rush. What am I to be called?" she asked.

"Mia."

Colonel Deena Mae walked through the streets of the city of Delma. She often spent the time she was not on duty walking amongst the people. There were many people in the city that needed help during the siege, and the help that was normally provided by the palace had been withdrawn. This meant that those who were the poorest in the city suffered the most during Kasnata's blockade.

Deena spent much of her time with these people. The orphans that had been created by the war saw her as a mother figure and would flock into the street the moment she approached the district.

Being an infertile woman in Delma was a difficult burden to bear. Not only would she never be able to raise her own family and fear being ostracised by her own, but it had forced her to take a path in life that she never wanted to walk.

In her childhood, she had dreamed of what it would be like to be the Duchess DeLacey, to spend her days raising the children of Kelmar, teaching them to read and write; teaching them the manners of court and teaching them how to fight in political arenas whilst their father taught them the art of war.

She also thought she would be the ally that Kelmar needed in court, defending his name and reputation from the machinations of his enemies.

When she had reached the age of sixteen, she was sent to be examined by the royal physician. He had declared that she was barren and would never bear children. She was then given the choice of joining the order of the Seven Stars, the ancient religion of Delma that had been all but dead before King Baruch Delich had ascended to the throne, serving in the army or leaving the city, forsaking her title and position in society, to serve on the farms of the kingdom as a common labourer.

Her ambitions had fallen about her in tatters in a single moment and she had been forced to make a decision about her future in the same moment that her dreams had been taken from her.

She chose the army. She would never be allowed to marry, but she could still protect Kelmar. It took her more than a decade to accept her new life and grow accustomed to her role in the army, but she never quite let go of the dreams of her childhood.

Having so many in need in the city gave her the opportunity to be a mother to those that had been abandoned by everyone else. The younger orphans had begun to call her mother and Deena had made up her mind to petition the king to allow her to adopt the orphans of the city and retire from the military.

There was no guarantee that the king would allow her to take that course, but with Kelmar returning to the city with the princess of the Order in his custody, she had an opportunity to petition the king with the support of the Duke.

"Colonel Mae!" *one of the older girls called out and waved manically as she watched the colonel approached.*

"Good morning, Kayla," *Deena smiled.* "Where are the others?"

"They have gone to try and get water. People have been talking about rations and needing slips of paper to get food and water, but no one has given us any," *Kayla rang her hands together nervously.*

"You don't need to worry about rations. I wanted to talk to you about something, but I don't want the others to know about it yet. Walk with me?" *Deena asked as she placed a comforting hand on Kayla's shoulder. The girl nodded enthusiastically and fell into step beside the colonel.*

Nasus rushed into the compound of the fortress. Night had fallen hours earlier than it should have and the alarm bells were ringing. The bells hadn't been a cause for alarm in a fortress that was so heavily defended by the skilled warriors of the Order; however, the sound of the gate being destroyed caused more panic in the daughter of Epoch than she would care to admit.

She looked around the fortress; warriors were lining the walls, bows drawn and firing at a rapid rate. Yoav, the General of the Order of the Wolf was staggering back to his feet. The Eight were stood in a fan formation behind Condor General Samara.

Nasus looked for her sister, but she couldn't see Haras anywhere in the compound. She let her eyes move to where the gate had stood. Neesa stood amongst the splintered wood. An aurora of tremendous power was emanating from her. The blood moon hung low in the sky, it was three times larger than it should have been and was the colour of freshly spilt blood.

"Give me the children," *Neesa demanded.*

"You'll have to pry them from our cold dead fingers," *Samara spat back. The warrior had her Cedema Coxan drawn and her shield raised.*

"You traitorous fools," *Neesa laughed.* "The power I wield is far greater than the usurper could ever hope to hold. Yet you would stand against me instead of joining me against her?"

"Children of Ashpa, defend the Order," *Scattergood replied.*

Yoav brushed the dirt off his trousers and patted down his cloak.

"Last Heir of Valia, today your bloodline ends. Your people will no longer plague mine," *he growled as he charged forward.*

Neesa looked at him with disdain. The arrows of the Order warriors were falling about her, all missing their mark, her power bending the air around her, distorting the flight of the arrows.

"As long as I have the blood moon, you cannot stop me."

The Eight followed behind Yoav in a spear formation that Neesa swept aside with a wave of her hand.

"Do you know how to stop her?" *Samara asked Nasus as she approached the general.*

"No, but she is only this powerful whilst the blood moon is in the sky, as powerful as she believes she is, she cannot stop the sun from rising," *Nasus replied.*

"But the Wentrus days are so short; she doesn't need to have constant night," *Samara replied.*

"She will be weakened during the day, and there is only so much punishment that her body can take before the power of the blood moon will force her to rest. We just need to hold her off until she retreats."

"Then we track her whilst she tries to recover?" *Samara sighed as she watched Yoav roll onto his feet and charge again.* "There must be another way."

"I can slow her down, but I can't stop her. I need some time to prepare, and I need Haras." *Nasus said firmly.*

"She is protecting the children," *Samara signalled to the warriors on the wall to stop wasting their arrows.*

"The children will be safe. You must delay her until we are ready," *Nasus said sadly.*

"We'll hold," *Samara said firmly.* "Warriors of the Condor to me!"

Chapter 3

The spire of Asuna could be seen on the horizon long before they reached the sealed city. Cassandra, Tola, Shamgar and the lost boy Shamgar had found approached the city from the north.

They had struck south from the Ballo Fortress and avoided crossing through the lands of Nosfa in order to reach the city of the Oracles.

It was impossible to gain access to Asuna without the permission of the Oracles, equally it was impossible to leave the city without their permission. Only those of the Order and of the Free Cities approached the Oracles for guidance. In the past, the rulers of other kingdoms had come and begged for the wisdom of the occupants of Asuna, but as rulers had changed, so had the way in which the kingdoms were governed. Rulers turned from seeking outside wisdom and trusting the counsel of those within their own countries.

The four dismounted in the trees that surrounded the city and secured their horses before approaching the walls. Cassandra placed her hands against the stone walls and waited. Shamgar, Tola and the boy watched as fingers of smoke seemed to seep out of the walls and coil up the arm of the Guardian of the Wilds.

The boy clung to Shamgar as he watched the smoke engulf the body of Cassandra and begin to creep towards him. He blinked and found himself transported into a large round room. Shamgar smiled down at the boy as he looked around in wonder.

There were eight chairs laid out in a circle around where Cassandra, Tola, Shamgar and the boy stood. Behind each of the chairs were doors that seemed to be made from coloured crystal.

"Welcome, Cassandra, Guardian of the Wilds and granddaughter of the Goddess. We have been expecting you," a voice came from the walls. The crystal doors swung open but only three people appeared.

One was a woman and the other two were old men.

"Omandia, Waldo, Wendell," Cassandra greeted each of them in turn. "Are the others not with you?"

"No, there are other matters that require their attention at present," Omandia said as she sat on one of the chairs. She was dressed in an orange robe that floated about her as she moved.

"I see. You know why we have come?" Cassandra asked.

"We do," Waldo said as he looked at the boy huddled next to Shamgar. "But there is little we can tell you that you do not already know. The blood moon is not responsible for the madness in Delma and it is not the portal beneath the city that has corrupted their minds."

"It isn't the portal or the blood moon?" Tola frowned.

"No," Waldo replied.

"What is it then?" the hero of the war of the east asked crossly. He had been dragged out into the wilds by Cassandra when he should have been seeking revenge for Renta.

Renta had been Kasnata's Condor General before Samara. She had been murdered by Kelmar and Tola had sworn to avenge her. He had loved the general, and seeing her cut down so brutally had driven him to be consumed by grief.

"The Seven Stars," Cassandra sighed and ground her teeth as she thought.

"Yes, you know what must be done, Cassandra," Omandia said firmly.

"*I do,*" the guardian confirmed.

"*Boy, step forward,*" Wendell barked as he squinted at him. The boy tried to hide behind Shamgar as the Oracle approached.

"*It's okay,*" Shamgar said, trying to reassure the young boy.

"Dona. Seria dos gras,*" the boy said, shaking his head.*

"Heral. Seperila gon lam,*" Cassandra replied. The boy looked at her. He nodded and slowly moved so that Wendell could see him.*

"*Do you know who this boy is?*" Waldo asked, looking at Tola, Shamgar, and the guardian.

"*No, he was wandering alone; we couldn't leave him out there on his own,*" Shamgar said, frowning at the Oracles.

"*He's the son of dragons, the one that the prophecy of Oran spoke of,*" Omandia said.

"*The prophecy of Oran?*" Tola asked.

"*It's of little consequence,*" Cassandra said dismissively.

"*What does the prophecy say?*" Shamgar asked.

"*That the son of dragons will become the spirit of destruction,*" Waldo said seriously.

"*The prophecy is unclear,*" Cassandra countered.

"*Prophecy is a useful tool, but it is often misinterpreted, and the predictions can be prevented from coming to pass,*" Wendell agreed.

"*What does this mean for the boy?*" Shamgar asked, looking between the Oracles and the guardian.

"*It means that he should be kept out of the reaches of those that would corrupt him. General Shamgar, will you permit the boy to remain here with us?*" Omandia looked at the General of the Order of the Bear with expectant eyes.

"No, I can't just abandon him. I will keep him with me for now," Shamgar said slowly.

"Very well," Waldo said as he bit his lip and dismissed his train of thought.

"What can you tell us about the Seven Stars?" Tola asked.

"They worship the dead goddess and would gladly give their lives to see her resurrected," Wendell explained.

"There is no such thing as a dead goddess," Cassandra tutted to herself.

"Of course, but they believe they worship a dead goddess that they can bring back to life to reign over all existence, which is what makes them dangerous," Waldo looked meaningfully at Cassandra, who nodded.

"And their practises are what are causing the king of Delma to lose his mind?" Shamgar asked.

"Yes, but they are not simply the practises of those under his rule. He is the one that has revived the worship of the dead goddess."

"Then it is the king that has to be stopped," Tola said firmly.

"It is, but be careful, young hero, your desire for revenge is a cold fury that may dull your pain now, but when it finally ebbs, you will be left with the guilt of your actions and no way of relieving it," Omandia warned. Tola glowered at Omandia, but didn't respond.

"Thank you, we will leave you in peace. Grace of Arala be with you," Cassandra said.

"Grace of Arala be with you," the three Oracles replied as the smoke began to rise around the four companions. A moment later, they were outside again.

"*To Delma?*" Shamgar asked.

"*To Delma,*" Cassandra agreed.

The city of Afdanic had gladly welcomed the Gibborim into the city. The city belonged to Lord Haston Bird and had prospered under the guidance of the family. Haman had been given a letter that Haston had signed to present to two different officials in the city.

The king had attempted to have Lord Bird assassinated as he returned to Afdanic, but the Gibborim had intervened. The people of the city had been informed that their lord was dead, but few believed it. Many thought he was being held prisoner by the mad king and refused to accept the rule of the Baron of Fintry, the king's closest ally, who had been placed in Lord Bird's seat.

Haston had written to his two former aides in the city, informing them of the needs of the Gibborim and all that had happened since the day that he had been delivered from the machinations of the king.

The city had rejoiced at the news that Haston was alive and the Gibborim were given quarters, spreading them across the city, making the arrival of so many newcomers at once much less noticeable. There were also those in Afdanic that were friends of the Gibborim and had readily welcomed their friends into their homes.

Many of the children born into the Gibborim had never lived above ground and found exploring the city an exhilarating experience. They had been warned not to speak of where they had come from to others in the city for fear of spies that would report their presence and existence to the king.

Haman had been given rooms in the castle of Afdanic and though he worried over the safety of Haston and Hermia, the majority of the Gibborim was out of the reach of the king for the moment.

Lord Haston Bird sat in the dark of the tunnels beneath the city of Grashindorph. Lady Hermia, the mother of King Mercia, was sat beside him. They had been sat in silence for days. They sat and listened to the noise of men that had become lost whilst searching for evidence of the Gibborim beneath the city.

"We should go find them," Haston said quietly.

"No, it's too dangerous," Hermia and Haston had discussed searching for the lost men and inviting them to join their cause. Hermia thought the risks were too great, especially as her Shield and Shadow were not there to protect her.

"If they are men that are loyal to the kingdom and not the madness of the king, all they will need is to see you are alive and they will fall on their knees and swear fealty to you," Haston countered.

"What if they think they are hallucinating?" Hermia asked.

"They are unlikely to attack the queen mother, even if they do believe that they are hallucinating," Haston said dryly.

"And what if they believe I am a ghost, come back to haunt them in their despair and misery for not serving me better?" Hermia looked sideways at Haston.

"I will be with you," Haston shrugged.

"A lord that has been reported as dead at the hand of bandits? I'm not

sure that will convince anyone they are not being haunted."

"Then we simply sit here and wait until Layla and Jephthah return," *Haston asked.*

Lavinia, Lacenta and Muse were not formerly received in the camp. Kasnata and her generals were all busy overseeing the rebuilding of the camp of Nosfa, the disposal of the bodies and making plans to try and make the camp more secure.

Lavinia took it as an insult that the queen refused to greet her. Abendigo had been the one to meet them and show the three women to the quarters that they would occupy whilst they were Kasnata's guests.

"Have you ever heard of the realm having guardians?" *Quisla asked Misna as the two women inspected the perimeter of the camp.*

"Yes, but as far as I knew they never left their fortress. They aren't known for their love of people. In fact, they care far more for the balance of the natural world around it. I've only read the records that others have left behind." *Misna replied.*

"What do the records say?" *Quisla asked, casting her eyes away from the camp and towards the city of Delma.*

"The Guardians have a habit of using people, putting them in danger in order to serve their own agendas," *Misna frowned.*

"You trust the records?" *Quisla asked in an off-hand voice.*

"No. Records are some of the most unreliable sources of information, but I don't like the idea of them being in the camp," *Misna pursed her lips.*

"You think they need a camp escort?" *Quisla sounded amused as she spoke.*

"I think that Methanlan is at a loose end," *Misna shrugged.* "There isn't any harm in giving the poor man something to do."

"Whose division does he belong to now?" *Quisla said looking back to the Raven General.*

"Does it matter? He seems to obey whatever orders he's given and none of us are that precious about our warriors," *Misna smiled.*

"Well, Hesla was," *Quisla folded her arms and shook her head,* "Though I suppose it is our warriors that are precious about whom they serve under."

"Indeed, fortunately enough, Methanlan and Shaul seem to be the exception to that. I will speak to him when we are done here," *Misna replied.*

Methanlan and Jack carried Harry's body out of Payne's healing tent. The two had spent half a day building a funeral pyre for him. They were the only ones present as the fire was lit. The stood silently, Methanlan had attended the funerals of so many of his fallen comrades that he knew the value of silence whilst watching the flames.

Jack was lost in his thoughts. Harry had been his closest friend for many campaigns. He had other friends in the ranks of Nosfa, but after the attack on the camp, he didn't know how many of them were still alive.

They stood in the cold of the snow, staring at the fire until the pyre had burnt down to mere cinders.

"I've made a decision," Jack said, his eyes fixed on the glowing embers.

"Oh?" asked Methanlan.

"I'm leaving, I'm going to Nosfa," Jack sighed.

"Someone will have to make sure you are listed among the dead then," Methanlan smiled to himself.

"It's the least you can do," Jack replied curtly.

"What will you do in Nosfa?" Methanlan asked as Jack turned away from Harry's ashes.

"I'll get my family and Harry's family out of the country. I don't need your friends to help me get them," Jack said firmly.

"Where will you go?"

"I don't know; somewhere far away from war," Jack shrugged.

"Go to them at night. Pack everything you can and go to Tulna. Tell them who you are, they'll help you. They aren't part of the Order, so you don't have anyone to hate there. Even if you don't want to stay, you'll be safe there until you know where you want to go," Methanlan said without moving away from the embers.

"Thank you," Jack said coldly.

"Take care of yourself. You may not think of me as a friend, but it has been an honour serving with you," Methanlan listened to Jack's footsteps crunching in the snow as the soldier walked away.

The warrior didn't expect a response; Jack had been through a lot in the last few days, more than most experienced in a lifetime.

"That was unexpected," *Misna observed as she joined Methanlan by the dying fire.*

"His departure?" *Methanlan asked.*

"No, you paying such a high compliment to someone outside of the Order," *Misna replied with a smile.*

"What is it you want, general?" *Methanlan said, ignoring the jibe.*

"There are some visitors to the camp that are in need of an escort," *Misna said with a wry smile, curling the corner of her mouth.*

"People you don't trust?" *Methanlan asked lightly.*

"You think I trust anyone?" *Misna shot back with a smile.*

"Who are they?" *Methanlan asked.*

"The guardians."

CHAPTER 4

The streets of Grashindorph were full an hour before the king was due to make his proclamation. Helez hadn't seen the streets as busy as they now were since he was a boy.

The atmosphere in the city, however, was not one of festival and excitement. It was an atmosphere of fear. People pushed their way along the streets to the square below the old palace's battlements, skirting away from the guards that were scattered through the crowds, their eyes fixed low.

One of the inns at the back of the square had set up a bar outside his inn with kegs lined up on a long, makeshift table against the wall of the inn and another a few feet in front of it. The front table had stools lined up on one side for people to sit and drink at.

Helez slipped through the crowd, a few people he had spoken to over the last few weeks in the city nodded abruptly to him as they passed, but nobody stopped to talk. He walked into the square and sat down at the makeshift bar, ordering a pint of ale so he could slowly sip the liquid whilst he took stock of the area.

Most people in the square were pushing together in the centre, trying to be as close to the palace battlements as possible. The palace itself was a crumbling monument to the prosperity and the line of great rulers that Nosfa had enjoyed and a bitter reminder of the terror and fear under which it now trembled. The battlements and barracks of the palace were well maintained though. The battlements ran around the old palace, the barracks, the guard's training grounds and the prison.

Though the king lived in his palace outside the city, he still made proclamations from the old palace battlements that overlooked the square. The king had yet to appear, but the crowd was subdued as the Baron of Fintry was stood looking down at them, his cold eyes making note of those that were in attendance and making a mental note of notable people that were absent.

"Bloody politics," a woman clicked her tongue against her teeth as she pushed through the crowd to the bar. She ordered a half pint of ale and collapsed on the stool next to Helez. She was finely dressed; the cloak that was draped around her shoulders was worth more than everything that Helez owned.

"Madame Ella, you should keep your voice down," the bartender warned under his breath.

"Madame Ella?" Helez asked.

"Yes, and by the looks of you, young man, you couldn't afford a minute of my time," Madame Ella said coldly.

"Don't worry, I don't want to trespass on your time or look down on your profession," Helez replied with a smile. Madame Ella turned and looked at Helez properly.

"Attractive, polite and in possession of at least half a brain, why are you wasting your life sitting in a city as doomed as this?" she asked.

"You don't like Grashindorph?" Helez asked with surprise.

"I did, when Rosla was king and when Lord Bird was the steward. Even when the barbarian queen was in the city, she did a lot to keep the king's madness in check, but now. No there is nothing but fear and insanity," she tutted.

"What do you expect when a man like the Baron of Fintry is the second most powerful man in the kingdom?" the bartender asked.

"The Baron isn't a concern. Men like Lieutenant Regus are," the madam replied. "A man with no remorse and despicable appetites."

"He comes to your house?" Helez asked.

"He does. Only one of my roster will service him and the scars she bears mean that there are now only a select number of people that are even interested in availing themselves of her services," Madame Ella said, shaking her head.

"He leaves scars?" Helez frowned.

"Burn marks from pokers. You can hear her screams all over the house," she replied sadly.

"Why don't you stop him?" Helez asked forcefully.

"She seems to enjoy it. The stupid fool had fallen in love with him; I don't think there is anything he could ask of her that she wouldn't willingly give at this point. It's the only reason I am here," Madame Ella sighed.

"He's at your house now?" Helez asked.

"Yes, been there three days already, from what my girl has said, he'll be there for at least seven more — finish out the week," Madame Ella said, throwing back the contents of her tankard.

Horns sounded on the battlements that heralded the arrival of the king. He stepped up with Mia beside him. She was wearing a long sleeved, high neck dress. Her hair was piled on her head, and she was accompanied by the guards from her cell.

"By the seven stars, that's Lady Mia Bird," the bartender said softly.

"People of Nosfa, I am here to share glad tidings with you," the king announced. "I am to wed, I present my future bride and your future queen, Lady Mia Bird." Mercia said without emotion in his voice as he looked down at the people assembled before him. Some glanced nervously about, clearly

confused and others stood simply staring up at him in shock.

"Long live King Mercia!" the Baron of Fintry cried.

"Long live the king," was repeated in muted voices across the square but they barely carried to where the king stood. Mercia narrowed his eyes and scowled as he turned and swept from the battlements, the guards pushing Mia along behind him.

"That bastard," Madame Ella slammed her tankard down on the table.

"What?" Helez asked.

"He gave her to Regus," she said, shaking her head.

"What makes you think that?" he asked.

"Those long clothes to hide the marks he left, and her spirit is broken. That poor child never did anything to harm another living being and ends up losing her father to bandits, her brother is sentenced to death as a traitor, and she winds up as a mistress to that cruel, sadistic bastard," the madam half-shouted.

"Keep your voice down," the bartender warned. Helez leaned in to the madam and dropped his voice to a low whisper.

Madame Ella was a woman in her late fifties, though her figure was that of a woman in her early thirties. She was dignified and a consort to powerful men. She had spent her life manipulating the lust of men and women to advance herself and was jaded when it came to love and had dismissed the idea that any individual, no matter how attractive, could have any effect on her.

Yet, as Helez's lips brushed against her ear and he ran his fingers through her hair in such a gentle manner, Madame Ella felt passion surging in her chest. His voice, low and rich pouring into her ear sent a chill down her spine, and instinctively her hand had moved so that it was resting on the inside of his thigh.

"I have a proposition for you," he whispered.

"Many men had made propositions to me, what makes you think I will accept yours?" she teased. Helez shifted his body closer to her.

"Because no man has ever been able to offer you what I can," he replied.

"Many men have made the boast and then had little to back up their claim," Madame Ella replied, twisting again from Helez so she could catch her breath and compose herself, but she found her body checked by Helez's hand on her waist.

"Meet me for dinner tonight, and I will do all that I can to induce you into accepting my proposal," Helez looked her straight in the eyes as he spoke. Ella swallowed and took a deep breath before replying,

"Come to the house. Ring the jade bell four times. Don't keep me waiting."

The journey from Asuna to the siege camp was long, but uneventful. Shamgar had passed the journey quietly lost in thought. The words of the Oracles rang in his ears. It was hard to believe that the boy he had found in the wilds was destined for such catastrophic things. He had tried asking the boy his name, but the boy didn't seem to have one.

Tola felt his hatred rising as he grew closer to the camp. The chance to avenge Renta made his mouth water and his pulse race.

As they rode into the centre of the camp, the boy leapt off his horse and started shouting,

"Belona! Belona!"

"*What's wrong with him?*" Shamgar asked.

"*The guardians are here,*" sighed Cassandra.

"*You've met the guardians before?*" Kasnata asked as she approached the riders. She had the boy by the hand. He was looking at the queen with wide eyes and he had stopped shouting.

"*We were at their fortress, your highness,*" Shamgar replied as he dismounted.

"*Who is the child?*" Kasnata asked.

"*The son of dragons, we found him in the wilds, majesty,*" the general of the Order of the Bear said as he moved to his horse's head.

"*Son of dragons? Does he have a name?*" the queen asked, kneeling down beside the boy.

"*No, not that he will tell us,*" Cassandra replied.

"*Dragonious. Do you like that?*" Kasnata asked the boy. He tilted his head and nodded. "*Dragonious it is,*" she smiled.

"*You should be careful, your highness,*" Lavinia warned as she stepped from inside her tent.

"*Oh?*" Kasnata asked as she rose back to her feet. The boy hid behind the queen's legs.

"*The boy is dangerous.*" Lavinia explained.

"*I have far more pressing concerns than the danger that a child presents.*" Kasnata said, giving the guardian a cold look.

"*What brings you to the camp, Lavinia?*" Cassandra asked with a deadpan expression.

"*Terrible things are unfolding; we are here to offer wise counsel to the queen,*" *Lavinia replied, her voice dripping with condescension.*

"*What a revelation that must be,*" *Cassandra shot back.*

"Cave Dweller, take Dragonious and feed him. He looks like he's not eaten properly for a few years,*" Kasnata said.*

"Of course, your majesty,*" Shamgar said, he led his horse and the boy away from the guardians and queen.*

"Tola, Princess Kia wanted to talk to you when you returned,*" Kasnata said, staring at Lavinia with a stony expression.*

"As you wish, your highness,*" Tola said, glad of an excuse to leave. He was still on his horse, so nudged the beast forward.*

"*Cassandra, Guardian Lavinia, please follow me,*" Kasnata said in a light tone. Cassandra left her horse in the care of one of the warriors by the corral and followed Kasnata to the war room.*

"*Ladies, morale in this camp is fragile. The blood moon is causing concern and panic. We are recovering from an attack that decimated the army of Nosfa and has left those that survived in a state of mourning that will not be helped by rumours spreading of two guardians bickering in the camp.*" Kasnata scolded the two women as she sat upon her makeshift throne.*

"*You presume to lecture me?*" Lavinia asked in an indignant tone.*

"*You presume to enter my camp without invitation to provide advice and then argue like a child with a woman that is well respected by those of the Order,*" Kasnata replied in an even voice.*

"*My apologies, your highness,*" Lavinia said with a slight sneer.*

"*What did you discover on your journey?*" Kasnata enquired, turning to Cassandra.*

"The madness in Delma is not caused by the blood moon. King Baruch Delich has resurrected the religion of the Seven Stars," the Guardian of the Wilds replied.

"Then we will need to send someone into the city," Kasnata sighed and rubbed her forehead.

"I will gladly go," Cassandra offered.

"I appreciate the offer, but before I send in spies, I believe sending an envoy would be best. I will talk to Avner, Baruch is his son-in-law; he will know the best envoy to dispatch," Kasnata replied and left Cassandra to go in search of Avner.

Layla sat on the rooftops of a line of abandoned houses. The Shadow preferred to be sat amongst the chimneys instead of walking amongst the people. She could see more for the rooftops than she could from the streets.

Jephthah was exploring the taverns of the city. It was a task that the man mountain had eagerly accepted. He could gather news and gossip from the drunks in their less guarded moments, whilst Layla watched the movements of individuals that struck her as being somewhat out of place in the city.

The announcement in the square had caused the city to plunge into a deeper state of despair. The people were shocked and scared. Some worried that the king trying to take a second wife would bring the wrath of the barbarians down upon the city. Others were terrified that the king had lost his mind.

What was more terrifying was what was now happening on the streets. Layla had watched a group of soldiers for four hours. They had gathered shortly before dark and seemed to be waiting for something.

The bells in the church tower chimed the hour and the soldiers moved. They marched in groups of four to seven houses. In unison they kicked the doors open and burst through them. The soldiers dragged people from their homes, the people screamed and begged to be set free, but the soldiers ignored their plea.

A cart was drawn up to where the soldiers were stood holding their prisoners. The prisoners were thrown into the cart and then taken off into the night. The soldiers dispersed and Layla frowned. She carefully climbed down from the roof and went to find Jephthah.

"What is it?" Jephthah asked as Layla stepped through the door to the tavern.

"People are being snatched from their homes," Layla said in a low voice.

"I see. We should find our friends," Jephthah said, yawning and stretching his arms over his head.

"Helez and Asahel?" Layla sounded surprised.

"They have been in this city for a long time now. They may know why," Jephthah said with a smile.

"You miss them," Layla smiled at the man mountain.

"Of course," Jephthah shrugged and staggered to the door of the tavern.

Helez rang the jade bell four times. He felt somewhat out of place in the brothel, but he was excited about seeing the madam again.

Madame Ella swept down the staircase in a long gown that made her look far more elegant than Helez expected.

"Good evening," she said with a warm smile. She offered her hand to the young man. Helez gently took her hand and kissed it, his lips only lightly brushing against her skin. His eyes were fixed on hers.

"My lady," he greeted her. Madame Ella silently turned and led Helez up the stairs to the top floor. She led him past the room that Regus was occupying, shuddering slightly as she heard a soft scream of pain coming from inside the room.

She took Helez to the end of the corridor and showed him into her rooms. Helez hadn't known what to expect, but he was pleasantly surprised.

The rooms were tastefully furnished, the looked like the rooms that Hermia had described when she talked of her life in the palace of Grashindorph.

A table was stood in the middle of the room and was laid out with dinner for two. There were candles in silver holders scattered across the room, casting a soft glow about the room.

"Can I offer you something to drink?" Madame Ella asked as she closed and locked the door behind her.

"Wine?" Helez asked.

"Of course," Madame Ella smiled. Helez watched her glide across the floor and pour two glasses of wine into two silver goblets.

She moved back and handed the young exile one of them.

"You said you had a proposition for me," Madame Ella teased as Helez drank the wine.

"I do, but wouldn't you prefer to enjoy dinner before we discuss it?" he asked with a smile.

"Dinner will keep," she said, fluttering her eyelashes at the young man.

"I think I can provide you with a solution to your Regus problem," Helez

said, putting his goblet down on one of the small tables that littered the room.

"Oh?" Madame Ella felt a sinking feeling of disappointment in her chest.

"Lord Haston Bird. He isn't dead. General Rathe Bird is not a prisoner of the king," Helez said quietly. He took the goblet Madame Ella was holding and put it down next to his. He led her to one of the low sofas that faced the window and was as far from the door as you could be in the room.

"What makes you think that?" Madame Ella looked at Helez with an expression of pity.

Helez opened the windows and looked out to the street below. A moment later he had a rope in his hand that he tied to one of the wall hooks. A few moments later, Asabel climbed through the window, followed by Mathias and Rathe.

Madame Ella gasped and fell backwards onto the sofa.

"How can you be here?" she asked, staring at Rathe.

"My friends freed me, and they saved my father," Rathe replied.

Helez collected Ella's wine and sat beside her on the sofa.

"Here, you look like you need this," he said kindly. Madame Ella gladly accepted the goblet and drained it in a single gulp.

"What is it you want from me?" she asked, looking between the four men.

"We want Lieutenant Regus. He has information about the king and Mia that we need," Rathe said seriously.

"I can help you," Madame Ella said quietly.

"How long will dinner keep?" Helez whispered to her.

"I think the moment has passed," Ella sighed sadly.

Chapter 5

Princess Kia spent three hours talking to Tola about what had happened in the camp when Kelmar had attacked. The hero of the war of the east had told Kia what they had discovered and about the boy Shamgar had found.

Light was starting to seep back into the sky when Kia made her way to her tent to try to sleep for a few hours. She stepped inside, stifling a yawn, and was surprised to see Shaul sat waiting for her.

"Good morning," Kia said, covering her mouth as she yawned again.

"Good morning," Shaul replied. "I'm sorry, I know you must want to sleep, you have worked so hard over the past few days, but I noticed you hadn't eaten today." he said nervously.

"No, I guess I didn't," Kia smiled and sat down on a small pile of cushions in the corner of the room.

"Here," he said. "It's not much, and it's cold now, but it's better than nothing." Shaul handed the princess some meat on the bone. He watched as she greedily devoured the meat and laughed to himself.

"I guess I was hungry," Kia shrugged and lay back on the cushions.

"I'll leave you to sleep," Shaul said, standing and stretching out his back.

"You don't need to go," Kia sat up suddenly.

"It's very late and you need to rest. There is still a lot of work that needs doing in the camp of Nosfa, and the men are looking to you for leadership," Shaul said gently.

"They are expecting me to lead them as a princess," Kia sighed.

"You are their princess," Shaul said warmly.

"I was a prisoner that no one ever expected anything from. This is all very new and more than a little overwhelming," the princess replied. Shaul sat down beside her and wrapped his arm around her shoulders.

"You are doing well," he said quietly. "The men are not expecting you to be your mother or your father. They are grateful you care for them."

"I should hate them," Kia said, shaking her head.

"Why? What have these men done to you?" Shaul asked.

"They are men that serve my father and do terrible things on his behalf," Kia rubbed her eyes and leaned her head against Shaul's shoulder.

"I have lived amongst these men since your mother joined with the army. These men are good people. They are no different from the men and women of the Order. You shouldn't judge them because they belong to the army of your father," Shaul said kindly.

"Thank you for not treating me like they do," Kia said, closing her eyes.

"What makes you think I treat you differently to them?" Shaul teased.

"You don't call me princess or your highness. Everyone else, except mother, does," Kia said, looking up at Shaul.

"Ah, well, princess-" Shaul began, but Kia elbowed him in the ribs. "I guess I deserved that."

"You did," Kia said in a satisfied voice. "Are you not tired?"

"I am," Shaul admitted.

"Then why did you wait here to feed me?" Kia demanded.

"Because you aren't used to life in the camp yet and I like taking care of you," Shaul said, taking his arm from around her shoulders. "Sleep well, princess."

Shaul stood and left Kia's tent. The princess watched him go with a smile on her face and curled up on the cushions, quickly drifting off to sleep.

Avner, General of the Order of the Hound, rode up to the gates of the city of Delma under a flag of parlay. It had been years since the general had entered the city. The last time, he had been invited. His grandson, Prince Jayden Delich was being dedicated and shown to the people for the first time.

To Avner it seemed like a lifetime ago. His grandson was dead; killed by Kasnata in a skirmish between the Order and the nation of Delma. The death of his grandson weighed heavily on his heart, but any guilt he felt or anger towards his queen had been erased by the attitude of his daughter.

Queen Adina Delich, queen of Delma and a daughter of the Order, had turned her back on her father and those who shared her blood in favour of her husband.

Since Shamgar's return to the camp, rumours had begun to spread of the Seven Stars being revived in Delma. And the thought that his daughter was now held under the sway of the dark religion brought a cold, sinking feeling to Avner's chest.

When Kasnata had summoned the general and tasked him with infiltrating the city as an envoy. Avner had briefly felt relieved, but that relief had quickly been replaced by apprehension.

Now, as the Dog of War waited for the gates of the city to open, he dreaded what awaited him inside.

"Greetings, General Avner," *Colonel Mae stepped out through the city gates to meet him.*

"Deena, it has been a long time since we last met,*" Avner replied.* "I believe I am to congratulate you on obtaining the rank of colonel."

"Thank you, sir. I wish we could be meeting under more cordial conditions-*" Colonel Mae began.*

"But that is the life of a soldier,*" Avner finished her sentence for her.*

"Indeed. I have been bid to ask you what brings you to our city gates,*" Deena said as Avner dismounted.*

"I have been sent as an envoy by her royal majesty, Queen Kasnata Nosfa,*" Avner replied formerly.*

"An envoy? I would have thought that if Queen Kasnata were to send a spy it would have been Misna that was sent,*" Deena replied with a raised eyebrow.*

"If she were sending spies, I doubt you would know of it,*" Avner smiled back.*

"Then what business does an envoy have in the city of Delma?*" Deena challenged him.*

"I am here to discuss the siege, and the war, with King Baruch and Queen Adina. I believe that we can bring an end to the hostilities between our nations without further bloodshed,*" Avner said sharply.*

"A worthy cause indeed,*" Deena smiled.* "If you will follow me, I will show you to your quarters.*"*

Madame Ella had given Helez her keys. The madam had keys that

opened any door in her house of ill-repute, keys that were to be used only in an emergency.

Asahel had been surprised at the lack of coaxing that had been required in order to obtain the keys from Madame Ella. There was a considerable attraction between Helez and the madam, but Asahel had expected her to ask for something in return. Ella had handed over the keys and agreed to wait in her rooms without asking for anything. Helez had promised to return the keys when Regus had been dealt with.

Despite their number, Rathe had insisted that they retain the element of surprise for as long as possible. This meant waiting until the noise in the room was loud enough for the sound of the door being unlocked to go unnoticed.

The four men waited for two hours outside the door. It was evident that the two had fallen asleep, but Rathe refused to let them enter the room until the screaming started again.

Helez slipped the key into the lock and felt the resistance of the lock click open. He took hold of the handle and waited for the signal from Rathe.

The four men rushed into the room with blades drawn.

Regus was brandishing one of the heated pokers and the room reeked of burning flesh. The girl was tied to the bed with leather straps, screaming in agony. Her skin was blistering where Regus had pressed the glowing metal against her skin. Some of the burns hadn't blistered; instead they were some that oozed pus and blood, and others that were a day or more old showed clear signs of infection.

Asahel stepped between the girl and Regus, holding the point of his sword under the lieutenant's chin. Regus tried to bring the poker to bear against Asahel, but Mathias and Helez laid their blades across his wrists.

"Lieutenant Thomas Regus, what an unfortunate day it is when one is forced to converse with you." Rathe sneered from behind the odious man.

"General Bird, no, not a general anymore; traitor is the official title now, isn't it?" Regus spat without turning to face Rathe.

"Put down the poker. We have some things we want to talk to you about," Rathe said, ignoring the jibe.

"Is that an order?" Regus half-laughed.

"A suggestion," Rathe clarified. "As you said, I am no longer a general, though I should warn you that if you don't choose to release the poker, my associates will be glad to deprive you of both your hands in order to ensure that you won't brandish it against us."

"I see your time in the barbarian queen's bed has made you more savage. Infected with the taint of her," Regus sneered. Without hesitation, Mathias flicked his blade causing it to slice across the wrist and palm of the lieutenant. Regus shrieked in pain and the poker clattered to the floor.

"Perhaps learning to live without the use of the tendons in your hand will teach you a little respect for your queen," Mathias said lightly as he kicked the poker away.

"You bastard," Regus growled.

"Rumour has it you have been very busy recently," Helez grinned and pressed the sword point against Regus' other wrist.

Asahel turned away from the lieutenant and released the girl from her bonds. The moment she was free, she lunged at Asahel, scratching at his face and screaming for the men to let Regus go. Regus seized upon the momentary distraction and spun around to attack the ex-general.

Rathe raised his sword and rammed the pommel into the bridge of

Regus' nose before the man could raise a hand against him. The lieutenant collapsed backwards, grasping his nose with his good hand.

"Take the girl somewhere else," Rathe said coldly, Helez wrapped his arm around the girl's waist and lifted her up and threw her over his shoulder. She tried to squirm free, but each time she moved, the burns on her back stopped her. Helez took the girl from the room and delivered her to Madame Ella.

"Is she all right?" Ella asked as Helez dumped the girl on the madam's sofa.

"A few burns that need attention," Helez shrugged. The girl tried to get up and push past Helez, but the exile shoved her back onto the sofa with a lack of ceremony.

"You may need to restrain her. If she comes back to try to help Regus, she'll end up getting hurt," Helez warned.

He left Madame Ella to deal with her girl and returned to his comrades and Lieutenant Regus.

In Helez's absence, Asahel and Mathias had trussed the lieutenant to a chair using the leather straps he had enjoyed using on the girl.

He strained against them as best he could, but the throbbing in his nose, hand and wrist made it difficult to endure any violent movement.

"What did you do to my sister?" Rathe demanded in a quiet voice.

"What she deserved to get," Regus replied with a cruel grin. Mathias slapped Regus across the face.

"Did the king tell you to do it?" Rathe asked. Regus laughed and Mathias hit him again.

"Do you know who these men are?" Rathe sat down opposite Regus and looked at the lieutenant with a cold, hard stare.

"Lackeys?" Regus asked in a mocking voice.

"These men have spent their lives training to oppose the king and those that support him. You may not think that I am capable of the cruelty necessary to get the information we want out of you, but I can assure you that they are," Rathe said with a dangerous edge to his voice.

"You don't scare me, traitor," Regus said firmly, his voice steady despite the pain he was suffering. Rathe shrugged and stood up.

"When you're done with him, cut out his tongue and break his fingers, if he's still alive. We don't want him reporting to anyone," Rathe said quietly to Mathias before he swept from the room.

Mathias looked at Regus, weighing the man up before he began.

"You like inflicting pain on others. Do you also enjoy it being inflicted on you?" the assassin asked as he walked towards one of the walls and began to remove whips and beating sticks from it.

Helez stood by the door, if anyone came into the room, past Rathe, he would dispatch them before they reached Regus and Mathias. Asabel picked up the poker and plunged it back into the fire.

"What I enjoy or don't enjoy is none of your business," Regus spat, and leaned back in the chair.

"I see," Mathias said, moving back to the lieutenant. "You clearly believe that there is nothing I can do to you that you can't endure, but that is a very foolish assumption to live under. You serve a corrupt and mad king, you follow the orders of a despot that has spent his life profiting off the misery of others. You have been protected by both for far too long. Neither of them can deliver you from us."

"I am a soldier. I follow orders," Regus replied with a smug grin.

"*Yes, you are a soldier, but you are still responsible for your own actions,*" *Mathias replied, shaking his head.*

"*And what actions are you holding me responsible for?*" *Regus asked coldly.*

"*You hurt Mia.*"

General Avner was to be given an audience with the king and queen in two days, until then, he was to be confined to his rooms. A guard had been placed on the doors, but Deena knew that they were no match for the general of the Order of the Hound is he chose to defy the king's command.

Avner's presence in the palace gave Deena a sense of hope. She had always thought that any way between Delma and the Order couldn't last for more than a few months, but as the war had dragged on into years, she had begun to worry that it would only end with the annihilation of her people. An envoy to bring an end to the war without further bloodshed was more than Dena could have hoped for, and the envoy was the father of the queen of Delma. Surely family ties still count for something in this mess, *she thought.*

"*Deena,*" *Kelmar's voice interrupted her thoughts. She had been so lost in them that she hadn't heard the duke approaching.*

"Your Grace," *Deena said, saluting her childhood friend.*

"*Enough of that nonsense,*" *Kelmar said, dismissing her salute,* "Come with me, I want you to meet someone."

Deena followed Kelmar back to his rooms in silence.

"Colonel Deena Mae, may I present, her royal highness, Princess

Kasna Nosfa," *Kelmar said as he shut the door. Kasna had been given a range of dresses to wear whilst in the castle. They were not dissimilar to the tight clothing that was worn on Grashindorph; the bodice cut low to reveal her cleavage and brought in sharply at the waist. The skirts were much slimmer though, tightly fitted to her figure so that it was difficult to walk.*

The first thing Kasna had done was take a knife to the skirts, cutting slits in the sides up to the knee so that she could sit and stand without needing assistance.

Kasna was sat on one of the large sofas in the room and leapt to her feet as the colonel was introduced. Deena bowed to the princess.

"Your highness."

"He said you would do that," *Kasna smiled as she walked over and took Deena's hands in hers.* "I'm a prisoner, I'm not sure the king and queen would approve of you bowing to me. Please, call me Kasna."

Deena looked up at the princess, not sure how to respond. She was clearly Kasnata's daughter in appearance, but Deena had expected a cold reception from the daughter of Mercia Nosfa.

"Kasna, it is nice to meet you," *Deena smiled as she straightened her back.*

"Come sit, Deena. I want to ask you some questions," *Kelmar indicated towards the large sofa in the room. The colonel did as she was asked and waited for Kelmar to begin.* "How has it been in the city since I left?"

"Worse than you thought it would be. The arrival of Kasnata's army and the blood moon have people panicking. Rationing of food and water wasn't implemented until it was too late. Though we have enough water to last for six weeks, we only have food for three. After that people will start to starve. People have already died due to the meagre rations and a lot of people in the poor quarter aren't being given access to rations,*" Deena said sadly.*

"How are they surviving?*" Kasna sounded horrified.*

"They aren't. Those that are desperate enough are turning to the sewers for their food and water,*" Deena explained.*

"Something that will kill them as surely as starvation,*" Kelmar sighed,* "What about the king and queen? The king seems to be aging at an alarming rate."

"He is. It's like the life is being leeched out of him. He barely speaks to anyone anymore, all the decisions that govern the kingdom are coming from Queen Adina,*" Deena shifted uncomfortably on the sofa.*

"What authority is she using to make her governance legal?*" Kelmar frowned.*

"No one has dared to ask her,*" Deena replied.*

"Why would she need authority? She's the queen, isn't that enough?*" Kasna asked sounding confused.*

"Not in Delma. The queen is a figurehead, she has respect as the mother of any heirs, but she had no right to rule. If the king is unable to govern, then it is Kelmar, as the Regent who governs,*" Deena said, looking meaningfully at the duke.*

"I doubt that Adina will allow that to stop her,*" Kelmar grunted.*

"The king and queen keep disappearing too, going beneath the palace for hours at a time. They don't offer any explanation for their absence either,*" Deena sighed.*

"Do they take anyone with them?*" Kelmar asked, leaning forward* onto his knees.

"No, just the king and queen. Prince Jayden went with them before he died, but no one goes with them now," *Deena looked at Kelmar expectantly.*

"I see, thank you, Deena," *Kelmar leant back against the cushions on the sofa and stared at the ceiling.*

"I should go. I need to get back to the poor quarter and see what I can do to help the people there," Deena said standing.

"Has the king given you permission to adopt the orphans?" Kelmar asked.

"Not yet, I was hoping you might help me talk to him," Deena smiled.

"I will do what I can," Kelmar said, returning the smile.

"There're something else you should know," Deena said, pausing by the door.

"Oh?" Kelmar said, sitting up and looking at the colonel.

"Avner is in the palace. Kasnata sent him as an envoy," Deena opened the door, stepped out and closed it behind her.

"That is interesting," Kelmar smiled to himself.

"It is?" Kasna looked at Kelmar with exasperation. It was clear to the princess that everything that Deena had to say meant much more to Kelmar than it had to Kasna.

"Your mother doesn't send envoys. She sends armies to crush her enemies. She knows more about what is happening in the city than I do," Kelmar grumbled and shook his head.

"That's a problem?" Kasna frowned, not understanding what it was Kelmar meant.

"I don't like not knowing as much as my enemies do in a war, especially when my enemies know more about my city than I do."

The Guardians interest in Kasnata's camp was not focused on endearing themselves to the queen. Instead, their attention was focused on Kia. The three seemed to avoid Shamgar at every opportunity and they had no contact with the boy, Dragonious.

They were never left unescorted in the camp; the only time Methanlan left them was when they retired to their quarters for the evening. In those instances, guards were posted outside the tent to prevent them from leaving. Methanlan reported to Misna every night. The Raven General felt a growing concern over their apparent interest in Kia. There was no immediate threat posed to the princess, but anyone who spent their time trying to ingratiate themselves to the royal line of the Order always made Misna suspicious.

Kia was by means unprotected either, Shaul had barely left the princess' side since she had been elevated to the position of general. She was not the youngest person in the history of the Order to hold the position, but she was one of the most inexperienced commanders and warriors to take up the mantle.

Shaul was not much older than the princess appeared to be, but he had more experience on the battlefield, and his time as a spy for the Order meant that he was the ideal man to protect the princess from those that wanted to manipulate the princess for their own gain.

No one had assigned Shaul to the position, though Misna was grateful that the man had taken up the position voluntarily.

Kia's mind was focused on other things. She spent most of her time with the men of Nosfa, helping to find them food and shelter in their camp. Most of the men of Nosfa had refused to enter the camp of the Order, after all they had endured; from the murder of their commanders at the hands of General Seaton, to the attack by Kelmar's forces from Delma, most of the men wanted to leave the siege camp rubble and return to their homes and their families.

Kia was slowly lifting their morale through her actions. When the members of the Eagle division were not training or performing their own camp duties, they were with their general, helping the men of Nosfa.

Shaul's presence at the side of the princess had been a shock to many of the men of Nosfa. Most had known him as Tam and Methanlan as Sidney, not realising the two men were spies for the Order. The revelation of the two men as spies meant that the men of Nosfa treated Shaul with distrust and it made it difficult for the princess to convince the men that she could be trusted. Shaul had considered asking Misna to provide Kia with a different bodyguard whilst she was in the camp of Nosfa, but Kia had insisted that Shaul remain with her.

It took a few weeks, but the men of Nosfa seemed to forgive Shaul for spying as he helped them to rebuild and survive the bitter cold of the everlasting Wentrus that the blood moon had brought to Celadmore.

CHAPTER 6

"You are sure they can't be trusted?" Shamgar asked in a low voice. Cassandra and the general were sitting in his quarters. Dragonious was asleep at the back of the tent and so the two spoke in conspiratol tones to keep from waking the boy as much as to not be overheard.

"I'm sure," Cassandra replied, crossing her arms and leaning back in the canvas chair that she was sitting in. Shamgar was pacing the tent in thought.

"What do you think they want?" Shamgar pursed his lips as he spoke.

"I don't know, but Misna is concerned with their behaviour as well," Cassandra shrugged.

"Misna spends her life concerned with the behaviour of all living things," Shamgar replied and shook his head, "Are they more of a threat than the other forces we are currently contending with?"

"Who can say, until we know more about what is going on inside Delma and why Baruch ordered Kelmar to capture the princess', it's impossible to say," Cassandra tapped her fingers on her chin.

"What have Kania and Nodarto said on the subject?" Shamgar sat down opposite the Guardian of the Wilds.

"Nothing you would find interesting. There are a few things I am certain of, though," Cassandra said, her lips pursed in thought.

"And they are?" Shamgar asked expectantly.

"That the war against Delma was launched because Mercia wants control over the portal under Delma as well as the one that sits under Grashindorph," Cassandra said flatly.

"There's a portal under Grashindorph?" Shamgar couldn't hide his surprise.

"Yes, but it's dormant right now. When Grashindorph was first built, they found a way to neutralise the portal. It is only a temporary state, but it can't be used at the moment," Cassandra explained.

"And the one under Delma can?" Shamgar frowned.

"Yes, though I have never heard of anyone wanting to use the portals to travel, I think Mercia means to use it as a power source," the Guardian of the Wilds mused.

"You still think Mercia is behind all this?" a new voice entered the conversation.

"Abbott," Shamgar greeted the newcomer with surprise in his voice.

"One day, you will learn to travel like everyone else," Cassandra said dryly. The holy man had appeared out of nowhere to join them in the tent.

"One day, you will learn that a degree of subtlety can be extremely useful and far from counterproductive," the Abbott replied, and Cassandra merely shrugged in response.

"You don't think it's Mercia who needs the portal?" Shamgar asked.

"Why would he? He has no magic of his own; nothing to augment," the Abbott shrugged.

"Then you think it is, Neesa?" Cassandra asked, leaning forward.

"She is the only one that makes sense. She needs the power of the portal to maintain her blood moon," the Abbott replied.

"Her blood moon?" Shamgar spluttered.

"Yes, my spies tell me that Neesa is moving against the small fortress General Samara has constructed near Roenca. Nasus and Haras are there as well as Yoav, the Eight and Kasnata's newborns," the Abbott replied gravely.

"She's after the children?" Shamgar growled.

"She needs the blood of the goddess as a sacrifice. She already has Leinad, but with Kia and Kasna escaping, she needs replacements," Cassandra said, slamming her fist on the table.

"Then why go after Mia?" Shamgar frowned.

"Placating the king. As long as he has an heir, he won't care about what happens to his other children," the Abbott was still stood where he had appeared.

"Then why was Baruch after the princesses? It can't be for the same reason," Shamgar rubbed his forehead in frustration.

"There is power in their blood, no matter what end it is to be used for. He seems to be concerned with securing the safety of his people and there are many forms of magic that require sacrifice," the Abbott reasoned.

"Dead magics," Shamgar said dismissively.

"Dead magic is only dead whilst there are those that don't practise it, but there are also many variations of blood magic that use sacrifices. The more potent the magic, the more blood that is required, for truly powerful spells, sacrifices are necessary if the caster doesn't want to die," the Abbott elucidated.

"Too many people with their own agendas," Cassandra moaned and looked at the Abbott. "Why did you come back? I thought you were needed at the Spire?"

"I was, but it seems that it was only whilst Kasna and Kelmar were there," the Abbott beamed.

"Kasna and Kelmar came to the Spire? Why didn't you bring them back here?" Shamgar demanded, his raised voice caused Dragonious to stir in his sleep.

"Because they both have a part to play in Delma," the Abbott said in an intentionally vague manner.

"You are as bad as your mother," Cassandra snapped with frustration.

"And you are far too impatient for your own good. Whilst Kasna is with Kelmar, she is not in any danger," the Abbott assured the Guardian of the Wilds and the General of the Order of the Bear.

"You are certain?" Shamgar asked with a raised eyebrow.

"The Spire tested them both. I am certain," the Abbott smiled.

After the fourth time Regus lapsed into unconsciousness, Mathias was convinced that there was nothing more that the lieutenant could tell them. As Rathe had instructed, Regus' hands were broken, and his tongue was cut out.

Rather than leaving him to be discovered at Madame Ella's house, Rathe and Asahel removed him and took his unconscious, bloodied and beaten form to an alleyway on the other side of the city.

"You have been busy."

Rathe spun round, his sword halfway free of his scabbard, but Asahel placed his hand on the ex-general's shoulder to check any attack.

"Consorting with exiles, Jephthah? What would Lady Hermia think?" Asahel grinned.

"You know him?" Rathe asked, releasing his blade.

"General Rathe Bird, may I present Jephthah, Shield of Lady Hermia Nosfa," Asahel said.

"Now is hardly the time for introductions and these streets are far from

safe," Layla said as she dropped down from the rooftops.

"Layla!" Asahel beamed at the woman and found her hand slapping the back of his head.

"Do you have somewhere safe where we can talk?" Jephthah asked.

"Of course!" Asahel beckoned for his former comrades to follow him. Rathe scouted ahead to make sure their path was clear. When they returned to the church tower, Helez and Mathias were waiting for them. Helez greeted Layla and Jephthah with the same mixture of surprise and joy that Asahel had.

"Did you have any trouble with the girl?" Rathe asked as the six sat down to talk.

"Ella is keeping her locked up until she has calmed down and will listen to reason," Helez explained. Mathias shook his head and looked at the ground. "Mathias thinks we should have made sure she couldn't talk either."

"He's probably right," Layla said with contempt for the former shield. "You are both far too soft when it comes to the danger that women present."

"For the moment, we are safe. If Ella thinks that the girl will talk, then we can take further measures, until then, there is the wedding," Rathe spoke up to keep an argument from breaking out.

"What did Regus tell you that was useful?" Jephthah asked.

"We know where men are to be positioned on the day, that Neesa is absent from the city and that they are struggling to find anyone willing to conduct the ceremony," Mathias said thoughtfully.

"Could any of us pose as the officiator?" Helez asked.

"If Mathias hadn't been held prisoner by the king, I would suggest that he could take the position, but as it is, only Rathe knows enough about the customs of a royal wedding, and he is not an option either," Layla said, *dismissing the idea.*

"That's true, but the priestess or priest of the church may well perform the ceremony if we ask them," Asahel suggested.

"That is worth considering. The wedding isn't legal under the law of Grashindorph, the king has a wife and the law only allows for one at a time. If they know the wedding would be interrupted before it could be completed, they may be willing to play along," Rathe replied.

"So you plan to stop the wedding and rescue Mia?" Layla asked.

"She's too well guarded the rest of the time and kept in the palace outside the city. Her wedding day is the best opportunity to reach her and disappear amidst the confusion," Mathias explained.

"Then we offer our help, on behalf of Lord Haston Bird," Jephthah grinned. Helez and Asahel had told Rathe that his father was alive, and the lordling had wept with relief, but hearing his father's name brought the former general close to tears.

"However, as we rescue Mia, we must also rescue Leinad from his father," Layla interjected.

"That is your one condition?" Mathias asked, sounding sceptical.

"Yes, that is our one and only condition," Layla confirmed. "Though I would like to talk to Helez and Asahel in private for a moment." Layla stood and climbed the ladder that led to the bell and the ledge that Asahel liked to sit on and observe the city. The two exiles followed the Shadow.

"A merry band you've formed," Layla said wryly.

"We did what was necessary to survive," Helez shrugged.

"You did more than that. You rescued two men from the king's prison and have managed to elude the soldiers searching for them. You've come a long

way since being exiled," Layla flashed a rare smile at the two men.

"I never thought I'd live to see the day when Layla willingly praised us," Asahel said dryly.

"I didn't bring you up here to praise you. Where is Joab?" she asked, her face returning to its usual sullen expression.

"He's dead. The Baron of Fintry killed him whilst he protected Mia," Helez said sadly.

"I see. Mathias told you this?" Layla asked.

"Yes," Asahel replied.

"I see. Does Mathias remember you?" Layla frowned.

"No, he doesn't remember meeting either of us before," Helez confirmed in a soft voice.

"Have you told him?" Layla asked, looking between the two men.

"No," Asahel said, folding his arms.

"Good. There's no need to tell him now," Layla pursed her lips as she thought.

"You think him knowing is a bad idea?" Helez asked.

"I think it will serve as a distraction. He was raised in Roenca, not among our people for good reason, but trying to explain those reasons now is an unnecessary distraction. There are two children that need rescuing, and they are our priority."

Each time Neesa was attacked, she easily repelled each one before any of the defenders got close enough to harm her, but she couldn't advance. Samara had organised her warriors to attack in rolling waves that were punctuated by the Eight, the general, and Yoav, launching their own attacks.

Neesa was kept in the gateway, but Samara knew this was not a battle strategy that would result in victory. It was a delaying tactic at best, and an obvious one at that.

Yoav seemed to be enjoying goading Neesa, so each time he was flung across the compound with more force. It was clear that despite Neesa's boasting, she was getting tired. No matter how much power she now had at her command, it was limited by her body.

The angrier Yoav made Neesa, the more power she used and the more she drained her body. As the night turned to morning, Neesa's powers waned, and the witch was forced to retreat, however, the defenders were in no condition to pursue her.

"Repair the gate," Samara ordered, when the general was sure that Neesa had retreated for the moment. The Eight took up defensive positions on the wall so that Samara's warriors could all work on replacing the gate Neesa had destroyed. Some of her warriors grumbled at the futility of such work, but none of them dared to disobey the general.

Neesa and Haras were making preparations in the small hut that Samara had been using to sleep in. Gildow and Deshanna were sleeping soundly on the bed, the two babies blissfully unaware of the danger that stalked them.

"How much longer do you need?" Samara asked as she and Yoav entered the building.

"Two days," Nasus replied firmly.

"Two days?" Samara demanded, her exasperation clear in her voice.

"Yes," Haras snapped.

"*What is it you are preparing?*" Yoav asked as he checked on the children.

"*A barrier of sorts. It will form a cage around Neesa. She won't be able to attack, she'll simply be suspended in the barrier,*" Nasus explained.

"*But you won't be able to attack her either. You'll be able to flee if you want or come up with a plan to stop her based on what you learn from fighting her over the next two days,*" Haras didn't sound convinced that either option would work in their favour.

"*How long will the barrier last?*" Samara asked as she checked her blade for damage and removed her armour to check it.

"*As long as out combined powers can hold her. Without knowing the limit of her power and how it compares to ours, we have no way of knowing,*" Nasus said sadly.

"*Send Warner to Roenca. The people there will be able to send riders to find reinforcements. I doubt Kasnata can march her army to you, but the Gibborim and the Roencian spies in Nosfa may be able to help,*" Samara suggested to Yoav. Wolfblood grinned at the general.

"*Sprite, you're not supposed to know about either the Gibborim or the Roencian spies in Nosfa,*" he said with a sly tone, Samara flashed Yoav a knowing smile. "*I'll send the boy. He can rest in Roenca for the night before returning. I'm not sure he'll be able to survive a second onslaught without taking some time to recover.*"

The injuries Mia had sustained at the hands of the king and the

lieutenant had healed quickly. The bruises no longer showed on the surface of her skin and the bones that had been broken had begun to knit themselves back together.

However, her spirit hadn't recovered. The Lady of Afdanic was a hollow shell of the woman she had once been. The loss of her father, and her mother at a young age, had been more than enough grief for one as young as she was to bear. But Mia had suffered more.

The loss of the man she loved, Joab, murdered before her eyes as he tried to save her from capture. Her brother taken prisoner and sentenced to death as well as the abuse she had received at the hands of Regus and being forced to marry the king, had left the young woman completely devoid of hope.

She spent her days crying bitterly and begging Joab to come back from wherever he had gone, to save her from the terrible fate that awaited her at the hands of the king. She raged at Arala for allowing Joab to be taken from her, for allowing the king and the vile men that served him to exist, that her father and brother were taken from her when they were both good men.

She begged for an end to her suffering, but each morning, the Lady Mia awoke to find that nothing had changed, and her depression deepened.

Each night, the servant assigned to bring her food also brought a sleeping draft to help the lady sleep, but she never drank it. Instead, Mia poured the draft into a vase in the corner of the room, until it was almost overflowing.

The draft was not particularly strong, but in the quantity that Mia had collected, it would bring an end to her suffering. She didn't imagine that it would be quick or a pleasant way to die, but it was far better than the slow, drawn-out death she would die at the hands of the king.

She waited until the morning of her wedding, after the maids had *arranged her hair and sewn her into the ridiculous gown that she had been ordered to wear, before she drank the draft. It would take several hours to kill her, but for the first time since Joab had died, Mia felt at peace.*

The palace in the city of Grashindorph was the chosen venue for the wedding of Mercia to Mia. The Hall of Kings lay at the centre of the palace. It was the throne room and meeting room of the kings that had ruled Grashindorph since it had been built. It was a room that was steeped in history and the room where the ceremony would be conducted.

The hall had been cleared of weeds and the marble façade had been patched so that looked as though the room had not been left abandoned for so long. The faces of the kings of Grashindorph from centuries past stared down at those who had assembled for Mercia's wedding.

The cold stone eyes judged those that stood and talked in hushed voices. Some stared back at the statues and shuddered, though all avoided looking at the statue of King Rosla Nosfa.

Those of his court knew that Mercia's father would never have approved of his son's actions, and though he was only made of stone, none in the room could face the disappointment that they would read etched into his lined marble face.

Guards were posted around the hall so that every door and window was heavily manned. The priest from the church of Arala stood on the top of a dais that had been erected at the far end of the room. No one had told the king that one of priests of his wife's religion would be performing the ceremony, and the

Baron of Fintry had made sure that those who knew had been threatened to keep their mouths firmly shut.

The Baron was to escort the lady down the aisle as her father was not there to do it. The king had yet to enter the hall, but Prince Leinad was sat to the left of the priest, two guards stood beside him.

The boy was dressed in the clothes of his mother's people and had an expression that showed he was far from happy about the wedding. Leinad knew that he would be punished for trying to embarrass his father and reminding everyone in attendance that his mother was still the queen of Grashindorph.

Asahel and Helez had managed to slip into the hall with the rest of the crowd and were stood a few feet away from the young prince. Asahel had thrown Helez a smile and nodded to Leinad when he had seen what the prince was wearing.

"Braver than all the people of Grashindorph, and he's not even old enough to shave," Helez whispered.

"Let's hope he lives long enough to learn," Asahel replied in equally hushed tones.

Mathias had found an opening in the roof of one of the rooms adjoining the hall and crept silently through the rafters so that he and Layla could look down on all the guests that were in attendance.

Trumpets sounded from the corridor outside the Hall of Kings and announced the arrival of the king. Mercia entered wearing the clothes he had worn to marry Kasnata. Gold glittered in the crown he wore, in the medals that were pinned to his chest, on the rings that he wore and even in the hilt of his sword and its scabbard. His cloak was blood red and trimmed with white fur. Under the cloak he wore robes of royal blue that hung loosely from his frame.

As he walked to the dais at the head of the hall, he looked around at all those who were attending. As he passed, he made a mental note of those of his court that were absent. His eyes fell on his young son and a snarl curled at the corner of his mouth.

He felt an overwhelming urge to draw his sword and run it through the boy for his impudence, but he still needed the child as an heir and as a bargaining counter against his barbarian wife and her army.

Silence fell over the hall as the trumpets sounded a second time. Outside in the hall, Mia could feel the effects of the sleeping draft beginning to take hold of her body.

"Stand up straight," the Baron of Fintry hissed as he tried to drag Mia to the door. The Lady of Afdanic could feel her muscles growing heavy and their sluggish response made it difficult to move or even stand.

The doors to the Hall of Kings opened and the Baron tried to walk her down the aisle.

"That's not good," Helez hissed as he watched Mia struggle to stay on her feet.

The Baron guided Mia to the dais and handed her over to the king.

"May all those here bear witness to the joy that flows between those who are in love," the priest began.

"May all those here bear witness to the failing rule of a king beset by madness," Rathe's voice rang out. The assembled guests and the king all turned to see the former general stood in the doorway to the hall, his sword was drawn and was wet with blood. Jephthah stood beside him, the bodies of three soldiers piled on his back and two more being dragged in his left hand.

The two men walked slowly down the aisle. Most of the guards were frozen in fear at the sight of the man mountain and the general that was supposed to be in prison. Those that chose to try and attack the two men fell where they stood, the guards of the palace could brawl in taverns, but they were not warriors, nor had any of them ever seen a real battlefield.

"A wedding present, your majesty," Jephthah announced as he dumped the bodies of the men at the feet of the king. "A man so sluiced in the blood of innocents deserves nothing more than corpses."

"How dare you," Mercia spluttered as his eyes widened with rage.

"Your reign is a disgrace to your father's name," Rathe said loudly. "A black mark on the history of this once proud and great nation. I will not see you disgrace my sister or my family." the former general raised his sword to the king.

"Kill them!" Mercia cried as he launched himself at Rathe. He dodged the king's frenzied attacks. Jephthah roared as the guards rushed to fight him. The man mountain knocked them easily aside.

The Baron of Fintry skirted round the edge of the fighting, watching for an opening left by either man, waiting for an opportunity to strike.

"The shadows are my domain, Fintry, you have no place in them," Layla hissed as she appeared behind the baron, distracting him from what was going on around him. The wedding guests panicked as the fighting broke out. They screamed and rushed, trying to remove themselves from the danger that Rathe and Jephthah presented.

Mia watched with horror filling her chest as her brother fought the king. She could feel pain slowly starting to spread through her limbs, the effort of trying to stand becoming increasingly unbearable.

Mathias slipped through the crowd to Mia's side and carried her from the hall in the confusion.

"Prince Leinad, come with us," Helez breathed quietly as he and Asahel took advantage of Jephthah distracting the guards.

"Who are you?" Leinad demanded.

"Friends of your grandmother," Asahel replied as he picked up the prince and retreated, Helez preventing any of the guards not fighting Jephthah from following.

"You will die here, you foolish boy, your house will end. Your children will not live to see the end of the blood moon; your whore will bleed to death on the icy plains of Delma. Your sister will be my new queen and there is nothing you can do that will change these fates, just as there was nothing you could do to save your father," Mercia snarled as he launched a wave of unending blows against Rathe.

"My father is not dead. Kasnata will destroy whatever machinations you send against her; Kia is safe in her camp and Kasna is in the city of Delma. Your daughters are far beyond your reach, as are my own children, my sister and your son," Rathe spat as he parried each strike.

Mercia stepped back from Rathe and looked around the hall, the guests had fled, and Mia and Leinad were nowhere to be seen.

"FINTRY!" the king bellowed. The baron looked over at the king, allowing Layla to slice her blade across his left eye and down the length of his cheek.

"For Joab," Layla growled. The Shadow looked over at Rathe, who nodded and grabbed Jephthah's shoulder.

"Stop them!" the king ordered as the three ran from the hall. Rathe had spent years poring over the plans for the palace of Grashindorph as he listened to

his father tell stories of the adventures that he had in his youth. The lordling knew where to go to enter the sewers and leave no trace of their presence.

He had shown his five companions the way from the hall to safety, just in case he fell to the king's blade. Jephthah, Layla and Rathe ran for the entrance to the sewers that Helez, Asahel and Mathias had already used. The sound of the king's voice followed them down the corridors.

"Come on, something's wrong with Mia," Helez urged them as they rounded the final corner to where they could slip through the opening in the floor that had been made by removing one of the stones.

"Go," Layla commanded. "I'll put the stone back and find you down there. There are plenty of entrances outside the palace I can use."

Jephthah, Rathe and Helez dropped through the floor and Layla heaved the stone back into place before fleeing from the palace.

"What's wrong?" Rathe demanded as he knelt beside his sister.

"She's been poisoned," Asahel shook his head as he held a lit torch over the figure of Mia.

"Poisoned? Who would poison her?" Rathe asked angrily.

"She did it to herself," Mathias said quietly. He was clutching Mia's hand and stroking her hair. "She didn't know we were coming. She tried to escape a different way."

Jephthah pushed the men aside and picked Mia up with one arm.

"What are you doing?" Rathe half-shouted.

"Keep your voice down, they'll hear you up there. We take her to Lady Hermia. She'll know what to do," Jephthah said firmly as he strode through the sewer without the help of any light.

"Excuse me, general, but what is going on?" Leinad asked, pulling at

Rathe's clothing.

Jephthah moved quickly through the tunnels. He didn't need light to navigate underground. He had spent most of his life living under the city of Grashindorph and could rely on his nose and his ears to tell him which direction to go.

By the time he reached Hermia and Haston's hiding spot, Mia's skin was deathly white, and her breathing had all but stopped.

"Mia!" Haston cried as his daughter was laid on the cold stone of the tunnel. Mia's eyes widened and filled with tears as her father knelt beside her. and Jephthah found light so that Hermia could examine the Lady of Afdanic.

"What happened to her?" Hermia asked as she tried to keep Haston out of her light.

"She poisoned herself," Mathias panted as the rest of the party caught up with Jephthah.

"I see. Where is Layla?" she asked.

"Coming via a different route, she made sure we weren't followed," Helez replied.

"I see," Hermia said looking between Asahel and Helez with a quizzical expression. "I need water, plenty of clean water and as many dried biscuits as you can find in our old stores."

Helez, Jephthah and Asahel moved quickly to find what Hermia had asked for. Mathias knelt beside Mia.

"I'll help too!" Leinad shouted as he chased after the three men.

"My grandson is safe from his father at last," Hermia sighed with relief, almost forgetting the dying girl in front of her.

"You're going to flush the poison out of her body?" Mathias asked,

focusing Hermia's attention back on Mia.

"I am going to force her to drink and then purge as much of it from her system as I can before I flush the rest of it from her body. When I am done, she will need to eat something that is easy to digest and that will soak up any of the poison still left there," Hermia confirmed.

"Will it be enough?" Mathias asked.

"I don't know." Hermia said quietly.

"Father, I'm sorry, I should have rescued her sooner," Rathe said as he stood behind his father. Haston had been so consumed with worry for his daughter, he hadn't realised his son had been reunited with him.

"Rathe?" he asked as he stood and turned to look at the man his son had become. "You rescued your sister? You dared to anger the king?" Haston gasped as he threw his arms around his son and hugged him tightly.

"Rescuing Mia is the least of my crimes as far as the king is concerned," Rathe smiled as he hugged his father just as tightly.

"Haston, take your son and share tales of your life in the Gibborim with him, when I have done all I can for Mia, I will send for you both. Then I would be interested to hear what adventures you have had, General Bird, that have upset the king and how it is that you, an assassin from Roenca and two exiles from the Gibborim were thrown together in a city as desperate as Grashindorph," Hermia said without taking her eyes off Mia.

Chapter 7

The Gauntlet was one of the most mysterious places on all of Celadmore. The labyrinth of rocks had led to formation of many myths and legends that had slowly grown over time.

There were tales of ghosts, ghouls and other mystical beings inhabiting the area. This meant most people avoided the Gauntlet. Those that weren't afraid of the supernatural worried they would become lost in the labyrinth and never be heard from again.

For this reason, the leaders of the Free Cities chose to meet there. In a realm beset by war, it was the one place that was free of fighting, and one pace where only those invited would be able to find the meeting.

The Free Cities of Fotheringhay, Uffington, Tissington, Capel Curig, Gump, Tilford, Roenca, Thaxted, SwafthamPrior, Appledore, Honeydon, Schendo, Wellow, Chesil, Repton and Eyam met when one of the leaders called for a meeting. Aftport had once attended, but Nosfa's army had conquered the city. A governor had been appointed to oversee the daily running of the city and the former leaders had been executed.

When Aftport had been attacked and conquered, a meeting had been held to forge new alliances. A treaty had been created that bound each of the Free Cities to the preservation of the others. If a city fell, then the other cities would liberate it and offer whatever aid they could to the refugees from the city.

Kania and Nodarto had called for that meeting, as they had for the one the leaders now gathered. In the last ten years, all the leaders had met three times. Each time it had been meetings that Kania and Nodarto had requested.

Other leaders could request meetings, however only a handful of leaders ever attended the smaller and less significant moots.

The camp for the meeting was set in a small canyon at the heart of the Gauntlet. A brook ran through the middle of it and a small amount of wildlife inhabited the area, though most of those attending brought their own food with them, the fresh water was a blessing.

The date of the meeting had been set to coincide with the Wentrus Festival of the Living, but most of the leaders had arrived in the closing days of Antompne. Kania and Nodarto were the first to arrive and begin setting the camp that would host the meeting.

The leaders of Eyam and Chesil arrived two days later and the leaders of Repton, Honeydon, Appledore and Schendo a few days after that. The remaining leaders trickled into the growing camp in the ten days before the Wentrus Festival of the Living. Each leader brought a small entourage of delegates with them. Tissington brought the most, a party of forty five, whereas Kania and Nodarto came alone.

The camp was more like a shanty town than a moot by the time all the attendees had finished erecting their tents Some of the leaders of the Free Cities brought merchants with them, the moot providing an opportunity to trade with the other cities before the meeting began.

At sunrise on 4th Wentrus, Kania rose and stepped out into the centre of the makeshift town. She banged a small gong three times and waited.

The leaders of the Free Cities emerged from their tents and made their way over to where Kania stood. Nobody spoke. Instead they followed the leader of Tulna to a large, round canvas structure that stood a short way off from the rest of the camp.

The outside was adorned with the flags of each of the Free Cities. Inside, there were chairs and large benches that were set a few feet away from the canvas walls. Behind the chairs and benches there were cushions that the merchants and entourage could sit on and watch the meeting, though they were forbidden from speaking.

Nodarto was the last of the leaders to enter the tent. He walked to the centre of the ring of chairs and cleared his throat.

"Friends, may the grace of the Goddess always shine and the light of the Seven Stars dim," he smiled at those gathered.

"For life and the glory of Arala," the response rippled around the tent.

"Thank you for coming, we are here to discuss the siege of Delma and the blood moon. The war that rages between the nine kingdoms cannot continue. We have asked you to meet to discuss sending out combined forces to aid the forces of Kasnata. We shall talk for five days and vote on the sixth day," Nodarto finished speaking and walked to sit beside his wife.

"Kasnata is a tool of Nosfa, sending her our forces is the same as turning over control of our cities to the king," the leader of Uffington spoke first.

"Kasnata is controlled because Mercia holds her children hostage, she is not his ally," Akiva of Roenca replied. "She has done more to hamper his efforts than any here and risked her children to do so. Some of us here have already committed resources to help General Samara build Kasnata's new outposts for the Order. Why should our support of the Order fall short of fighting alongside them?"

"Why should the burden of helping the Order fall to the free people?" the leader from Swaftham Prior asked.

"If our people wish to remain free, then surely, we should be sending out support to those who are fighting to bring an end to tyranny, not sitting back *and declaring it is not our responsibility. What happens if the Order falls? Who will the nine kingdoms turn to conquer next?" Wellow's leader replied.*

"We need our own forces to protect against bandits and raiders. Look at what happened to the Free City of Ashpa, we do not want our people to share the same fate," the leader of Tilford shot back.

"There were eight children that escaped from Ashpa, Kasnata took them in, and they have pledged themselves to her service. Why should we not do the same?" asked the leader of Capel Curig.

"What about the people of the desert and the wilds? Why are they not here too? Surely their horsemen would be of more value than the handful of warriors that each of our cities has," the leader of Honeydon enquired.

"The people of the desert and wilds have agreed that whatever decision we come to, they will do as we do," Kania replied.

"Where are Cassandra and the Abbott?" the leader of Repton asked with a raised eyebrow.

"They are with Kasnata; they have chosen to her aid her, and her children, without the support of Tulna, the other Free Cities, or the people of the deserts and wilds," Nodarto said from behind steepled fingertips. He could feel his head beginning to throb already. Nodarto glanced over at Kania. She was sat listening to each of the leaders as they voiced their opinions. She said nothing else for two days. The conversations and arguments had become circular and Nodarto had to threaten to expel more than one party for threatening behaviour.

When Kania was sure there was nothing new that could be added to the conversation, she silently stood and left the tent. The other delegates were shocked into silence and looked helplessly at each other, searching for an explanation for her behaviour.

She appeared a few moments later with a young boy by her side.

"Leaders of the Free Cities, may I present Warner of Ashpa. He was sent to the village of Roenca with a request for aid, but as Akiva had left for this moot, he was forced to ride through the Gauntlet to search for us. He brings a message you should all hear," Kania said as she indicated that Warner should speak.

"I bring the compliments of Lady Nasus and Lady Haras, General Yoav, General Samara, the Eight of the Order, formerly of Ashpa, and of Queen Kasnata. Great leaders, our enemy has revealed herself. The witch, Neesa, the Last Heir of Valia, assassin for the king of Nosfa and mistress to the king – she is the source of his madness and the source of the blood moon," Warner said formerly. He was shaking, nervous at having to address so many strangers at once.

"What happened?" the leader of Appledore asked, jumping to her feet.

"Neesa attacked the fortress of Kasnata, which has been constructed close to Roenca. The child of General Rathe and Queen Kasnata had been brought to the fortress to keep them safe from attempts on their lives by King Mercia's forces. Neesa came to kill them. She tore the gates off the fortress with ease, she threw General Yoav to the ground as if he were a rag doll and not one of the warriors in the fortress could injure her. They sent me to find help," Warner explained.

"Riders from Roenca have already been dispatched to the city of Grashindorph to reach our allies and spies within the city walls," Kania confirmed and tried to soothe the panic that was beginning to rise around the room.

"If Neesa is the one behind the madness, then the war of the nine kingdoms is her work. We must stop her," the leader of Thaxted said in an agitated manner.

"Peace," Kania said holding up her hand.

"Rathe Bird is in Grashindorph along with members of the Gibborim. They will be more than equal to dealing with Neesa. The blood moon is not the only danger we face," Nodarto said firmly.

"What other danger is there?" the leader of Fotheringhay asked.

"The rise of the waning Seven Stars," Akiva said bluntly. The other leaders stared at the leader of Roenca.

"Akiva, the floor is yours; tell us what your spies have discovered about the Seven Stars," Kania said as she steered Warner to some cushions and Akiva stepped forward to speak.

Kelmar and Kasna slipped silently through the palace of Delma. Kelmar had spent most of his life in the palace, he knew the location of each of the guards, where the secret passages were and hot to remain hidden if one of the guards left his post.

Kelmar had paid one of the guards to inform him when the king and queen were going down into the catacombs.

The door to the catacombs had always been locked for as long as Kelmar could remember. As a boy, he had tried to break through the door on several occasions, but the giant hunk of wood and metal had refused to yield to him.

Kelmar took hold of the handle and pulled the door, gently at first, and then with more force. Despite being used by the king and queen, it was very stiff – the hinges in desperate need of oil. Eventually the duke had pulled the door wide enough for the two to squeeze through.

On the other side of the door, there was a staircase that led down into the catacombs. Torches hung on the walls, all of which were lit. Kasna's chest tightened with an overwhelming feeling of dread. Kelmar was trying to express the boyish excitement he felt at finally being able to explore the catacombs he had been kept out of for so long.

The two descended into the bowels of the palace. There were no guards set in the winding corridors that lay below the palace, so their progress was unimpeded. Kelmar was glad of the lack of guards. The corridors were narrow and had smooth walls with no alcoves to hide in, should the two be discovered.

The corridors were a maze of crisscrossing chaos, somewhere that anyone unfamiliar with their layout could quickly become lost. Kasna bit her fingertip so that a short spring of crimson seeped from it. She used the blood to mark the wall so that they could easily track where they had been and created markers they could easily follow out again.

After what seemed like hours, Kelmar and Kasna could hear low murmuring coming from up ahead. They advanced more slowly, keeping as close to the walls as they could.

The corridor opened up into a large round room that was sunk into the ground. There was a gantry that ran around the top of the room that several corridors opened onto. The gantry was carved out of stone, as where the steps that led to the floor of the room below. The steps ran in a sweeping curve twice around the whole of the room before they reached the ground.

The murmuring was coming from the room below. Kelmar and Kasna both dropped to their stomachs and crawled forward on their elbows. They stopped just short of the edge of the gantry and looked down.

Below there was a ring of people stood wearing purple wraps around their waist, but nothing else. The wraps hung at an angle, sweeping up from the knee to halfway up the opposite thigh. The king was among their number, his regal clothes lay piled to one side of the hall.

In the centre of the circle was a stone altar that the queen was stood upon. Her face was streaked with oils and blood. She wore the same wrap, but her body was covered with symbols that have been painted on with fingers and blood. Behind the queen the air shimmered and distorted, colours sparked from within it like small lightning bolts.

The group were chanting in low voices and the queen was stood silently, waiting for something. Kelmar grabbed Kasna by the arm and pulled her back to the safety of the corridor. He motioned that they should leave.

The two made their way back through the maze of corridors, neither spoke until they were within the confines of Kelmar's rooms.

"Who were all those people?" *Kasna asked.*

"Nobles and public figures. They all have some standing in the nation. What on earth were they doing?" *Kelmar said, shaking his head.*

"It sounded like they were worshipping something," *Kasna replied, she was shaking as she sat down on one of the sofas and pulled a cushion into her arms.*

"Worshipping what?" *Kelmar frowned and paced around the room.*

"I don't know, but it felt bad," *Kasna screwed up her face and shuddered.*

"Felt bad?" *Kelmar stopped pacing and sat beside Kasna.*

"I don't know how to explain it. The chanting, the atmosphere, it made me feel sick, like it wasn't natural," *Kasna convulsed at the thought.*

"There was an atmosphere?" *Kelmar asked with a raised eyebrow.*

"Yes, you didn't feel it? It was like my mind was being crushed beneath the weight of something evil, tearing at my skin, like it was trying to get into my body," *Kasna explained.*

"That makes sense," *Kelmar said slowly.*

"It does?" *Kasna didn't sound at all convinced.*

"Yes, it sounds like we might have found the source of the madness in Delma," *said Kelmar as he lapsed into silent thought.*

With Kelmar returning to Delma without being seen by any of Kasnata's forces, the queen and Misna were concerned about what might be lurking to the north of the city. A scouting party was organised, Princess Kia was elected to lead the party to gain more experience in the field.

Shaul had volunteered to accompany her along with twelve other veteran scouts. Lavinia and Lacenta had also requested to join the scouting party, Muse electing to remain behind in Kasnata's camp.

The party had set out before dawn and were due to return in ten days with a report of any signs of Delmarian activity. The fresh snow and frozen ground made progress slow for the first few days.

Shaul and two of the scouts went ahead each night to find somewhere that was suitable to camp and begin preparing the area. During Shaul's absence, Lavinia took the opportunity to talk to Kia.

On the third day, the party reached the low hills that led to the small mountains and the mines that provided Delma with much of its wealth. The party had found signs of patrols and carts travelling towards Delma, the snow covered any tracks almost as soon as they were made. However, where patrols and carts had driven through the snow and the freeze had come before fresh snowfall, there were tracks that could be seen when the snow was dusted away. Broken branches, animal signs and snagged hair and furs on bushes told the scouts where to look for the tracks.

The tracks led through the hills to a farm. From the outside it seemed to be abandoned, but Kia ordered caution and only after two of the scouts had confirmed that no-one was there and hadn't been for several days, did the party venture into the farmyard.

"We can sleep here tonight. The horses won't be able to travel on the mountain paths, if we put them in the stables and leave a few of the party here to guard them, they should be safe until we come back," *Shaul whispered to Kia. The princess nodded. The orders were passed and volunteers to remain behind were called for.*

To Shaul's surprise, Lavinia and Lacenta volunteered to stay behind with the horses. The next morning, the rest of the scouting party started to climb the mountain path. Kia and Shaul took the lead; Kia was searching the rock face for something, examining the mountain side carefully as she moved.

Shaul was focused on the path ahead and the weather, until they reached a plateau, there was nowhere to set camp if the weather turned against them. He didn't notice that Kia wasn't beside him anymore. When he turned back to look for her, he saw the princess was climbing the sheer rock face.

He watched as Kia hauled herself up with her arms, trying desperately to reach the next handhold. It was clear that no one had ever taught the princess how to climb. Shaul was transfixed by the sight. Her hands were being scratched and torn by the sharp rocks, but she tried to climb higher.

Once Shaul recovered from his initial wonderment of watching her climb, the spy began to question why she was climbing the rock face. He started back down the mountain path.

"General, what are you doing?" he called out. The other members of the scouting party had come into view further down the path. Some were pointing at the princess with mouths open. Others laughed at the sight.

"Climbing," she replied. Shaul chuckled to himself.

Kia grunted as she tried to lift herself up further. Her arms were aching, her fingers were beginning to cramp and her whole body felt exhausted. It's worth it, she thought, and momentarily lost her concentration. Her feet slipped out from underneath her so that she was dangling from the cliff face by her fingertips.

She tried desperately to find new footholds, but her feet simply slipped off the face of the mountain.

"Kia, hold on," Shaul yelled as he tried to negotiate his way quickly back along the treacherous ledge to where the princess was struggling to keep her grip. The rest of the scouting party was too far away and could only watch as the daughter of Kasnata turned her fingertips white as she desperately clung to the slippery rock.

Shaul moved as deftly as a mountain goat, he reached Kia's side and pulled the princess over to where the footing was better. Kia wrapped her arms around Shaul's neck and wept with relief. Shaul held onto the princess with one arm and the mountain with the other until the princess was ready to move *higher up, somewhere the two could sit and wait for the rest of the scouting party to join them.*

"Whatever possessed you to take that route?" *Shaul breathed once the two were safe on the road above.*

"Lavinia, she told me that there was something hidden within the rock that would help destroy the blood moon," *Kia rested her head on her knees as she caught her breath. Shaul frowned.*

"Did she say what it was?" *the Queterian asked.*

"No, just that I would know it when I saw it," *Kia replied.*

"I see," *Shaul pursed his lips.* "Wait here. If the guardians and the rest of the scouting party arrive before I get back. Stay here. No matter what any of them say, wait here for me," *Shaul said firmly, and Kia nodded in agreement. The spy climbed back down over the ledge to where Kia had been struggling.*

He looked at the rock as he moved down the mountain until something caught his eye. It wasn't far from where Kia had been struggling. It glinted in the sunlight like something forged from metal.

Shaul traversed his way across to it. What he found was a small alcove that contained a small metal box. He stuffed the box inside his armour and made his way back to Kia.

He said nothing about the box to the princess. Kia recovered quickly from her ordeal and the scouting party followed the tracks until they reached an abandoned cabin that sat on the mountain peak, looking down at the city of Donamecca below.

"They brought supplies from Donamecca and hid them here in the mountain," *Shaul shook his head and smiled.*

"They knew about the siege?" *Kia asked as she looked down at the peaceful city below.*

"They prepared for one. The path to this outpost has been cut by a landslide, there won't be any aid from Donamecca until this eternal Wentrus ends. The rocks and earth will be too difficult to lift until there is a thaw. Delma is cut off for now. We should go back and report," *Shaul said, leading the way back down the mountain.*

The more time Shamgar spent with Dragonious, the more that the Queterian was convinced that he was not safe as long as he remained in the camp of the Order. The way the guardians reacted to him was nothing compared to the way that the younger members of the Order treated him.

In the Order, warriors were sent to the battlefield from the age of seven. They were trained to fight almost as soon as they could stand. Though the seven-year-olds were not thrown into the heart of every battle, it was essential that the children of the Order understood what it was to fight in a battle. It was not romantic; it wasn't the way that the songs of bards told them it was. Battle was a brutal and bloody business. There was no room for heroics, there were those who fought beside you, there was following the orders of the generals and there was adapting to whatever situation you found yourself in.

The children of the Order were trained to fight, and they looked down on other children that weren't. The Eight had earned the respect of the children and had proven to be far superior in skill. Dragonious was not a warrior. He was clearly powerful, but Shamgar knew he was not a man to fight with a sword.

"Where are you from?" *Shamgar asked as he sat alone with the boy.*

"Nether Roth," *Dragonious had learned the language of the Order quickly, but his own form of speech caused the words to sound almost foreign. Shamgar had to listen carefully to even understand what the boy was saying.*

"I've never heard of it. How did you end up by yourself?"

"I was cast out. I was not what the masters wanted,"

"You were a slave?"

"No, not a slave. There is a master in Nether Roth, he has generals. If you are not the master of Nether Roth or a general, you must call them the masters. There was another boy. His name was Aksoth. The master chose him. I was supposed to die," *Dragonious explained.*

"You escaped?" *Shamgar asked.*

"I don't know what happened. I prayed I wouldn't die. Then I was on my own. I didn't understand where I was. Then I found you and the woman that speaks my language."

Shamgar lapsed into silence. He needed time to think about what to do with the boy.

"If the masters of Nether Roth want you dead, then we must find somewhere safe for you to hide. I don't know where Nether Roth is, but you are here and Cassandra speaks your language, so I imagine she has been to your land before. Don't worry though; I will do everything I can to keep you safe."

Avner hated seeing cities under siege. The desperation and malice that surfaced amongst the population was not something that was pleasant to witness.

Neither was what an invading army did to a city that they had laid siege to. He was raised to fight on the battlefield, against those that had chosen to raise weapons and fought with honour.

There was no honour in a siege ravaged city. As an emissary of peace, he was restricted to the palace and was only allowed to visit certain areas of the palace without permission from the king and queen.

Deena came to visit Avner every day and delivered the same message,

"Their royal majesties apologise, but they cannot grant you an audience today. They crave your indulgence."

Every day that Avner listened to this message, he became more frustrated with his daughter and son-in-law. Every day that she delivered the message, Deena became less hopeful that the siege would end with a peaceful agreement.

So Avner waited and looked out of the windows of the palace at the city below.

Chapter 8

There were not many commanders remaining amongst the men of Nosfa. One colonel, four majors, twelve captains and thirty lieutenants were all that remained of the officers. There were more sergeants and corporals, but they were busy seeing to those who served under them and making arrangements for some of the bodies of the wealthier soldiers to be taken back to Grashindorph.

The commanders of the men of Nosfa had little to do whilst the sergeants and corporals worked. They had spent hours discussing who was now in command of the army, what they were supposed to do in order to fulfil their oaths as soldiers and retreating from the siege altogether.

There were many amongst the Order who would have been glad to see the army of Nosfa departing from the battlefield, however Kasnata's generals felt the men of Nosfa still had a role to play in the war against Delma.

The commanders were summoned to a meeting with Misna, Amalia, Quisla, and Kia twelve days after Kelmar had attacked the camp.

The meeting was held in the newly erected tent at the centre of the camp of Nosfa. The four generals arrived on horseback, accompanied by the fanfare of an honour guard marching in full ceremonial armour.

The warriors of the Order marching into the heart of the camp of Nosfa caused rumours and gossip to be spread through the ranks like wildfire. The honour guard formed a perimeter around the tent and stood with their spears in hand and their swords sheathed at their side.

Misna led the four generals into the tent. The commanders were stood around a table, all muttering in low voices and looking sullen.

"Good morning," General Kia barked, causing some of the men to jump.

"Thank you all for being here. We appreciate you must have many pressing matters to deal with, but we have come on behalf of her royal majesty, Queen Kasnata Nosfa, Empress of the Order and Queen of Nosfa," Quisla said in a brisk tone. She marched around the table and sat in the chair at the head of it.

"Empress?" one of the captains asked.

"Empress," Quisla confirmed in a dangerous tone. She held the gaze the captain had fixed her with until the man backed down.

"What does she want?" the colonel asked, clearly unhappy with where Quisla had chosen to sit.

"I would show more respect if I were you," Amalia said in a low growl. The colonel ignored her.

"She sent you here. What does she want?" the colonel asked again.

"He really should have shown some respect," Misna sighed as, in three strides, Amalia crossed to the colonel, hit him in the stomach and then knocked him over with a second punch that broke his nose.

"You have shelter, food and water because her majesty commanded it. You are alive because her majesty dispatched troops to defend you. She is royalty by birth and by marriage. You will show her some respect," Amalia said flatly.

One of the majors helped the colonel to his feet and steered him towards a chair.

"Forgive the colonel, he hasn't slept well since General Bird was recalled to Grasbindorph," the major explained. "We are grateful for all her highness has done for the men of Nosfa and we are willing to listen to whatever message you bring from her."

Quisla glanced over at Misna, who gave her a slight nod.

"You are Major Fitzsimmons?" Quisla asked.

"I am," the major replied.

"Good, we are here because Queen Kasnata wishes to restore order to your ranks. She will address the men of Nosfa herself, but asked us to meet with you in private to discuss your own feelings on the matter first," Quisla said, resting her feet on the table.

"What matter is that?" one of the lieutenants asked.

"Her majesty will appoint a new commander to the army of Nosfa; he will be from among your people, and another to act as his second. The men of Nosfa will fight under the banner of the Order and bring an end to this war in the way that the Queen of Nosfa dictates," Kia explained.

Misna watched each of the commanders' faces as they reacted to Kia's words. She made a mental note of those that she would have to watch carefully.

"Of course, those of you who do not wish to serve in this army; you will be returned to Grashindorph with a letter for the king explaining what has happened here," Quisla said with a smug expression on her face. Any man that returned to Nosfa carrying such news would be executed. The commanders all knew this as well as the generals in Kasnata's army.

"You have three hours to decide. Whether you wish to serve or return to Grashindorph. Major Fitzsimmons, please write down the names of all the commanders, and their decisions, and bring it to her majesty once the three hours has passed. If you fail to deliver it, all of you will be sent to Grashindorph," Amalia said curtly. The four generals left the men to decide which path they wanted to take.

"Do you think any of them will be a problem?" Quisla asked Misna in a low voice as the women mounted their horses.

"A few, do you think we should have mentioned that the queen will

decide who goes and who remains, regardless of what they decide?" Misna asked with a broad grin.

All of the commanders chose to stay to serve Kasnata; however, those that Misna had suspected would be problematic were told that they were returning to Grashindorph with the men that refused Kasnata's offer of serving under her flag.

Only a handful of men wanted to return to their families, the rest chose to stay to see their fallen comrades avenged.

Major Fitzsimmons was appointed to the position of second-in-command and Tola was named as the commander. Order returned to the camp, training resumed, as well as patrols. Most of the men were pleased at Tola being placed in command. He had the reputation of a hero and was respected by the warriors of the Order as much as by the men of Nosfa.

Those that were unhappy with the appointment were being dispatched to Grashindorph. If they chose to return, they would be executed by the king, if they went anywhere else, they were no threat to Tola and his command.

Misna went to bed that night marvelling at how well Kasnata had done in removing those that opposed her from amongst the men of Nosfa and bringing the rest of the force under her command, all without spilling any blood.

Hermia spent all night with Mia; by the morning she was sure that the Lady of Afdanic was no longer in any danger. Mia slept for four days after she had been rescued from Mercia.

When she finally awoke, her father was sat by her bedside.

"Mia, oh my child, you're finally awake," he smiled at his daughter and gathered her into his arms.

"Father?" Mia asked groggily. "It can't be, you're dead."

"No, he's as alive as you or I," Rathe grinned from the doorway.

"Rathe? This isn't possible," Mia said clutching her head as her father let her go.

"It's alright, Mia," Mathias soothed. The assassin was sitting at the far end of the room, reading. Mia looked over at him and shook her head.

"I don't understand. I must be dreaming," she sighed.

"With all that sleeping draught you drank, you should be grateful you aren't resting eternally," Hermia said with a matter-of-fact tone as she pushed past Rathe to examine Mia.

"Queen Hermia?" Mia collapsed back on her pillow.

"Too many ghosts," Mathias chuckled to himself. Hermia threw him a reproachful look.

"What is the last thing you remember?" Hermia asked Mia as she fussed over her.

"Drinking the sleeping draught before going to the wedding," Mia said, screwing up her face.

"Well then, you will be pleased to know you didn't marry Mercia and you aren't dead," Hermia said abruptly.

"But all of you –" Mia began, but Mathias cut her off.

"Mia, if you were dead, who else would you expect to see?" he asked gently.

"Joab," she said quietly.

"He's not here. Your father wasn't killed; he was rescued by the Gibborim. Lady Hermia wasn't murdered; she escaped and started the resistance against her son. Your brother was rescued by two men called Helez and Asahel. They rescued me too. They helped us to rescue you and Prince Leinad," Mathias explained.

Mia looked at the assassin and started crying. Haston took his daughter in his arms and held her whilst she sobbed.

"Where are we?" she asked when she calmed down.

"Under the city of Grashindorph. We're safe down here for now. There are only a handful of us here not but in a few days' time, the rest of the Gibborim will have returned to the city. The king has finally gone too far, and it is time for us to act," Hermia said stoutly. Mia stifled a yawn.

"Rest, little sister," Rathe said as he walked over to her and kissed her on the forehead. "You don't need to worry about any of that. You're safe now and that is all that matters. Mathias will keep you safe." he smiled.

"What about you?" Mia asked as Rathe turned to leave.

"I am going back into the city with Helez and Asahel. We have people to protect on the surface, we'll be here for a few days yet, but once the rest of the Gibborim has arrived, we will be gone. With so many to fight for freedom, our swords are needed elsewhere," Rathe grinned at his sister.

"You're going back to Delma?" Haston frowned.

"Someone needs to tell Kasnata that Leinad is safe and that I am alive. I'm not sure she will believe it from anyone else," Rathe shrugged.

"Asahel and Helez are going with you?" Hermia asked.

"Yes, they were exiled and don't want to overstay their welcome. They will be assets in the war against Delma rather than wasted as mercenaries,"

Rathe replied.

"Thank you," Hermia sighed.

"I owe them a great debt, they saved my life, the least I can do is offer them both the chance of a new one," Rathe said and left Hermia and Haston to look after Mia. Mathias sat in the corner, reading his book, feeling a great sense of relief.

There was no trace of Mia in the city of Grashindorph. The king ordered all homes and business to be searched until Mia was found.

No building was left untouched, even the church of Arala was searched, yet no one claimed to have seen Mia. The priests and priestesses of the church of Arala were arrested by the Baron of Fintry for questioning after witness reported seeing General Bird near the church.

The baron didn't care whether the priests and priestess had been harbouring the general; he needed to make an example of someone.

Homes were burned when soldiers were refused entry, people dragged into the streets to be executed and tortured.

The fear that had gripped the hearts of the people of Grashindorph began to turn to hate and talk of rebellion and the Gibborim in quiet whispers became more and more common.

Regus had been found in the alley and taken back to the barracks, where the surgeon had nursed him back to health. His hands were ruined, he *couldn't grip anything properly and he could make only base and guttural sounds.*

The lieutenant wanted revenge on Helez, Asahel, Mathias and Rathe, but above that, he desired retribution against Madame Ella.

Regus knew that nothing happened in the madam's house without her knowledge and consent. He had spent enough coin in her house to purchase some loyalty from the whore, but she had readily sold him out to traitors.

In Regus' eyes, this made Madame Ella a traitor as well. He didn't knock on the door of the brothel, or open in carefully; instead, he kicked it off its hinges and stabbed the man that sat in front of the curtain. He had a dagger sewn into a gauntlet that he wore on his right wrist. He couldn't carry a sword, but we wasn't going to walk about the city unarmed.

The man collapsed to the ground, clutching his belly that was oozing bile and blood. Regus didn't break his stride as he tore down the curtain and marched up the stairs to Madame Ella's rooms.

From the other side of the door, he could hear the madam moaning and the grunts of the man that was rutting with her. He tried the door and found it was unlocked, so he slowly opened the door and crept inside the room.

Madame Ella was lying on her bed, the man on top of her, neither of them aware that Regus had entered. Ella normally locked the door when she was entertaining a client; however, she had taken to leaving the door unlocked in a vain hope that Helez might visit her.

Regus sat on a chair that was behind the screen that Ella used to change. He couldn't be seen by either the madam or her client from where he sat. He waited, listening to them, enjoying the arousal that came from the noises they made.

It didn't take long for the man to finish, pay the madam and bid her goodnight. He left the room quickly and shut the door behind him.

Ella sighed and walked to the window to look at the city. Since she had met Helez, she had found her work somewhat less satisfying than it had been before. She often imagined the young man returning to make love to her, the fantasies often her only inspiration when it came to slaking the desires of her patrons.

Regus moved quietly to the door and locked it. He walked deliberately towards her; every step increasing his anticipation of what was to come.

Ella felt his breath on the back of her neck and turned, expecting to see Helez stood behind her. Regus stared into the madam's eyes with hatred. Ella quailed under such a terrible glare; she was so terrified she couldn't scream.

Regus slashed at her skin, grazing wounds designed to hurt, but not to kill. Ella tried to run, but Regus pinned her body to wall with his.

The madam screwed up her eyes and shuddered as she felt the lump in Regus' trousers pressing against her. She refused to beg or apologise as Regus raped her and stabbed at her flesh with his dagger.

He cut her eyes from her head when he was finished and left Ella lying on the floor, bleeding, barely able to move. He took her eyes with him as a trophy. He took cushions and throws from the room. He lay them on the stairs in the brothel and when he was satisfied with their placement, he set fire to them.

Every room in Madame Ella's house was occupied and the only escape from the brothel was the staircase. Regus watched with satisfaction as the house burned. He listened to the men and women inside screaming for help.

The window to the room that belonged to his preferred whore was flung open and the girl looked through it desperate for help. She saw Regus and tried calling out to him, but Regus ignored her pleas for help. He watched her intensely as panic took hold and in a desperate attempt to escape the flames, she jumped from the window onto the street below.

He watched as the whole house became engulfed by the flames, the heat so unbearable that he had to take a few steps back as the blaze grew. Satisfied that he had his revenge against the madam, Regus returned to the barracks to collect his belongings before going to his own apartment.

CHAPTER 9

Asahel, Helez and Rathe made ready to travel to Kasnata's camp. Layla provided them with food rations as hunting was becoming increasingly difficult in the wilds as Wentrus dragged on.

The three men made repairs to their weapons and Jephthah managed to find horses for the men. Rathe missed his own mare, but he was sure that the Baron of Fintry would have taken her as a prize.

The Gibborim returned to Grashindorph without ceremony and life filled the tunnels below the city once again. Helez and Asahel said their goodbyes to Mathias and left without a word to anyone else. They were exiles and had no place among their people any longer.

Rathe said goodbye to his father and sister, to Mathias, to Layla and Jephthah, and to Hermia. Jephthah led the three men through the tunnels and out of the city to where the horses were waiting.

"Be careful," Jephthah warned as the three men mounted and made ready to leave.

A rider burst through the trees on a horse that was too big for him. He was clinging tightly to its neck and was clearly exhausted from riding. There was sand frozen in his hair and on the coat of his horse.

"Whoa, boy, where are you going?" Jephthah asked as he caught the head of the horse and pulled it to a stop.

The rider fell out of the saddle and landed on the ground, breathing heavily.

"I am looking for General Rathe Bird, I have a message from General Yoav and General Samara," he said quietly.

Rathe leapt off his horse and raced to the boy's side.

"Who are you, boy?" Jephthah asked with narrowed eyes.

"I am a man of Roenca. I was sent to find Rathe Bird, please do you know where he is?"

"I'm here, what is the message?" Rathe demanded.

"Neesa attacked the fortress of Kasnata that has been constructed close to Roenca. The children of General Rathe and Queen Kasnata had been brought to the fortress to keep them safe from attempts on their lives by King Mercia's forces. Neesa came to kill them. Send help," the boy said with a great deal of effort.

"Roenca isn't far; it won't take you long if you go now. They will know where the fortress is. We'll take care of the boy," Jephthah said. Rathe nodded and remounted his horse.

His heart pounded in his chest at the thought that his children were in danger. He didn't wait for Helez and Asahel; instead, he kicked his horse into a canter and headed south towards Roenca.

Kia's scouting party returned within ten days of setting out from the camp. Kia reported that supplies from Donamecca had been smuggled through the mountains to Delma, but there had been a landslide that would make all further aid impossible. She left the incident on the mountainside out of her report.

Misna was waiting for Shaul when he entered her tent. Shamgar, Cassandra and the Abbott were waiting with her. He had sent a message to

Misna asking her to assemble them all.

"What is it?" Misna asked as Shaul slipped through the gap in the canvas.

"Lavinia was after something in the mountains," he said quietly as he sat down opposite Shamgar.

"What were they after?" Cassandra asked.

"This," Shaul said as he pulled the metal box from inside his armour. He slowly opened the lid. Inside were a handful of pebbles with runes carved on them.

"Tell us what happened," the Abbott said sharply. The note of concern in his voice caused Shaul to shut the box.

"Lavinia told Kia that there was something in the mountains, something that could destroy the blood moon. They told her to find it. She nearly killed herself climbing the side of a mountain to get to it," Shaul said crossly.

"Does Lavinia know you found it?" Shamgar asked.

"No, Kia doesn't know I have it either. Only you four know," Shaul said more calmly.

"Good," Cassandra sighed and leaned back to lie on the floor of the tent.

"What are they?" Misna asked, looking at Cassandra and the Abbott.

"Not something that can destroy the blood moon," Cassandra replied with contempt.

"They are stones," the Abbott shrugged.

"They are not normal stones," Misna said dryly.

"No, they're augment stones. They're used to absorb power from a great source. Once the stones have absorbed the power, they change into different stones – depending on the power they have absorbed. They are extremely *powerful and extremely dangerous," Cassandra said, staring at the ceiling of the tent.*

"Why would Lavinia need these?" Shaul asked, looking down at the box.

"She shouldn't. Not unless she is planning to do something to make herself immortal," Cassandra tutted. The Guardian of the Wilds sat bolt upright and looked at her brother.

"She wouldn't dare," the Abbott said calmly.

"She would," Cassandra retorted.

"So, the stones are useless against the blood moon?" Misna sighed.

"Not useless, but they won't destroy it. The magic used to create the blood moon isn't the right type of magic for these stones," the Abbott said.

"There's only one type of magic," Shamgar said, rubbing his forehead.

"No, there is only one type of magic in this realm. These stones react to a different type of magic. They'll absorb power from anything once they are activated, but their full potential can only be realised when they absorb the right type of power," the Abbott said patiently.

"Then why would Lavinia want them?" Misna asked.

"To extend her own life. If she has these, then when the new guardian is born, she will have her own power to sustain her life, even after her powers have been transferred," Cassandra said bitterly.

"That's a problem?" Shamgar asked.

"It's forbidden. Using blood magic in augment stones to prolong her life, she won't remain as she is now, the magic will twist her will and her body, she'll become something completely different and entirely dangerous," the Abbott pursed his lips.

"She endangered Kia's life to try and extend her own?" Shaul asked

looking down at the box.

"It seems so," the Abbott shook his head.

"We should have locked her up centuries ago," Cassandra spat as she got to her feet.

"Where are you going?" Misna frowned.

"To remove their inglorious presence from the camp," Cassandra said hotly.

"I'll do it," the Abbott called after his sister.

"You will?" Cassandra sounded surprised.

"Of course, I will take them to Asuna. They will be kept there until one of the blood takes them from there," the Abbott smiled. Cassandra nodded her agreement and sat down again.

The Abbott swept from the tent. The sound of raised voices could be heard not long after. There was a bright flash of light and the voices ceased.

"What was that?" Shamgar asked blinking several times.

"That was the guardians leaving," Cassandra said with a small measure of satisfaction.

"What do we do with these augment stones?" Shaul asked. He still held the box in his hands, but didn't feel comfortable holding onto them any longer.

"I'll take care of them for now." Misna said, holding out her hand. Cassandra made no objection as the box was handed over.

"How is Kia?" Shamgar asked as Misna put the box in the chest in the corner of her tent.

"Alive. She did well, but she is still very inexperienced," Shaul said mechanically. Misna and Shamgar exchanged a wry smile.

"Experience comes as long as you are alive to gain it. Make sure she stays *alive, and she will gain the experience," Shamgar grinned at Shaul.*

Kelmar was lost in thought. The discovery of what lay beneath the city pressed on his mind. Kasna's life was in danger as long as she remained in the city and there was little he could do to protect her.

He was so consumed with his thoughts that he didn't hear the guards pounding on his door.

"Kelmar, the door," *Kasna said gently touching his arm.*

"Enter!" *Kelmar shouted and smiled an apology at Kasna.*

"Your Grace, a woman appeared on the battlements. She came out of thin air. The men are worried, they think she's a witch," *the guard spoke hurriedly, he was shaking violently and barely able to hold the spear he carried.*

"Arrest her and bring her here," *Kelmar said dismissively. The guard bowed and retreated quickly.*

"You aren't worried about witches?" *Kasna asked.*

"No, I only know of one witch, and she isn't in the city," *Kelmar shrugged.*

"How do you know?" *Kasna asked with a raised eyebrow.*

"She can't appear out of thin air, she just thinks she can," *Kelmar replied.* "I need you to stay out of sight whilst I deal with the prisoner."

"If you insist," *Kasna shrugged.*

"Come, hide in here," *Kelmar said. He took the princess by the hand and led her into the bed chamber, closing the door behind him.*

"You shouldn't worry," *she whispered as he hugged her and kissed her forehead.*

"I'm not worried," *Kelmar gave her a weak smile.*

"Liar," *Kasna said as she kissed his cheek. He stood for a moment, holding the princess without saying a word.*

"I don't know what to do," *Kelmar sighed.*

"Remember what the Abbott said?" *Kasna smiled up at him.*

"Yes, but it's of little comfort," *Kelmar shook his head and released the princess.*

"She's here," *Kasna said. The doors to Kelmar's apartment opened and the two could hear the guard giving instructions to the prisoner.*

"Stay here," *Kelmar ordered. He turned to face the doors and took a deep breath. "You shouldn't have come here." he poured all of his frustration and fears into the words he spoke, all the anger he felt towards the king and the helplessness he felt.*

"Why?" came the reply. He opened the door and stepped through, closing the door behind him. Cassandra stood in Kelmar's room, the Guardian of the Wilds hadn't changed since the duke had first encountered her on the outskirts of Tulna, save for her clothing. She was no longer wearing the leather and furs that she had been clothed in. Instead, she wore tight fitting trousers and shirt in a style that Kelmar had never seen before. He tried to hide the surprise he felt at seeing her stood in the palace of Delma.

"You foiled my attempts at Tulna once, but I took what I came for regardless. You will die before you take her from here," Kelmar looked over the *immortal and frowned. "Why are you dressed like that?"*

Cassandra smiled to herself and shook her head.

"You brought me here," she said simply. "For reasons I am not sure you are even aware of yet."

Kelmar shifted uncomfortably and glanced at the doorway he had emerged through. Following his gaze, Cassandra took a step towards the door.

"Move one more step and I will make sure that it is your last," he said defensively as he drew his sword and threatened the Guardian of the Wilds with it.

"Kasna?" she called with trepidation and the Princess of the Order and the kingdom of Nosfa opened the doors and stepped into the room. Kelmar looked desperately between the princess and the guardian. Cassandra smiled warmly at the girl.

The immortal felt her eyes welling up with tears as she looked upon the princess she loved like her own daughter, but she managed to maintain her composure.

Kasna looked at Cassandra suspiciously and moved quickly to Kelmar's side. The duke sheathed his sword and took the princess into his arms.

"That's not who you think it is," Kasna said quietly and gently kissed Kelmar.

"It's not the same woman from Tulna?" He asked sounding slightly confused.

"Yes and no," Cassandra said with a smile. "You always were more intelligent than any gave you credit for," she said with pride to the princess.

"What do you mean, were?" Kelmar frowned and reached for his sword again.

"Peace. It is not a threat, but an observation. One that I should have realised I knew and saved myself this trip," Cassandra sighed and shook her head. "Weakness of heart is a terrible thing at the best of times, but in moments like these and with the dangers that we face, it is unforgivable," the guardian chided herself.

Kelmar gently pulled himself from Kasna's arms and slowly walked towards Cassandra.

"What dangers do you know about?" he asked as he reached out and placed a hand on the guardian's shoulder. Pain seared through Cassandra's mind as she collapsed on the floor. Kelmar pulled his arm back instantly, but the guardian had vanished.

"What happened?" Kasna asked, looking terrified.

"I don't know," Kelmar said helplessly. "She spoke of dangers."

"Do you think she means the dangers that we stumbled onto beneath the castle?" Kasna asked.

"Possibly, but for now, we need to create a body. There is enough panic in this city without the guards spreading rumours of a woman that can appear and disappear out of thin air," sighed Kelmar.

"You would rather they think that you brutally murdered a prisoner?" Kasna gave Kelmar a wry smile.

"It will be much better for morale," Kelmar smiled back.

General Shamgar didn't want to keep Dragonious in Kasnata's camp any longer. With the guardians removed and incarcerated in Asuna, the Ballo Fortress stood empty.

Cassandra agreed that it would be safer for the boy at the fortress than *it would be if he remained in the siege camp. Shamgar waited until dark before he set off with the boy. He rode to the edge of the Ballo Sea and then rowed to the island. There was no attack from vicious creatures as they approached the island. They landed on the beach and Shamgar pulled the boat up and out of the water.*

The boy jumped out of the boat and gazed up at the fortress. He didn't look back at Shamgar, instead he ran around the fortress until he found some stone steps that led up to the gate.

Shamgar watched as the boy disappeared from sight. He half-expected the boy to reappear and beckon for the general to join him, but the boy was gone.

Cave Dweller smiled to himself as he pushed the boat back into the water and climbed in. He'll be safe here, a place he can call home, **he thought as he rowed back to the far shore.**

Dragonious watched Shamgar rowing away from the island from the battlements. The boy liked the general, but he felt nervous around the people of Celadmore. They weren't like the people of Nether Roth, they were much softer and if the masters were looking for him, he would rather face them on his own.

CHAPTER 10

2432GL 17th Wentrus

The Guardian of the Wilds was not a patient woman. Though she had lived for centuries, patience was a virtue that still escaped her. Avner hadn't sent any news from inside the city since he had been dispatched as an emissary.

Cassandra wasn't concerned for Avner's safety, but she was anxious to find out what was going on within the walls of Delma.

As she was not under the command of any of the forces that were settled in Kasnata's war camp, Cassandra was free to come and go as she pleased.

The guardians were no longer able to influence Kasnata or Kia, Misna had the augment stones secured and Shamgar had removed Dragonious, this left the guardian of the wilds with nothing except the mystery of Delma to occupy her mind.

Kia's patrol had found no sign of how Kelmar and Kasna had entered Delma without being discovered, but the guardian suspected that there were a few secret entrances scattered around the edge of the city, however, walls were not something that slowed down a creature like Cassandra.

She was one of the four immortals of Celadmore, the mother of Anagura, a direct descendant of the Goddess Arala. Her powers, like those of her brother, were limited, most who came across the guardian of the wilds never dreamed that she or the Abbott were demi-gods, however, she was infinitely more powerful than most of the inhabitants of Celadmore.

She didn't need to wait for the cover of darkness in order to infiltrate the city. Instead, she closed her eyes and took a small black stone out of a bag that she carried at her waist.

When she opened her eyes, she was stood on the upper floor of a small, run down house. It seemed to have been empty for a while. The small black stone had crumbled to dust. She wiped her hands on her shirt and slid out of the window.

She dropped down to the street below and moved through the people that were crowding towards the market. The guardian of the wilds slipped towards the palace.

No one challenged her as she wandered around the outside of the building. The steps were heavily guarded, but the rest of the palace seemed to be severely undermanned.

When she was certain that no one was watching her, she opened one of the palace windows and climbed through.

"Looking for someone?" *Avner greeted Cassandra. He was sat on one of the large sofas in the room. The general had set up several training dummies in the room to keep him occupied whilst he waited for the audience with his daughter, but despite this he still looked bored.*

"You've been here for a while. I thought I would come and find out what you discovered," *Cassandra replied with a grin.*

"Nothing, save for my daughter is most definitely not an ally to her people any longer. I am still awaiting an audience with her and the king," *Avner sighed and stretched out on the sofa.*

"Have you seen Kasna?" *Cassandra asked as she looked around the room.*

"No, but Colonel Mae has told me that the princess is safe for the moment. She is with Kelmar; the duke has become her protector as well as her captor," *Avner answered the guardian of the wilds as he stifled a yawn.*

"Kelmar is protecting her? Well, that is certainly interesting," *Cassandra smirked.*

"They are on the floor above. If you want to visit her, I am sure you can find a way to see her without the guards noticing," *Avner closed his eyes and sighed. When he opened them again, Cassandra had gone.*

When Neese had tried to step through the gates of the fortress, Nasus and Haras had sprung their trap. There was no warning for the witch that she was in any danger until the moment the barrier engulfed her form.

It took the form of a perfect sphere as the two daughters of Epoch cast their spell and the assassin was lifted into the air.

The moment the spell was triggered, Yoav led Samara and the remaining seven members of the Eight from the shards of the fortress' defences and out into the forest around it. They carried the young prince and princess with them as they made for the village of Roenca.

In the back of his mind, Yoav wondered if Warner had managed to find anyone to come help, but he had to assume that they were on their own for now.

"Riders approaching from the north," *Samara hissed. Yoav didn't want to slow their progress, but riders would mean danger. Any spies in Nosfa wouldn't be able to ride in numbers and most would have no choice but to travel on foot or as part of merchant caravans.*

"Sprite, take two of the girls and try to lead them off. We'll head for the village and meet you there when you've dealt with them," *Yoav replied.*

The horse that Yoav's party rode had barely recovered from their journey to the fortress. The three horses that Samara, Lucinda and Merinda rode would be ruined by the diversion. If they couldn't find the help they needed in Roenca, or fresh horses, three of their number would have to stay behind and sacrifice themselves whilst the others escaped.

Scattergood and Adino carried the babies at the centre of the riders. Yoav rode in front of them, whilst the others formed a protective shell around them.

"If the women can't draw off the riders, be ready to flee for all you are worth. If we have to stand and fight, get back to Kasnata. Tell her what happened," Yoav ordered over his shoulder. Scattergood and Adino nodded in reply.

Yoav strained to listen for the sounds of battle and horses over the sound of his own horse's hooves.

"Hello, the column!" a voice called out from the trees in front of them.

Damn*, Yoav thought.*

A moment later, six horses crashed through the trees and fell into formation with the six riders of the column. Yoav glanced to his left and roared when he recognised the face of the man that was riding beside him.

"Camsa!" Yoav cried with delight, "I feared we'd lost you to the madness of the king!"

"His hospitality was somewhat lacking," Rathe replied. "Though he is certainly not lacking in insanity."

"What of Grasbindorph?" Yoav asked.

"Rebellion and revolution," Rathe grinned.

"Forged by your hand?" Yoav enquired lightly.

"By my friends, late of the Gibborim. Introduction will wait until we are finished with this flight. Your messenger found us on the road. He told us of the danger to my children," Rathe said, his tone changing from light-hearted to serious.

"So like a fool that falls in love with the wife of his king, you charged down here to protect them?" Yoav asked with a grin on his face.

"Something like that. The blood moon is Neesa's doing?" Rathe asked.

"It seems that way. The Last Heir of Valia is who she really is. She's behind Nosfa's madness, the murders in our midst, the traitors that sought to use you, and the blood moon," Yoav replied.

"So she needs killing." Asahel asked from behind Yoav and to the right.

"Not as simple as it sounds lad. We have been fighting losing battle since she first appeared. That infernal moon gives her power beyond measure," Yoav grunted.

"Is there any way to destroy the moon?" Helez asked from the other side of the pack.

"Destroying the moon would damage our world far more than even Neesa can," Samara replied.

"Where is Neesa now?" Rathe asked.

"Caught in a trap that Nasus and Haras of Benadrocca set. They can only maintain it for a few days at most," Samara said.

A split second later, the general was flung from the saddle as her horse collapsed. A long gash ran the whole side of the horse that now lay twitching as it died.

"Go!" Yoav roared, peeling around to the right to allow Scattergood and Adino to ride through.

"You hoped to hold me for a few days? Pathetic witchcraft from the daughters of lesser beings could only ever hope to last for minutes," Neesa crowed from behind the riders.

The riders all circled around to face Neesa, a single line arrayed in a horseshoe about the Last Heir of Valia.

"You have even brought the general into the bargain. What sweet ecstasy it shall be to carve his body into pieces and deliver them to the feet of the pretender. I should reward you for such service, Wolfblood," Neesa danced with glee as she slowly advanced on the party.

Behind the riders, Samara shook her head and staggered back to her feet. She watched as Neesa drew closer to her allies and began to chant under her breath.

Neesa felt the tug of other magic around her and desperately looked to find its source.

"Well, who would have thought a pawn like you would know spells like that," Neesa said with a nasty tone in her voice.

"There is so little you know about our people," Samara replied. Neese laughed and sent a wave of energy peeling towards Samara. The moment the blast left her hand, the Last Heir of Valia felt all her power drain from her body. She collapsed to her knees and Yoav sprang forward.

Helez was struck by how much the old man's movements resembled a wolf's. He attacked without mercy with a single killing stroke.

Yoav's sword struck Neesa through her side, piercing her lungs so that blood began to choke her almost instantly.

"Fool," she spat. "You don't know what you've done."

"We know," Yoav replied sadly. "Camsa, you look after my queen.

She's a rare woman, but you, well, you are an even rarer man. Whatever is waiting in Delma, she'll need you with her." *Yoav smiled at his protégé.*

"What is he talking about?" Rathe asked as Samara walked between the horses.

"Nasus and Haras knew of a way to kill Neesa, but it needed the ancient magic of this part of the forest. This is where all healing magic and blood magic were born. Here, any who know the incantations can cast the most powerful spells with no harm befalling them.

"They taught me a spell to drain Neesa's power from her for a short time. Their trap was set to buy enough time for us to reach this point. They told us that one of us would cast the spell, but in order to destroy Neesa and her magic, a sacrifice had to be made. When one is so strong in blood magic, they can recover from even the most devastating wounds. Blood willingly split as a sacrifice negates the power of blood magic that has been gain from slaughtering others," Samara explained.

"And I am glad to do it. I didn't think I'd be seeing you before the end, Camsa, but I'm glad I did. Sprite, it's up to you now," *Yoav said.*

Rathe watched in horror as Samara drew a dagger and in three swift steps, slit the throat of his teacher and friend.

"No!" Neesa choked.

"The line of Valia ends here. May your treachery never stain the ground of Celadmore again," Samara spat in disgust as Neesa tried to scream.

The blood magic she had gained control of through spilling the blood of so many others was now destroying her from within. Her body turned to dust before the riders' eyes and as the last of it was swept away by the wind, the blood moon finally faded from the sky.

"Resha, ride after Scattergood and Adino. Make camp with them. We will join you shortly," Samara ordered. "I'm sorry, General Rathe, he knew what he was doing."

"But why did he do it?" Rathe asked.

"To protect the children of a woman that was as close as a daughter to him, and of a man that was as near to him as a son. He died for his love of both of you, those babes in arms, and to save Celadmore from the madness of one that should never have been allowed to gain such power," Samara replied.

"With Neesa dead, does that mean Mercia's mind is free?" Asahel asked.

"No. Whatever she did to his mind is damage that cannot be reversed, and it is not responsible for the madness that seems to have grown in Delma," Samara sighed.

"Then our work is far from over," Helez groaned.

"It is. We will return to Kasnata's camp. Her majesty will want to see her children are safe and she will want the body of General Yoav so he can be honoured. There is no one that is more suited to give both to her than you, general," Samara said.

The riders watched as Samara picked up Yoav's body and carried it across her shoulders. She took hold of the reins of Yoav's horse and walked through the trees until they found Scattergood, Resha and Adino.

Rathe was finally reunited with his children. He held them both tightly and thanked Arala that they were safe.

"We should carry Yoav's body on one of the horses." Rathe said to Samara as he watched the Condor General preparing Yoav's body with a shroud made from the saddle blanket on from his horse.

"No, he is my burden to carry. As is the judgement and punishment I

will face for what I have done," Samara replied.

"Judgement and punishment? You brought an end to the blood moon and Neesa's influence in this world," Helez frowned.

"I broke the laws of my people to do it. It was necessary, but it is equally necessary that I face the consequences of doing so," Samara smiled in spite of herself.

"Too many people ignore the consequences of what they chose to do instead of accepting responsibility for them," Asahel murmured to himself, and for a reason that Helez couldn't explain, he found his mind slipping to thoughts of Madame Ella and wondering whether she was all right.

The Gibborim was alive once more below the city of Grashindorph. Haman had been glad to lead his people back to their home after having to abandon it so quickly.

The people were overjoyed to find Hermia was unharmed and after she told them what had happened during their absence, there was a renewed sense of hope amongst the people.

Leinad found that life in the Gibborim was much more fun than his life in the palace of Grashindorph. Every morning he woke and was trained in sword and stealth by Layla and Jephthah. The lessons were hard, but the blood of his mother meant that he was unusually gifted when it came to learning about combat.

Hermia enjoyed watching her grandson grow and took time to teach him about the duties of a king and the culture of Nosfa when he wasn't being *trained to fight.*

Haston spent all of his time nursing his daughter. Mia was still weak after the ordeal she suffered at the hands of the king and the shock of seeing so many who were supposedly dead alive and well had also taken its toll on her body. Mathias sat in the corner of the room watching over the Lady of Afdanic and her father, just in case any of the Baron of Fintry's men had infiltrated the Gibborim.

Layla dispatched agents into the city above, agents that looked for those being persecuted by Mercia's men, people who gathered at night and plotted to overthrow the king and those that were simply fed up with living in fear.

All these people were brought to the Gibborim. Those that were brought below the city were kept away from the main body of the Gibborim, it was a separate camp in the sewers. None of them knew that Hermia was still alive, or how big the Gibborim was.

As the weeks went by, more and more camps were set up throughout the tunnels under the city of Grashindorph until it became clear that water and food supplies would become a serious issue if new supply lines weren't created soon.

Hermia left the practical side of maintaining the day-to-day welfare amongst the rebels to Haman. His skills at foraging and maintaining order were seemingly unequalled in any man that Hermia had ever encountered.

Even though there were lots of camps spread out through the sewer labyrinth that held several thousand people, Haman made their smooth-running look effortless.

So, Hermia plotted her revolution with Jephthah and Layla, waiting for the right moment to strike.

Cassandra returned to the camp of Kasnata without visiting Kasna. She didn't like the idea of letting an enemy like Kelmar know how easy it was for her to infiltrate the city undetected, let alone the palace.

Knowing that Avner had discovered nothing new but was there to watch over the princess was all that Kasnata would need to be told. But there was something else that Cassandra needed to do.

Misna greeted the Guardian of the Wilds upon her return and the two spoke at great length about what needed to be done in Delma. It was a conversation that wouldn't be repeated. General Misna knew what needed to be done to ensure Kasna's safety and she was more than capable of making all the necessary preparations without involving anyone else.

Kasnata was in her war tent when Cassandra returned.

"What news do you bring?" *Kasnata asked as Cassandra entered. Princess Kia was sat with Shaul and Tola a short distance from where her mother was looking at maps.*

"General Avner hasn't been able to discover anything about what is happening in Delma, save for an interesting development with Kasna," *Cassandra replied. Kia looked up sharply at the mention of her sister's name.*

"Where is Nini?" *Kia demanded.*

"She is in Delma, in the palace. She is under the protection of Duke Kelmar DeLacey," *Cassandra sounded amused as she spoke.*

"So, he was telling me the truth on the battlefield?" *Kia asked.*

"I cannot say whether he was telling you the truth or not. I only know that he is protecting Kasna now,*" said Cassandra with a shrug.*

"With the death of Prince Jayden, Kelmar became the heir to the throne, if you ignore the politics that would interfere with the line of succession. Even if the king ordered him to turn over Kasna, as regent, he has the right to refuse and hold her as his prisoner rather than a prisoner of the king,*" said Shaul.*

"You have learned a lot about the politics in Delma,*" Kasnata smiled at Shaul.*

"Cold nights around fires with soldiers, your majesty, they make for excellent learning experiences,*" Shaul replied.*

"The murdering bastard has the princess, and you are all acting as though she is perfectly safe!*" Tola shouted. He had been sat quietly brooding, but the mention of Kelmar's name had caused all his anger of Renta's death to surface again.*

"She is perfectly safe,*" Cassandra said firmly.*

"How can you say that? You know what he did, Kia you were there, you saw what happened to Renta," Tola said turning to the princess for support.

"Enough, Tola. I know what he did to Renta, but Avner is in the palace, he has a better vantage point than any of us to judge what danger my daughter is in. I trust his judgement,*" Kasnata said firmly.*

"Majesty, please, let me go into the city. Let me go and rescue Kasna from Kelmar,*" Tola begged.*

"No, Tola,*" Kasnata shook her head and fixed Tola with a hard stare.* "Until there is a direct threat to her life, I would rather focus on gathering information and searching for the hidden entrances into Delma. There must be several, especially when the duke was able to slip past our lines with the princess and enter the city without being seen."

"But your majesty!" *Tola tried to argue.*

"She's right, Tola," *Princess Kia sighed.* "We'll get to Kelmar soon enough, but there are other things we need to focus on."

"Indeed, there are, princess," *smiled Cassandra.* "One of which is that I need you to come with me, your majesty." *the Guardian of the Wilds bowed slightly as she spoke.*

"I see. Where are we going?" *Kasnata asked.*

"Far to the north, majesty, but it won't take long," *Cassandra replied with a twinkle of glee in her eye.*

"Very well, Kia, Misna and Amalia are to command the army of the Order in my absence. The men of Nosfa are willing to follow Tola, so you will command them under the direction of my daughter and generals. Whatever happens, I trust that the four of you will do what is needed," *Kasnata spoke to her youngest daughter and Tola firmly. Kia nodded in agreement as Shaul left the tent in order to tell Misna and Amalia what was happening.*

"But what about Kelmar?" *Tola demanded.*

"The city is surrounded. He has nowhere to escape to," *Cassandra shrugged.*

"He got into the city without us seeing him," *Tola spat back.*

"Then perhaps you should be spending your time trying to find out how he did that instead of screeching for an assault on the city," *Cassandra said through gritted teeth. Her time with Tola in the wilds had evaporated the little patience the Guardian of the Wilds possessed.*

Kasnata moved to stand beside Cassandra and a moment later the two had vanished.

The world around Kasnata was completely dark and her head was swimming. She felt the air ripping past her, and her feet were not touching the ground. The sensation didn't last for long. With a thud, Kasnata landed on hard stone. Her feet made contact first, but she was unprepared, so the queen collapsed in a heap.

"Sorry, I should have warned you," *Cassandra said sheepishly, offering a hand to help Kasnata back to her feet.*

"Where are we?" *Kasnata asked as she was hauled back to her feet.*

"On Anamoore. We're in the temple of Arala," *Cassandra replied as she led the way done a long stone corridor.*

"No one is allowed to set foot in the temple, save for the priests and priestess. Not even those of royal blood," *Kasnata hissed as she followed Cassandra.*

"That is true, but there is one other reason that people are allowed to set foot here and that is when the goddess has called for them," *the Guardian of the Wilds stopped at the entrance to the central chamber of the temple.*

The room was made from grey stone, but at the centre there was a bracer made from the purest white marble and was surrounded with carvings of the Goddess Arala. In the bracer, there was a giant flame that was burning without any fuel.

"The fire of Aisimecca," *Kasnata breathed.*

Around the bracer, the priests and priestess of Arala were gathered and seemed to be waiting for something to happen. Cassandra didn't enter the room, instead, she hung back by the door as Kasnata walked towards the fire, her vision completely fixed on the flame.

"Child of fire, you are welcome here," *the worshippers chanted as Kasnata passed them, but Kasnata couldn't hear them.*

The queen walked forward until she was within a fingertip's reach of the bracer. Before she could touch the marble, the fire in the font flared and engulfed the room. As the fire swept over Kasnata she didn't feel afraid, instead she felt completely at peace.

"Welcome, child of my blood. Not since the days of Anagura has there been a queen such as you," *a voice spoke in the fire. It was no more than a whisper, but there was such power in the words that Kasnata began to tremble.*

"You summoned me, what is your will?" *Kasnata asked.*

"Clever child, there is much that I would tell you, but time is not your ally. You have done well thwarting the plans of the dark ones, but there are more of them still to be defeated. The realms must be kept separate but there are those who are beyond these borders that threaten the balance of the worlds. Never has there been such a queen as you before, you are one who can keep those forces at bay, your allies will help you, but those who are joined to you by bonds of love will suffer. Even when all hope seems lost, there will be a way to bring an end to the darkness. Remember this, no matter how many centuries may pass."

Kasnata collapsed on the ground as the fire slowly retreated into the bracer. The queen felt a hand on her shoulder.

"Are you alright?" *Cassandra asked quietly. The priests and priestesses were all bowing on the ground, facing towards the bracer.*

"Yes, I'm fine," *Kasnata said shakily.*

"What did She say?"

"That no matter how dark it seems there is still hope. That I need to remember that no matter how many centuries pass. What does that mean?" *the queen asked, looking up at the Guardian of the Wilds.*

"If I knew, I doubt I'd be able to tell you. Come, we should return to the camp," *Cassandra said warmly.*

"Yes, but I feel I should remain here for a few days and attend to some matters," *Kasnata said pursing her lips.*

"Very well, I will wait outside the temple for you. Come to me when you are ready to leave," *Cassandra replied.*

CHAPTER II

The first few weeks in the Gibborim Mia spent asleep. She had come so close to dying that Hermia had decreed she needed to rest until her body had recovered. Haston came to sit with his daughter whilst she was awake, but their conversations were stilted, and Mia sat staring at the walls whilst her father tried to elicit some reaction from her.

Mathias knew that Mia had suffered greatly at the hands of the king and his men, but he also knew that the death of Joab played a part in her depression. Haston did what he could to help his daughter, but the torture she had endured was not something that Mia could tell her father about.

Haston knew there were things that his daughter was keeping from him and grew more and more frustrated by the silence he elicited from her.

Mathias sat quietly in the corner of Mia's room. He spent his time reading the piles of reports and messages that Layla allowed him to have access to whilst Mia slept. When she was awake, Mathias sat and watched the young woman out of the corner of his eye and listened to the conversations that her father attempted to have with her.

During the night, Mia would awake screaming and Mathias would move to her side and comfort her until she was calm enough to go back to sleep. When Mia woke in the mornings, she didn't remember her nightmares or the assassin comforting her. All she felt was the emptiness that losing Joab had brought and the shame of what the king and Regus had done to her.

"There must be something that we can do to help her," Haston said with frustration as he sat with Hermia and Haman.

"She has gone through more than any of can imagine and most of it was

at the hands or by the order of my son," Hermia said, shaking her head.

"Those that have endured so much, so young, they must find their own way to deal with the pain of loss and the agony of being broken by the cruelty of others," Haman sighed.

"I am her father; there must be something I can do to help her," Haston growled.

"It is precisely because you are her father that you can do nothing to help. A daughter never wants to disappoint her father, she will do all she can to make him proud. She will cry in his arms when she is hurt, but she will never tell you anything that she thinks will make you ashamed of her," Hermia said gently.

"There is nothing she could do to shame me," Haston spat back defensively.

"She doesn't feel that way. Her spirit has been broken and it will take time for the damage to be repaired," Hermia soothed.

"Give her time, you may find that Mathias can help her more than you can," Haman offered.

"You think that Mathias will be able to fix this for her?" Haston grunted.

"Fix? No, everything that she has seen she will have to deal with herself and learn how to move on from it. But he won't harm her. He has been with her a long time. He may not say anything that will make things better, but his continued support could do more to help her recover than you can imagine. His presence alone will do more for Mia than any of us can," Haman observed as he leaned back in his chair and closed his eyes. Haston opened his mouth to reply but was quieted by Hermia.

"Haman is right, they have shared fires through these battles they have survived and a lot of what is hurting her, he already knows. There's nothing that she has to explain to him, his companionship endures and gives back a sense of stability. There is so much that Mia is going through and trying to process that she can't even begin to explain it all. Having someone beside her that she doesn't need to ask questions, that won't ask what it was that caused such a change in her, that shares part at least part of her pain. Mathias sat beside her will do more for her sanity than all that we can offer," the former queen said sagely.

"Then all I can do is wait and see what my daughter chooses to do?" Haston asked.

"That is all any of us can do, and when she is ready to be helped, we can be there," Haman replied.

Joab opened his eyes. His chest felt as though a hot poker was resting on it and every breath he took sent searing pain shooting through his body. He felt weak and the light that filtered into the room stung his eyes.

"So, you are finally awake," the voice of the Abbott greeted Joab.

"Where am I?" Joab asked, the words catching in his throat and making it more difficult to breathe.

"Try not to speak, you don't have the strength yet," the Abbott said as he helped Joab sit up and gave him a cup of water to drink from. "You are at the Spire. Some of my brethren saw the Baron of Fintry riding to Triban and discretely followed him.

"They saw what he did at the inn. Only you had a chance of surviving the wounds that were inflicted by Fintry and his men. They did what they could to keep you alive and then brought you here. The wound to your chest was badly infected, you were delirious for days. You have been in and out of consciousness for weeks now. I was beginning to wonder whether you would ever fully regain yourself," the Abbott finished and lay Joab back down.

"What happened to Mia?" Joab rasped.

"I told you not to talk," the Abbott chided the Shadow. "The last I saw, Mia was taken to Grashindorph. The king was to marry her."

Joab tried to sit up. The thought of Mia back in the hands of the king revolted him. He didn't care how badly he was injured; all that mattered was rescuing Mia.

"Be still, you fool," the Abbott said, forcing Joab back down with very little effort. "The news from Grashindorph says that the wedding was interrupted and that Mia vanished with her brother, Mathias and members of the Gibborim."

"Mathias is still alive?" Joab asked, feeling his breath catching in his chest again.

"Yes, and if the reports are true, then he and Mia are both safely out of the reach of the king. There is nothing for you to do until you have fully recovered. So, rest and no more talking until your chest has healed," the Abbott insisted.

Joab smiled and closed his eyes. Knowing Mia was safe meant that he could rest easy and recover his strength, as there was a debt that he owed to the Baron of Fintry that Joab intended to repay.

Kelmar awoke to the sound of soldiers marching down the corridors of the palace of Delma. The sound of clanging armour made him feel sick to his stomach, especially as the sound of it was growing steadily louder.

Ever since he and Kasna had been down to the corridors beneath the city and seen what it was that the king and queen of Delma were doing, he had not been able to rest easily.

The slightest sound made him jump. He hadn't been able to sleep for more than twenty minutes at a time and any servant that entered his quarters was treated with suspicion.

Kasna hadn't said a word about what they had witnessed in the catacombs, and any time that Kelmar attempted to broach the subject with her, the princess immediately changed the subject.

Kasna had changed since their journey beneath the city. Instead of teasing and laughing with Kelmar, she was sullen and silent unless Kelmar asked her a direct question. She did nothing except lie in Kelmar's bed and stare at the canopy of silk above it.

"What is it?" Kasna asked as she sat up next to Kelmar.

"I don't know, but it doesn't sound good," Kelmar replied. The duke climbed out of his bed and walked through to the sitting area. As he walked into the room, the doors to his apartments were thrown open and Colonel Deena Mae walked in at the head of twenty guards.

"The king demands the presence of Duke Kelmar DeLacey, the Regent of Delma and the prisoner, Princess Kasna Nosfa," Deena said formerly.

Kelmar's jaw tightened.

"Are you here to escort us?" he asked.

"We are. We will wait while you dress. The king is not concerned with the state of undress that the prisoner may or may not be presented in," Deena said as she looked sadly at Kelmar.

"I see," Kelmar said shortly. He turned back to his bedroom and shut the door behind him.

"The king wants to see us both?" Kasna asked. She had dressed whilst Kelmar had been out of the room.

"He does, but why send for us so late in the night?" Kelmar asked in a low voice.

Kelmar dressed quickly, making sure that he hid a dagger at his ankle and had his sword at his waist. He took Kansa by the hand and led her from the bedroom.

"The king says you won't need your sword, your grace," Deena said as the two emerged. Kasna felt Kelmar's grip on her hand tighten momentarily.

"If that is what the king says," Kelmar tried to sound offhand as he removed the blade and its scabbard from around this waist and dropped it on the sofa.

"If you will follow me," Deena said, bowing slightly. The colonel walked slightly ahead of Kasna and Kelmar, the rest of the soldiers falling into place behind the duke and the prisoner.

They walked in silence. Deena didn't date to turn round to look at Kelmar. She didn't like her orders any more than he did, but she was a soldier, and her duty was to serve the king. Whatever he commanded, she was sworn to carry out his wishes.

Kasna looked straight ahead as they descended the stairs to the floor below, making more noise than the princess thought was acceptable for the time of night.

"Greetings, Colonel Mae," General Avner was standing at the bottom of the stairs waiting for the procession.

"Good evening, General Avner, it is a little late for you to be roaming the halls, isn't it?" Deena asked, trying to sound light-hearted.

"It's a strange thing, but I found that for some reason I couldn't sleep tonight. I thought a walk through the corridors of the palace might help me to relax and low, I meet with you on my journey," General Avner smiled.

"How fortuitous. I believe you know Duke Kelmar DeLacey?" Deena asked, standing slightly to one side.

"Of course, Kelmar, how are you?" Avner asked with a strange look on his face.

"A little restless, like yourself," Kelmar replied curtly. His grip on Kasna's hand got tighter.

"It seems to be a plague affecting us all tonight. I was asked to pass on best wishes from a mutual friend if I came across you during my visit," Avner said with a false smile on his face.

"Oh? And who is the mutual friend?" Kelmar asked with a tinge of frustration to his voice.

"Tola," Avner said pointedly. Kelmar released Kasna's hand and instinctively reached to where his sword should have been. Avner watched the action and looked at Kelmar with disappointment.

"General, I am afraid we must be moving along now," Deena said gently, trying to step between the general and the duke, but Avner brushed past

her and knelt at Kasna's feet.

"Your highness, your mother is worried for your safety. Have you been mistreated at all?" Avner asked in a low voice.

"I am well, thank you, general. My mother has no need to worry," Kasna smiled and gently touched the general on the shoulder. Avner rose back to his feet and looked the princess in the eye.

"I am glad to hear it," Avner said with a grin, but his smile vanished when he noticed the sadness in Kasna's eyes. "Princess?" he frowned.

"All is well, general. There is nothing on the surface of this realm that has the power to harm me," she said, holding the general's gaze. Kelmar shot a worried look in Kasna's direction.

"General, the king is waiting for us," Deena whispered in Avner's ear.

"I see, well it will not do to keep the king waiting, and I will accompany you, to apologise for the delay I have caused," Avner smiled.

Deena opened her mouth to protest but wasn't given the opportunity to respond as Avner strode off towards the throne room of the palace.

The procession of soldiers, nobles and a prisoner entered the throne room with almost no ceremony. Avner threw open the doors and marched without any care to the dais where the king and queen both sat on their thrones.

"What is the meaning of this?" King Baruch Delich demanded with a snarl as Avner bowed before him.

"I was responsible for delaying this party enroute to your majesty, I felt it was my duty to apologise for and explain the delay," Avner said as he rose back to his feet and watched Deena lead the princess and the duke to where he stood.

Avner waiting at the foot of the stairs had made Kelmar even more nervous. The noise of the soldiers marching in their armour had no doubt awoken most of those that lived in the palace, but Avner was restricted to his quarters and was only allowed to leave them at the instruction of the king.

The general had chosen to break one of the strictest protocols in Delmarian etiquette, and also dared to come before the king without invitation or leave for an audience.

In ordinary circumstances, the breach of custom would be cause for at the least imprisonment, and at the most execution, yet the king was merely glowering at his father-in-law.

"Your majesty, Duke Kelmar DeLacey, the Regent of Delma and the prisoner, Princess Kasna Nosfa," Colonel Mae saluted and moved to stand beside General Avner. The two stood to the left of the king leaving Kelmar and Kasna facing the king and queen with the detachment of soldiers fanned out behind them.

"Princess Kasna Nosfa, step forward," the king commanded.

"You are charged with attempting to escape from your confinement, acts of sedition and the poisoning of the city water supply," the queen said abruptly. "Do you have anything to say in your defence?"

"Your majesty, my deepest apologies, but I don't know what you are talking about," Kasna stammered. The king and queen were looking at the princess with foul expressions that made Kelmar's skin crawl.

"Ignorance is not a defence under Delmarian law. Two nights ago, you were seen sneaking out of the duke's quarters and heading into the city. You then poisoned the well in the centre of the square. A well that had only just been dug down to a deeper level to provide water for the city to help the people of Delma to weather the siege of your mother and her army.

"*You have also been seen meeting with those that oppose the rule of our king, Baruch Delich, and have been heard trying to turn our own regent against us. You have tried to seduce him, corrupt him and have even snuck spies into the palace,*" *the queen sneered at the princess as she spoke with an acidic tongue.*

"*Your highness, I must protest –*" *Kelmar stepped forward and tried to intervene.*

"Silence, DeLacey," *the king boomed. Kelmar stared at the king with a helpless expression.*

"*For your crimes, the king is ready to pass sentence,*" *the queen continued.*

"*Please, your majesty, I haven't done any of those things,*" *Kasna begged.*

"*Princess Kasna Nosfa, daughter of King Mercia Nosfa VI and Queen Kasnata Nosfa, you are sentenced to death for your crimes,*" *the king said flatly.*

Colonel Mae closed her eyes and dropped her chin to her chest. She had expected the verdict, but it didn't make it any less painful to hear. Kelmar stood, frozen to the spot, unable to hide the shock he felt.

"*Take her to the dungeons. The execution will be carried out on a date that has yet to be set,*" *the queen said coldly. Two of the soldiers stepped out of the fan and grabbed Kasna by the arms.*

"*Please, wait,*" *Kasna begged as they dragged her from the hall and down into the dungeons beneath the palace.*

"*As the Regent of Delma, you will carry out the execution,*" *the king said, addressing Kelmar without emotion.*

"*Sire, please,*" *Kelmar said quietly.*

"*If you do not, then you will be charged with treason and share her* sentence," the king threatened and watched as Kelmar meekly nodded.

"Am I dismissed?" Kelmar asked, doing his best to control the emotion in his voice.

"You are all dismissed," the king said lazily and slumped back in his chair. Deena and Kelmar both bowed and turned away from the dais, but Avner didn't move.

"When I was a younger man, I had a daughter," Avner began talking in a nostalgic voice. "She was bright, beautiful, kind and skilled with a blade. I didn't think there was anything on all of Celadmore that I could love more."

"I said you are dismissed," the king barked, but Avner ignored him.

"When her mother died, something in her changed. She didn't want her father to love her anymore. She pushed him away with every word she uttered and even chose to marry outside of her people to escape him. But when she got married, she was happy again; she started to act as though she still loved her father and wanted him to be part of her life again," Avner continued.

"I never wanted you to be part of my life again," the queen spat angrily.

"Had you asked me when I was a young man if there was anything that you could do that would disappoint me, I would have said there was nothing. That no matter what came in life, I would always be proud of you. I now find that my greatest regret in life is that the daughter I raised became you," Avner looked at his daughter, his heart had been broken by Adina long ago so now all he felt was shame as he looked at her. "I'm glad your mother never lived to see you like this."

"Arrest him!" Adina shouted and her father laughed.

"I come as an ambassador under a white flag, you can't arrest me," the general said scornfully.

"I will make you regret everything you have just said," Adina screamed as Avner turned away from his daughter and walked from the throne room.

"By the will of Arala or by the Seven Stars?" he asked over his shoulder. He didn't wait for the queen to respond. He strode past Kelmar and Deena and went back to his rooms without uttering another word.

The Baron of Fintry sat in the office of the Knight Marshal of Grashindorph. He had commandeered the office and was directing the search for Lady Mia, and for the rebels that had caused the disturbance at the king's wedding.

King Mercia had given the Baron free rein to deal with the rebels as he saw fit. The Knight Marshal had been unceremoniously ejected from his office by the Baron. Fintry had little time for the man. He had made no secret of his dislike either.

In the baron's opinion, the Knight-Marshal was woefully inept at keeping order in the city. The ring of traitors, that others called the Gibborim, had been allowed to flourish, and no matter how many searches the Knight-Marshal ordered, nothing had been found.

The baron held the Knight-Marshal ultimately responsible for the disruption of the king's wedding, as well as the escape of the former general, Rathe Bird, and the assassin, Mathias.

The Knight-Marshal hated the Baron of Fintry, and being thrown out of his office by the baron had done nothing to endear the man to him. After the baron had taken over his office, the Knight-Marshal had disappeared into one of the local taverns and refused to leave.

He slept with his head on the table and when he wasn't asleep, he drank tankard after tankard of ale, which he refused to pay for. The landlord didn't dare to throw the Knight-Marshal out into the street, so he was stuck with an unwanted guest.

The Knight-Marshal sat in the tavern for four days before anyone chose to disturb him.

"May I join you?" a dark-haired and dark-skinned woman asked.

"Of course, there is plenty of room," the Knight-Marshal said as he looked over the woman's figure. She was an older woman, but looked no older than forty. She was tall and slight in build, but there was muscle on her frame. "Time has been kind to you, Layla." he grinned as she sat down opposite him.

"Thank you, it seems that the same can be said of you," the Shadow replied. The Knight-Marshal was roughly the same age as Layla, they were both in their mid-fifties but neither looked anywhere close to their age.

The Knight-Marshal had only a few flecks of grey at his temples, the rest of his shoulder length hair was still jet black, even after years of serving as a soldier. He had broad shoulders and clear tanned skin that was only marred by the scars he had picked up in battle.

"What brings you out of the shadows?" he asked, leaning forward and placing his hands on the table. Layla smiled and leaned forward so her face was only a few millimetres away from the Knight-Marshal's and her hands were resting on top of his.

"I am looking for someone," Layla whispered. She had missed spending time with the Knight-Marshal. The two had been lovers for a time, but neither had been willing to sacrifice their duty for the sake of building a life together. "I *thought you might know where they are."*

"Your friends did an excellent job of ruining the king's wedding; there are a lot of people looking for them and for you. Are you sure this is the best time to be looking for someone?" the Knight-Marshal sounded concerned as he gently took hold of Layla's hands.

"It is the perfect time," Layla smiled dangerously and brushed her lips against his. "I'm looking for the Baron of Fintry." she whispered.

The Knight Marshal's heart leapt in his chest.

"And if I can help you to find the baron, what will I get in return?" he asked with a crooked smile.

"What do you want?" Layla asked coyly.

"The same thing I have always wanted," was the reply.

Layla slowly rose from the table and led the Knight Marshal up the stairs of the tavern to the rooms that were available to rent by the hour.

"Are you sure you haven't had too much to drink for this?" Layla giggled as she shut the door. A second later, the Knight Marshal had her pinned against the door and was gently kissing her.

Layla wrapped her arms around the Knight Marshal as he broke the kiss.

"I missed you," he whispered in her ear.

"Fool," Layla teased as she nestled her head into his shoulder.

"The baron's spies have been watching me since he came to the city, they will have already told him that you came to meet with me," the Knight Marshal sighed.

"I know. I expect he will send men to arrest us both," Layla replied.

"He'll come himself with a small number of men he thinks he can

trust," he rested his head against Layla's.

"He thinks he can trust?" the shadow asked, lifting her head.

"The baron has more enemies than he realises," the Knight Marshal replied.

The sound of shouting in the bar below told the two that the Baron had arrived.

"Where are they?" the Baron of Fintry demanded. The landlord was shaking at the sight of the baron and six soldiers in his tavern. He couldn't speak, but he raised a trembling arm and pointed in the direction of the stairs.

"You and you, come with me," the Baron said to the two soldiers that were closest to him. "The rest of you, secure the tavern."

The patrons of the tavern were grabbed by their collars and were thrown out into the street as the baron ascended the staircase, flanked by the two soldiers.

The doors of the rooms for rent were kicked open without ceremony until the baron found the room where Layla and the Knight Marshal were waiting.

"Kilaran Daken, Knight Marshal of Grashindorph, you are under arrest," the baron crowed as he stepped into the room.

"Is that so? What are the charges?" Kilaran asked with an amused expression on his face.

"Treason," the Baron shrugged. "The king does not take kindly to betrayal."

"After all that he has done to preserve his place on the throne? The king is guilty of far greater acts of sedition than any he has punished for it," Layla scoffed.

"You are a fool, Layla. Did you think that a meeting between the Knight Marshal and a fugitive wouldn't be reported?" the baron crowed.

"On the contrary, I was sure it would." Layla grinned.

"Soldiers, arrest them!" the baron ordered, but the soldiers didn't move.

"Knight Marshal?" one of the soldiers asked.

"Return to the barracks, men," Kilaran dismissed the two men. "And shut the door behind you."

The two soldiers saluted and closed the door as they left the room.

"The king will hear of this!" the baron shouted after the two men.

"I doubt that," Layla said as she sat down on the opposite side of the room to the baron.

"I don't need soldiers to arrest you; I am perfectly capable of doing that myself," the baron cried as he drew his sword.

"I have a few questions for you, baron, before we begin the open hostilities," the shadow said dryly. The Knight Marshal had his hand resting on his sword and stood between Layla and the baron.

"And they are?" the baron scowled.

"Did you turn Bracha against her own people?"

"I did."

"Did you kill Joab?"

"I did."

"Very well," Layla sighed as she stood and moved to Kilaran's side.

"You will both die here," the baron snarled.

"No, they won't," the door opened, and Jephthah stepped into the room, striking the baron across the back of his head.

The baron crumpled to the floor, dropping his sword.

"*Impeccable timing,*" *Layla said with a raised eyebrow as she looked down at the unconscious form of the baron.*

"*I should return to my post.*" *the Knight Marshal said as he watched Jephthah picked up the body of the Baron.*

"*No, you can't,*" *Layla said desperately grabbing his arm.*

"*You're worried?*" *Kilaran smiled at his former lover.*

"*The baron has allies as well as enemies; you will be in danger if you return to your post,*" *Layla argued.*

"*Then what do you suggest?*" *the Knight Marshal asked.*

"*Come with us, join us,*" *Layla said forcefully.*

"*I am sworn to serve the line of King Rosla Nosfa, I will not abandon that duty,*" *Kilaran said, gently placing his hand on Layla's.*

"*Your duty is to protect the people of Grashindorph; you won't be forsaking your duty by coming with us,*" *Layla countered.*

"*Whatever you are going to do, we need to go,*" *Jephthah grunted, "*Lady Hermia is waiting for the baron.*"

"*Lady Hermia?*" *Kilaran looked between Layla and Jephthah with confusion.*

"*Did you think that I would fail in my duty to protect her?*" *Layla asked with a slight smile.*

"*I don't understand,*" *Kilaran said, shaking his head.*

"*Come with us and you will.*" *Layla urged and the Knight Marshal begrudgingly agreed.*

CHAPTER 12

"Your highness?" *General Amalia whispered as she knelt down beside the bed of Kasnata. The queen had gone to bed early the last few days, ever since she had returned from her trip with Cassandra. She hadn't told anyone what happened or where they had been. The queen wasn't entirely sure what had happened or what it meant, so had decided to keep the events in the temple to herself for the time being.*

Kasnata had felt exhausted since she had returned, though, so she had left the running of the camp with Misna, Amalia, Kia and Tola, each in charge of the different aspects of the army.

The queen needed to rest, but it was also good for her daughter to gain experience leading her people without her mother's constant presence.

Cassandra had disappeared again without any explanation or apology for her departure, though Kasnata didn't doubt that whatever she was doing and wherever she was going was not something that the dark angel needed to know.

The queen had not left her tent since she had returned. She barely left her bed, spending her days wondering how her other children fared and fretting over the fate of both Mia and Rathe. There had been no word from Grashindorph since the messenger had brought news of Rathe's execution and Mia had set out to rescue her brother.

"What is it, Amalia?" *Kasnata asked groggily as she sat up and yawned.*

"You have visitors," *Amalia smiled at the queen. Kasnata frowned for* a moment and then looked past Amalia. Behind the general, there was a cluster of people waiting for her.

"Rathe!" the queen leapt from her bed and rushed into the waiting arms of the former general. Rathe held her tightly to him. "How did you escape?" Kasnata asked as she stepped back slightly from her lover.

"By the skill and cunning of these two men, may I present Asahel and Helez, formerly of the Gibborim. Asahel, Helez, her majesty Queen Kasnata Nosfa," Rathe smiled as he made the introductions.

"Your majesty," the two men bowed.

"Thank you both," Kasnata said with sincerity. "Mia, Mathias and Joab, what happened to them? They came to rescue you."

"Joab is dead. The Baron of Fintry killed him when he captured Mia and Mathias in Triban. But they are both with the Gibborim now," Rathe explained. "As is Leinad."

"My son is safe from his father?" Kasnata looked as though she was about to faint in Rathe's arms.

"He is. His grandmother is educating him, raising him to be the king his father should have been," Helez assured the queen as Gildow started crying. The two babies were being held by General Samara, who was standing behind Rathe.

"Our son and daughter have also been delivered from the hands of Neesa at the fortress near Roenca," Rathe said, as he took his son from Samara and handed him to Kasnata.

"You return to me with news that my son is safe and bring our children back with you," Kasnata sighed in wonder as she gazed down at their son.

"I live to serve," Rathe said, bowing slightly with his hand on his heart *before taking his daughter from Samara. Kasnata looked up from her son's face over those that were assembled. The Eight and Samara were stood silently behind Rathe, Helez and Asahel, all with grim expressions on their faces.*

"Where is General Yoav?" *Kasnata frowned.*

"If your majesty will follow me," *Samara said and led the queen out of her tent. Outside Haras and Nasus stood either side of General Yoav's horse. His body was hung over its withers. Abendigo and the warriors of the Order of the Wolf were stood in formation around the horse, all with their heads bowed.*

"What happened?" the queen asked as she handed her son to Amalia and walked over to the general's body.

"He gave his life to undo the power of the blood moon and to save your children, your majesty," Nasus answered.

"His throat has been cut," Kasnata looked to Samara for an explanation.

"In order to break the power that Neesa, the last heir of Valia, wielded, General Yoav agreed to sacrifice himself so that I could perform one of the forbidden rites of blood. The general has paid for breaking this ancient law with his own life. I am prepared to do the same," Samara said firmly.

"I see. Abendigo, see to the body of Wolfblood. General Samara, I will need time to weigh the consequences of your actions, but I shall convene a tribunal to hear of what happened in adherence to our laws," Kasnata spoke quietly as she watched General Yoav's body being carefully lifted from his horse.

Abendigo lay the general on the ground and knelt down beside him. He said something in a low voice that was only for the ears of the dead general. Kasnata stood silently crying as Abendigo rose to his feet and howled.

The other members of the Order of the Wolf joined in a mournful chorus. Helez and Asahel were surprised when Rathe began to howl with them. The sound of the howling wolves drew other members of the Order from their beds. Those of the Order of the Hound and Order of the Bear also joined the mourning chorus with howls of their own.

The night was filled with pain as the other generals of the Order appeared. Shamgar roared and collapsed beside the body of a man that he had thought he would die fighting next to. Misna stood next to Amalia, the two holding hands and showing no outward emotion, save for the white knuckles as they tightly clasped the hand of the other. General Kia led away the general's horse, using the animal to hide her pain. Quisla and Marissa wept in each other's' arms as the queen slowly walked forwards and placed a hand on the shoulder of Shamgar.

In the city of Delma, Avner could hear the mournful chorus and felt his heart break for the loss of a man that he had begun to think was immortal.

"I will see you in Halsanda, old friend. Save a place by the fire for me," *he whispered and softly howled his own lament.*

The camp of the Order didn't return to their beds that night. Fires were stoked and stories about the fallen generals, Renta and Yoav, were shared as the people mourned.

Tola lay staring at the canvas of the tent above his head and replayed the death of Renta over and over again in his mind. The sacrifice of General Yoav in the defence of Kasnata's children had ripped open the festering grief he nursed and now threatened to sink him into an even greater depression.

Princess Kia sat around one of the fires beside Shaul. She listened to the memories the man of Queteria had of sharing his years of war with two warriors that Kia had never had the opportunity to know well.

Payne came out of his tent to sit and listen to the others talking, though he said nothing of how he felt. Oswin, Cara, Anna, Serra, Horace and Benaiah sat with the healer, the normal jibes absent from their conversations as the laughed and cried.

Amalia sat with the children of Kasnata and Rathe as the former general and queen helped Abendigo with the preparations for the funeral of General Yoav.

Shamgar sat with Samara, Kia, Haras, Nasus, Marissa and Quisla, none of them spoke, but simply stared into the flames of the fire.

Misna didn't join with the others in sharing memories; instead the Raven General led the seven members of the Eight to the edge of the camp of the Order.

"I have news for you about the razing of Ashpa," the general said when they were far enough from the fires.

"What is it?" Merinda asked.

"I believe that we may have found the men who took your brother and some of the other children that survived Ashpa being burned. Slavers that are hiding in the woods to the north between the villages of Dono and Kela. There are lots of abandoned mines in those woods for them to hide in, but I am certain that you will find them there," Misna told the children.

"Slavers?" Scattergood frowned.

"Yes, I have reason to believe that the others weren't killed but were taken as slaves. There is a good chance that your brother is among them," Misna

replied.

"We must see the queen, the sooner we go, the better the chances we have of finding our friends and family," Colm said excitedly.

"I have already asked the queen for leave for you to go. You have as long as you need, and may leave as soon as you are ready. I would warn you that it has been some time since your home was burned. The slavers are unlikely to still have any of your kin, but you will be able to find out where they were sold and perhaps to whom. If the slavers do still have your kin, then prepare yourselves for the worst. They are not kind to those that they cannot sell," the Raven General looked across the hopeful faces of the children and sighed to herself.

"Thank you, general," Vaike said.

"Good luck," Misna gave the seven members of the Eight a half-hearted smile.

A branch cracked under foot in the darkness. The eight warriors all reacted instinctively. Swords were drawn in fluid movements as they turned to the direction the sound had come from.

"Stay your blades, young fools," the voice of an old woman drifted out of the darkness.

"Who are you?" Misna asked.

"I am an old woman from Delma. There are some that know me as the Mother of Dawn. My real name has been forgotten. I am here to see the queen," the old woman replied.

Misna laughed to herself and relaxed. The seven members of the Eight looked at her with puzzled expressions.

"Sheath your swords," she ordered. "Come forward Mother of Dawn, you find yourself amongst friends tonight."

"Most gracious of you," the Mother of Dawn said as she moved forward into the ring of light that was cast by the torches of the camp.

"I am afraid that you will have to wait a few hours to speak with her majesty," Misna apologised to the old woman.

"Ah, I feared that one of the generals had passed when I heard that chorus. Who was it?" the Mother of Dawn asked.

"Yoav," Misna replied sadly.

"Did he die well?" the Mother of Dawn looked at Misna with a curious expression on her face.

"He did," Misna nodded.

"Then he could have had no better end and could not have asked for a higher honour than to be mourned so by his people. I didn't come to you alone though," the Mother of Dawn said with a twinkle in her eye.

Out of the darkness children slowly walked forward. All of them were dressed in rags and were covered with filth. Most looked as though they hadn't eaten in weeks and some were clearly suffering from sickness.

"By Arala, what happened to them?" Lucinda asked as she looked at the children with horror.

"They are the poor and forgotten of Delma. They only have myself and Colonel Mae to care for them. They have no homes and in the siege they have been cut off from food and water, forced by the king and those of his court to scrounge in the sewers," the Mother of Dawn explained.

"Why bring them here?" Resha asked.

"Because there is something that is about to happen in Delma, something that needs to be prevented and something that these children need to be protected from. I do not come with glad tidings for any in this camp, save for

what is about to happen can be prevented," the Mother of Dawn said sagely.

"The Seven Stars?" Misna asked.

"They will not wane for much longer," the Mother of Dawn confirmed.

"Kasnata will want to see you as soon as the funeral has finished. I will fetch Payne to look at the children and General Kia will help me find food, water and quarters for them," Misna sighed and shook her head in dismay.

"Thank you," one of the children squeaked. Misna turned her head and looked at the young girl that was sat on the ground shivering.

"The ground is still half-frozen; you would be better sat by a fire," Misna said as she moved to the young girl and gently picked her up off the ground.

"I can walk," the girl chattered.

"I doubt that you could walk more than another five steps before collapsing," Misna laughed slightly as she spoke. "What is your name?"

"Kayla," the young girl replied.

At dawn, Kasnata called her generals together to hold the tribunal for Samara. The general explained the events that had led up to General Yoav being sacrificed to destroy Neesa and the blood moon.

Though the laws of the Order had been broken, all the generals agreed that there had been no alternative.

"Samara, though you were justified in your actions, I cannot simply pardon you for taking the life of another for the sake of magic. You will spend the rest of your life atoning for this act by serving the least among us. However, you will not forfeit your role as general,*"Kasnata passed sentence over the Condor General, relieved that she wouldn't have to lose another one of her officers needlessly.*

Misna had left the Mother of Dawn and the children of Delma with Haras and Nasus. The two women of Benadrocca seemed glad to have something useful to do in the camp.

The Raven General had instructed the two daughters of Epoch to keep the children and the Mother of Dawn out of the way until Yoav's funeral had been held.

It was the tradition of the Order to hold their funerals at sunset, when the body of General Yoav would be taken into a lean-to, which his men had built, and it would be sealed and set alight.

Payne had looked at the children and declared that they would be fine after some rest, food and water and that there was no risk of sickness being spread amongst the warriors of the Order and soldiers of Nosfa.

Instead of a feast to honour the fallen general, tales of his life were told, and cups of hot mead were poured out and toasted to his memory.

"There isn't any dancing or feasting?*" Rathe asked Abendigo as he helped to build Yoav's funeral pyre.*

"No, when a life is sacrificed or lost outside of battle, there is no dancing or feasting. Yoav sacrificed himself willingly and we honour him with mead. When Renta was killed, she was murdered. When it is murder, there is only mourning before the burning of the body. There will be dancing after,*" Abendigo explained.*

As the sunset, a horn sounded three times. It was becoming a familiar sound to Rathe. Helez and Asahel stood on either side of Kasnata, flanked by her female generals, Princess Kia and Shaul.

The two men of the Gibborim watched spellbound as General Yoav's body was carried to the small lean-to that had been built by the Order of the Wolf. His body was wrapped in linen and born on the shoulders of Shamgar, Abendigo, and Rathe.

As they stepped into the lean-to and laid the general's body on the ground, Rathe was struck with an overwhelming wave of emotion and couldn't hold back the flood of tears that came spilling out.

"It's alright, pup," *Shamgar said kindly.* "He's waiting in Halsanda for all of us. We'll see him again."

"Will you lead the singing? It's what he would have wanted," *Abendigo asked Rathe. The former general looked between the two Queterians and shook his head.*

"I don't know the song," *Rathe replied. Shamgar grinned and Abendigo laughed slightly.*

"When it is the funeral of an individual there are no set words. It is the tune that we sing to," *Shamgar explained.*

"But the verses, you sing them together," *Rathe frowned.*

"A beat or two behind the song leader," *Abendigo grinned.*

"Do you know the tune?" *Cave Dweller asked.*

"I do," *Rathe said slowly.*

"Then you'll be fine. When we step out of the lean-to, you need to start singing. Don't worry too much about the words; just let your heart choose them," *Abendigo patted him on the shoulder and stepped out of the pyre, followed by Shamgar.*

Rathe took a deep breath and did the same. As he stepped out of the lean-

to, he began to sing.

"Let him lie down, let him find rest. He battled for peace, may it be his, let him lie down. Let your hand guide his way, let him lie down. Let him find his place at your table, let him lie down," *he sang the haunting melody. He was weeping as he sang, but no one seemed to care.*

Shamgar and Abendigo joined him in the song before the rest of the Order took up the chorus.

"His body is spent, let him lie down. His blood spilt in willing sacrifice, let him lie down. For the love of his own, let him lie down. For our love for him, let him lie down."

The three men repeated the verses three times and silence fell over the funeral. General Kia, Amalia and Quisla lit three torches and carried them forward, handing them to the three men.

They turned and slowly walked towards the lean-to and the rest of the order began to sing.

"Let him be laid down, let him find his rest. He has warred for long enough; he has earned his place. Let your hand guide his way, let his feet carry him true. He is weary from battle; he has shed his blood. Let him be laid down, let him find his rest. Let the honour guard ride out to welcome him in, let the gates be flung open, let him come home. Let him be laid down, let him find his rest. He has warred for long enough; he has earned his place. Let your hand guide his way, let his feet carry him true. He is weary from battle; he has shed his blood. Let him be laid down, let him find his rest."

Helez and Asahel listened in wonder as the members of the Order bid farewell to General Yoav. The singing ended and Rathe, Shamgar and Abendigo set the funeral pyre on fire with the torches. Kasnata stepped forward and drew her sword.

"We live by the will of Arala, we die by the sword. Let those we give to her flames be welcomed into her arms and find peace."

"By the will of Arala, by the will of fire," *the members of the Order replied.*

Helez and Asahel watched as Rathe, Abendigo and Shamgar were joined by the other generals of the Order and Princess Kia, forming a ring around the burning pyre. Other members of the Order stepped forward until seven circles had been formed.

Shamgar looked at Rathe and nodded. The former general of Nosfa took a deep breath and let out a long, mournful howl that was taken up by those stood in the seven circles.

"No sacrifice shall be forgotten, no life is lost that we do not remember," *Kasnata said as the howling died out.* "For the love of each other, those we fight to protect, those that we would die to defend."

A roar erupted from all the warriors of the Order. It was a war cry that would curdle the blood of any that heard it on the battlefield, and it caused a shiver to run down the spines of Helez and Asahel.

The two men watched as the High Priestess of Arala stepped forward to lead the members of the Order in prayer. Music began to play and those in the seven circles began to dance.

The circles all danced slightly out of sync, so the two men could see a ripple effect coming from the centre.

"I would get some rest if I were you," *Kasnata smiled at Helez and Asahel.*

"But the funeral isn't over," Helez frowned.

"No, but they will dance until dawn, take the chance to rest," Kasnata replied.

"What are you going to do?" Asahel asked.

"I have a guest to greet. She has been waiting for a day to meet with me," the queen said with a sigh.

"Can we come too?" Helez asked.

Kasnata blinked several times and looked blankly at the two men.

"If you want to," she said slowly. "I don't know why you would want too though."

"We were both trained to protect Lady Hermia, as you are our queen and the one we are currently pledged to serve, it seems only right that we use our skills to protect you," Asahel grinned at the queen.

Kasnata laughed and nodded,

"Very well."

Asahel and Helez followed the queen through the camp to the tent where the Mother of Dawn and the children of Delma were staying.

"Well, a child no longer, I see," the Mother of Dawn greeted Kasnata as she entered the tent.

"I told you, she has grown well," Cassandra was sat next to the Mother of Dawn with one of the children asleep on her knee.

"You were right. I should know better than to doubt you," the Mother of Dawn sighed.

"Back so soon?" Kasnata asked Cassandra with a raised eyebrow.

"Yes, there was something I needed to check on. It didn't take long," Cassandra replied. Kasnata knew better than to press the Guardian of the Wilds *for more details.*

"Misna tells me that you bring news from Delma as well as refugees," Kasnata said, turning her attention to the Mother of Dawn.

"I am sorry to say that I do. Baruch has sentenced Kasna to death. She is to be executed by the Regent," the Mother of Dawn said grimly.

Helez and Asahel watched as the queen's face became a mask of rage, and she drew herself up to her full height.

"Then the siege is over. We march on the city and Baruch will watch his kingdom burn for daring to pass sentence on my daughter," Kasnata said through gritted teeth.

"That is one response, but if I might suggest a more subtle approach?" Cassandra said tactfully.

"This execution isn't to be public. Most people in Delma have no idea that the princess has been sentenced to death. Baruch intends to sacrifice Kasna in order to resurrect the seducer, Hyse. By having Kelmar sacrifice Kasna, the duke will become the slave of Hyse and Baruch will not only have brought back the dead goddess, but will have preserved his mind as well," the Mother of Dawn explained.

"What are you talking about?" Asahel asked looking worried.

"What do you know of the Seven Stars?" Cassandra enquired.

"That it is the religion that serves the dead goddess, Hyse," Asahel replied.

"That's it?" Cassandra frowned. Asahel nodded. "The Seven Stars serves Hyse, but she isn't dead, not really. She is sleeping and powerless unless the blood of the Goddess Arala is spilt in sacrifice to her. When Hyse rises, the Goddess Arala diminishes until she is sleeping and powerless in our world. When this

happens, all life is extinguished save for those that have pledged themselves to the Seven Stars," the Guardian of the Wilds explained.

"How do you know that?" Helez asked.

"Because it has happened before. There are many ancient texts that record eons before any of our peoples came to Celadmore. Plus, the Oracles are not really alive so they have survived each of these purges," the Mother of Dawn answered.

"But those who have pledged themselves to the Seven Stars are not safe. The one who has sacrificed the blood of the Goddess Arala becomes the slave of the seducer. His mind is completely lost and his entire purpose for existing is to serve the whims and desires of the seducer. Those who have attended the ceremony of resurrection are given whatever it is they desire for their part in aiding the seducer. But it doesn't last. The seducer cares only for destruction and uses the desires of the servants of the Seven Stars to ruin them until the only thing left is death. Eventually the slave of the seducer dies and with no one left to worship her, the Seven Stars begin to wane. Then life begins again, and the Goddess Arala takes up her place once more. Thus, the cycle begins again," Cassandra continued.

"So, if Baruch were to sacrifice Kasna, then we would all die?" Asahel asked.

"In fire and blood," the Mother of Dawn nodded.

"Which is why we must destroy Delma now," Kasnata said firmly.

"Peace, your majesty, General Avner is in the city, he will be able to delay the execution for a time. The Mother of Dawn and I agree that removing Kelmar and Kasna from the city would be the best thing to do in this situation," Cassandra tried to calm Kasnata.

"*General Avner is not your only ally in the city. Colonel Mae is loyal to Kelmar before the king. With the help of the Eight and Methanlan, I believe we can get them out of the city with almost no bloodshed,*" *the Mother of Dawn explained.*

"*The Eight have gone in search of the men that razed Ashpa; I don't know when they will return. Warner isn't with them either. We cannot delay,*" *Kasnata argued.*

"Venia, stay your hand," *Cassandra warned. Kasnata scowled at the Guardian of the Wilds.*

"*It is my daughter's life we are talking about,*" *Kasnata retorted.*

"*No, it is all life we are talking about and by rushing into battle you would risk every living thing on Celadmore and across the other realms to try to save your daughter,*" *Cassandra was losing her patience.*

Kasnata closed her eyes and tried to clear her mind.

"*If you can send word to General Avner, tell him we need him to delay the execution for two weeks from today. If the Eight are not back by then, we take the city by force,*" *the queen said with resignation.*

"*Very well, your highness,*" *the Mother of Dawn nodded.*

"*Have you decided who is to replace General Yoav yet?*" *Cassandra asked.*

"*Abendigo,*" *Kasnata replied shortly and left the tent to get some fresh air.*

"*Are you alright?*" *Asahel asked as he and Helez followed the queen.*

"*I will be fine. It has been a very intense day,*" *Kasnata sighed and stared up at the stars.* "*Four of my children and my lover are saved from the hands of my enemies, but General Yoav is lost and the whole of existence is threatened because the king, whose city I am laying siege to, has my daughter as his captive and though my army could reduce the city to rubble I am forced to wait.”*

“If I might, your highness, you are coping extremely well with it all,” Helez offered.

“Thank you, if you don’t mind, I need some time alone to think,” the queen said, excusing herself from the two men. She walked into the camp of the men of Nosfa and checked the fortifications that had been built to protect against any further assaults from the city.

As dawn broke, the queen walked back to her quarters and found Rathe waiting for her. It was the first time the two had been alone since he had returned to the camp. He didn’t say a word as she entered the tent, merely turned and opened his arms to her.

Kasnata collapsed into his arms and cried as the former general held her.

CHAPTER 13

Joab spent weeks in the Spire. He spent that time confined to three rooms so that he didn't disturb the others that lived there. The Abbott came to visit him every day, but Joab saw no evidence that there was anyone other than the Abbott in the Spire with him.

The young shadow was frustrated at being stopped from going to Mia and seeking vengeance against the Baron of Fintry, but he also knew that it took time to recover strength and even after seven weeks he had not fully recovered enough to fight a man like the baron.

There was little to do in the Spire save for sleep, eat the food the Abbott brought, examine the strange architecture and read the books the lined the walls.

The rooms in the Spire were unlike anything Joab had ever come across before. They seemed to be made from some sort of opaque crystal that created light. There were no windows in any of the walls and the doors seemed to open of their own accord as there was nothing that Joab could find that resembled a handle.

The light crystal provided wasn't constant either; Joab noticed that it would wane as night drew in and when he lay down to sleep the crystal would cease to produce any light at all. He knew that if he sat for too long contemplating why these things happened, it would quickly become an unnerving place to be. So instead, he read.

The books that lined the room he was held in were a strange mixture of books. Some were in languages he'd never heard of, some made him feel queasy when he touched them; others made him want to laugh. The books that he had read so far had been in the language of Roenca. One was a history of the village written a hundred years before Joab had been born. Another was a folk tale about how the City of Grashindorph had come into existence.

Every day, Joab sat in the same chair in one of the rooms and slowly read through one of the books.

"What are you reading now?" the Abbott asked as he brought Joab his breakfast.

"A book that I thought was a story but now I'm not as sure," Joab said as he turned to the next page.

"Oh?" the Abbott smiled.

"It seemed like it was the story of a knight who set of on a quest for one of the ancient kings of Grashindorph, but I'm being to think it is the diary of the knight," Joab looked up from the book.

"You're quite right; it is the diary of the First Knight of Grashindorph. He was sent into the gauntlet a long time ago and he wrote down everything that happened. He was surprisingly good with a pen as well as a sword," the Abbott said as Joab closed the book and moved to the small table that the Abbott was setting out his breakfast on.

"When will I be able to leave?" Joab waited for an answer before he started eating.

"I think you're strong enough now. You've been here much longer than you think," the Abbott said with a shrug.

"I can go today?" Joab blinked several times.

"You may, though there are a few things that you will need to know," the Abbott stood and beckoned for Joab to follow him.

The two walked out of Joab's three rooms and walked down the corridor *that lay outside of the room. It was a sloping corridor that slowly curved around a central column of clear crystal. The corridor reached from the ground to the top of the Spire and there seemed to hundreds of rooms that led off it.*

Joab stared at the doors as they passed, wondering what lay behind them. When they reached the grand entrance chamber, Joab saw there were hundreds of robe men stood waiting for them. They were men of different creeds and Joab was sure that some of them couldn't possibly have been born from any of the people of Celadmore.

"We have returned, Abbott," one of the brethren said stepping forward and bowing his head.

"Is everything prepared?" the Abbott asked.

"It is." the brethren chorused.

"Thank you."

The other monks all bowed to the Abbott and began to filter out of the entrance chamber into the many corridors that led off it.

"What is going on?" Joab frowned, but the Abbott didn't reply. He stepped passed the shadow and opened the doors of the Spire.

The land that lay outside the doors of the Spire was completely alien to Joab. There were plants and hills enough, but he had never seen any of them before. There were three suns and four moons hanging in a purple sky that was streaked with orange.

"We are not in Celadmore anymore," the Abbott said shortly.

"Then take me back," Joab shouted.

"I am afraid we can't," the Abbott sighed and looked at the shadow sadly.

"What do you mean, you can't?" Joab yelled, he felt his pulse quicken

and knew that his anger was overwhelming all rational thought. In Celadmore there was Mia, the Gibborim and the Baron of Fintry; his entire purpose for living.

"We have been here for weeks; it seems that the Spire has deemed that this is where you are to live," the Abbott explained gently.

"What do you mean, the Spire is not alive! It is a building," Joab spat.

"That isn't altogether true. The Spire is not simply a building it is magic and light that are held together by crystal and it changes as fate requires. It moves between realms, and I think it has even stepped across time when I haven't been looking as well," the Abbott tried to calm Joab with his explanation.

"So, you have no control over it?" Joab asked, not quite able to believe what he was hearing.

"A limited amount of control. As long as the doors are open then it will remain where it is. When the doors close then it is something of a mystery as to what will happen next," the Abbott admitted.

"I don't believe this, what am I supposed to do? Where am I supposed to go?" Joab stammered as he stared at the alien land before him.

"My brethren have been hard at work whilst you have been recovering. They have scouted the land. There appears to be plenty of water and a wide variety of food here. They have built a homestead for you. From what they have said it is very large and grand, far bigger than you will ever need it to be, and it is easy to defend should you be attacked," the Abbott said as he stepped out of the door and onto the stony ground of the alien realm.

"So, I am just to live here, in a homestead?" Joab asked, completely dumbfounded.

"It seems so for the moment, though I do not think you will be alone long," the Abbott replied.

"Do you even know what this place is like? Does it have a name?" Joab asked on the brink of tears.

"It is the land of Oran, and it is a land that has a feeling of destiny about it," the Abbott replied as he led Joab to the homestead.

Lady Hermia Nosfa sat looking at the Baron of Fintry. The man scowled at the Queen Mother and refused to speak. He had been beaten by Jephthah and tortured by Layla, but the man still refused to break.

"Do you know why I am here?" Hermia asked the baron. He raised an eyebrow in reply and tried to look bored as he leaned back in the chair he was chained to.

"I see, well I imagine you think that I am here to shock you into confessing your part in my son's schemes, but no. I think you have suspected that I wasn't dead for some time and that the appearance of Jephthah and Layla at whatever that mockery of an event was, confirmed it for you," Hermia rattled off.

Layla, Jephthah and Kilaran all watched the exchange from a distance, out of the eye line of the baron. When Kilaran had seen that Lady Hermia was alive, he had fallen on his knees and wept with relief, taking a vow to serve Lady Hermia in restoring peace to Grashindorph.

"You see, there is nothing we need from you, other than your presence. The blood moon has been destroyed and we have been sent word that Neesa is dead. There only thing we needed was to remove you from your position in

Grashindorph and watch everything descend into chaos," Hermia smiled.

The baron frowned and closed his eyes with a disdainful snort.

"Ah, I see, you don't believe me. Well, that is to be expected. Then let me say that Jephthah was allowed to beat you in retribution for what you did to his wife. Layla was allowed to torture you in retribution for murdering her son," Hermia said as she slowly stood and walked towards the Baron. Kilaran shot a glance at Layla.

"You didn't know that Joab was her son when he came to work in the palace, did you? What a piece of information for both you and Neesa to miss," Hermia said as she stopped behind the Baron.

"What's going on?" Mathias whispered as he appeared beside Layla.

"The baron is about to break." Layla hissed in reply.

"There are two who deserve to take a pound of flesh from you for what happened to Ilana, but they are far from here now, and Bracha bore the brunt of their wrath. So that must be enough for them. You see, with Neesa dead and you in our custody, there is no one left with any influence over the king in his court. How long do you think it will be until my son's mind completely unravels?" Hermia asked, leaning forward. "Especially when he learns that his Knight-Marshal has disappeared as well."

"You think you are so superior to my king," the baron snapped. "You think that he is a lesser man for wanting power, for wanting to make our nation greater? He is a great and glorious leader."

"No, he's a delusional creature that has become so focused upon himself that he has forgotten that his first and only duty is to his people," Hermia said in the baron's ear.

"The people love their king," the baron shot back.

"The people are seeking shelter from their king. Every day people flood into the Gibborim trying to escape him. The city above is emptying baron, the time of Mercia is over," Hermia stepped back from the Baron and turned to the men that were watching. "Mathias, bring her in."

Mathias nodded and disappeared, returning with Mia on his arm a few moments later.

The Lady of Afdanic was far from the creature that she had once been. She shrank to Mathias' side when she saw the baron. Her skin was a sallow colour, and her eyes were sunk into her skull – two effects of the sleeping draft that Hermia knew were permanent.

"It's all right, Mia. He can't hurt you here," Hermia assured the young woman as Mathias led her to the former queen's side.

"Lady Mia, the king will be pleased," the baron said as he looked the young girl up and down with lustful eyes. Mia shrieked and tried to run from the room, but Mathias bundled her to his chest and calmed her down.

Jephthah took two steps forwards and hit the baron across the back of his head. The force of the blow caused the chair with the baron in to fall forwards, the baron's head striking the floor with enough force to split it open.

"You'll pay for that, you, common thug!" the baron cried.

"No, he won't." Layla laughed as Jephthah picked up the baron, and the chair that he was in, and righted them both.

"Mia, he can't hurt you here," Mathias soothed as the woman whimpered.

"Mia, the Baron of Fintry has done far more to harm you than any of us. We are leaving what happens to him up to you," Hermia said as Mia lifted her head from Mathias' chest.

"Kill him," Mia sniffed.

"And you thought she'd want to show him mercy," Jephthah whispered under his breath to Layla.

"Very well," Hermia agreed, her lip curling slightly.

"You can't kill me!" the baron declared and struggled to try and get out of the chair.

"I want him to die like Joab did. He left him bleeding on the tavern floor. I want him to die knowing how Joab felt." Mia gasped between sobs.

"Layla," Hermia nodded to her shadow. Layla took her dagger from her belt and moved to stand in front of the baron.

"Cowards! All of you!" the baron's eyes were wide with fear as Layla slowly pushed the point of her dagger between the baron's ribs. His screams choked in his throat as blood started to fill his lung.

"Take Mia back to her room, she doesn't need to watch this," Hermia murmured to Mathias. The assassin nodded and gently steered Mia out of the room.

"What do we now?" Kilaran asked as he looked down on the baron with a small measure of satisfaction as he watched the man he hated die.

"We wait," Hermia replied.

"What for?" Kilaran frowned and looked at the Queen Mother.

"For the rioting to start," Layla replied.

The Baron of Fintry had died a whimpering mess, but none in the Gibborim had shed a tear for him. His body was left for the rats to find, and

Hermia had dismissed everyone for the day. Kilaran had been glad to finally steal a few moments alone with Layla.

"Joab was your son?" he asked when she had taken him back to her quarters.

"Our son," Layla said sadly.

"I see," Kilaran sighed and shook his head.

"I am sorry. I would have told you, only you would have wanted to be a family in the most conventional way, and it would have only caused us to resent one another. I did not want that for you or me. I am truly sorry that you did not have the opportunity to know your son," Layla explained.

"I understand, I do. And you are right, I would have insisted that you stayed at home to raise him as my wife, and I continued in my duties, and it would have destroyed us. I am glad that he was such a fine man. To spend his life dedicated to another and to protect Lady Mia for as long as he did under the watchful gaze of both Fintry and Mercia. I am proud to know he was my son," Kilaran said, offering Layla a weak smile.

"I thought that I had let go of him when he chose to train as a shadow, but the truth is that ever since I heard of his death, my heart has not stopped aching. He was part of us both, I could not be with you, but with him beside me it was as though you were standing somewhere just out of sight, watching over us," Layla admitted.

"I truly have missed you. There has never been another," Kilaran said as he took hold of Layla's hand and squeezed it gently.

"And I you. Perhaps now, as we both are in the service of Lady Hermia, it is our moment?" Layla shrugged and squeezed Kilaran's hand back.

"In the service of Lady Hermia, she will always come first. Can you *accept that she will always be before you?" Kilaran asked with a frown.*

"Yes. Can you?" Layla asked hopefully.

"To have you in my arms and bed again? Yes," Kilaran smiled and kissed her gently. "Come, we should go down to dinner."

"Dinner can wait," Layla said firmly as she kissed him passionately and took her lover to bed.

"Are you sure that we should be doing this now? I mean, shouldn't we wait for Warner to come back?" *Merinda asked in a low voice as the seven children of Ashpa moved through the trees.*

The forest wasn't particularly dense, but the melting snow made the ground difficult to negotiate, so the members of the Eight had chosen to leave their mounts at the edge of the forest and continue on foot.

"We don't even know where he is let alone when he is coming back. We know where the slavers are now, if we don't act now, we may never find them again," *Scattergood hissed in reply.*

"He's right, the longer we wait, the harder it will be to find out what happened to Jericho and Natalia," *Resha agreed.*

Vaike and Colm were scouting ahead of the rest of the party, searching for any signs of people having passed through the trees ahead of them. The other five members of the Eight moved slowly, making sure that they stayed low and made as little noise as possible.

After three hours of making steady progress through the forest, Scattergood, Lucinda, Merinda, Resha and Adino came across Vaike and Colm crouched behind a small clump of evergreen bushes.

"You've found something?" *Adino asked.*

"There are tracks leading in and out of the old mine ahead. Looks like horses, men and carts have all been going in and out of there quite recently," *Vaike replied.*

"Are you sure this is an abandoned mine and not an active one?" *Lucinda asked.*

"Positive. There's not sign of anything being brought to the surface. There are no rubble piles and no one is on the surface to check through what is being brought out," *Colm replied.*

"Then this is there the slavers are?" *Scattergood said through clenched teeth.*

"It's probable; they could be refugees hiding from the war and the Wentrus weather," *Vaike offered.*

"Have you been into the mine yet?" *Resha asked.*

"No, we thought it might be wise to wait for you, just in case," *Colm grinned.*

"Then it looks like we have a mine to explore," *Merinda sighed.*

"Vaike, you and Colm will go in as a unit, Lucinda and Adino as another and I will go with Resha. Merinda, you stay out here and watch for any signs of people coming or going. If it looks like we've been captured or killed, ride back to the Order and tell General Misna and Warner what happened," *Scattergood ordered. Each of the others nodded to show they understood what they needed to do.*

Merinda moved away from the group first, finding a tree she could climb and hide amongst the branches. The others drew their swords and moved cautiously towards the mine.

There was a single shaft that went down into the belly of the rock, but there were lots of different shafts that split from the main one and even with three parties, Scattergood knew it was going to take some time to find out who was in the mine.

Rather than look down every shaft, the children of Ashpa looked for signs that someone had recently passed that way. Most of the shafts were undisturbed, but there were six or seven different paths that looked as though they had been recently walked.

Adino and Lucinda took the first of the paths; there were torches on the walls that had been lit about halfway down the main shaft, just as the natural light failed. Each of the pairs had taken one of the torches to allow them to explore the mine.

If there was anyone living in the mines, then they would have to have torches and fires that would cast more light than the single torches that the pairs carried.

Vaike and Colm took the second path, marking the wooden support beams with a diamond so that if Adino and Lucinda came back without finding anything, they wouldn't waste time exploring the same path as Vaike and Colm.

Scattergood and Resha moved further in, the two moving all the way to the end of the main shaft before picking a route to explore. Some of the offshoots had some signs that people have passed down them, but there were only two that seemed big enough for carts to travel down.

As far as Scattergood was concerned, the route that was furthest in was the most likely to be the one that led to where the slavers had their main camp and where any slaves would be held.

Resha followed Scattergood without saying a word. She knew that Jericho disappearing had hurt Scattergood more than losing Ashpa had. He felt responsible for his brother and for Natalia. Resha was the same age as Jericho, and the two had been very close as they grew up.

There were some mornings when Resha woke up in the camp of the Order and her first thoughts were of Jericho. It was why Scattergood had chosen Resha as his partner for the mine. Whatever they found in the maze of man-made tunnels, he knew he could rely on Resha.

They walked for half an hour before Resha signalled they should stop. Ahead, she could see the dim glow that was cast by a large fire and the low rumble of voices gathered around it.

Scattergood set the torch in one of the empty brackets on the wall of the mine and crept forward behind Resha.

As they drew closer to the fire, they could hear the voices much more distinctly.

"We've been here for months, when are we going to leave these stinking mines and head to the market?"

"There is no market. The king in Grashindorph has completely lost his mind and people are being dragged off for questioning every night. The market has shut down."

"Then we go to Zenix or Hespan or Rentano or Sina, the other kingdoms always need slaves."

"No, we'd attract too much attention travelling with across the land with this many slaves when that barbarian horde is camped outside of Delma. We wait it out. When they've broken the siege, we go into Delma and sell the slaves. Until then, we sit tight."

"And where are we going to get the food from to last until then? The slaves are already looking too thin, and some are sick. We'll never get anything for them if they're all dead by the time we can get to a market to sell them."

"Fine, we'll thin the herd. Take the older ones and those that are sick and kill them. Make sure you do it outside and somewhere that the scavengers can pick the corpses clean. That way, the bloody moorin and wolves won't venture down here to look for any live prey."

There were five men sat around the fire, all of them rough-looking men. The fire was set in the middle of the carved-out cavern, and there were cages that were filled with people drawn in a horseshoe against the back wall.

From where Resha and Scattergood crouched, they couldn't see whether Jericho or Natalia were crammed in there with the other slaves.

They watched as two of the men walked towards one of the cages and heard the grating of metal as a key turned in the lock and the door was swung open.

The two men grabbed at the old and the sick, dragging them out of the cages without ceremony and throwing them at the feet of the other three men.

"We should do something," Resha hissed.

"Wait until they herd the slaves past us, we'll slip in amongst them and catch the off-guard when we get outside the mine," Scattergood replied.

The sound of shouting drew the attention of the two children of Ashpa. A young girl was screaming as she was being pulled out of the cage.

"Natalia," Resha gasped.

"Let her go!" a boy shouted from inside the cage.

"Jericho!" Scattergood shouted, the leader of the Eight completely forgetting himself as he rushed towards the cages with his sword drawn.

Resha was right behind Scattergood as the rough-looking men took up arms. They were slow to react though; none of the slavers had expected anyone to find them so deep in the mines.

The weapons they had to hand were knives and cudgels, something that they were adept at wielding, but Resha and Scattergood had been training with warriors whose pedigree lay in war and death.

Scattergood's sword cut easily across the throat of one of the men who was trying to skewer the young man with a blunt knife, as Resha flew past.

She wielded two short blades and easily dodged the wildly swinging cudgels of the two men that were still by the fire. The girl slashed at their legs, bringing both men to their knees so that Scattergood could deliver the killing blow to both.

"Stop!" one of the slavers yelled. Scattergood and Resha looked up to see the two men holding the slaves around them at sword point.

"Let them go," Resha warned.

"No, you're going to back away and leave here or we'll kill these slaves," the slaver replied.

"You can start to kill them, but we'll kill you before you get very far," Resha replied with a dangerous look in her eyes.

"Not before we've killed the people you came here for," the other slaver replied.

The air to the right of Scattergood and Resha rippled as two arrows flew past them and struck the remaining two slavers in the chest.

Scattergood turned around slowly to see Vaike and Colm stood and a little behind them.

"You certainly make a lot of noise," Vaike grinned at Scattergood as

be shouldered his bow.

"Scattergood! Resha!" *Jericho shouted as he limped out of the cage. Scattergood felt anger rising in his chest as he saw the condition his brother was in.*

The boy was nothing more than skin and bones. His leg had clearly been broken and left without any splint, so it had set at an odd angle, making it difficult for him to walk.

Resha watched as the two brothers embraced and smiled to herself. She turned and walked over to where Natalia was sat crying and picked the little girl up and carried her away from the other slaves to calm her down.

"Adino and Lucinda are clearing the rest of the mineshafts, we found food, water and horses, there are a couple of carts too," *Vaike reported to Scattergood.*

Colm was searching the bodies of the slavers. He took the keys off one of the men and unlocked the remaining cages. The slaves were crying with joy and relief as they fell out of their iron prisons.

Some were too weak to stand, others openly wept in each other's arms.

"What do we do with all these people? We can't leave them here," *Colm said as he walked back to where Vaike, Resha and Natalia were sat.*

"We take them back to the camp of the Order. Even if we knew where they all came from and their homes were all still there, with the war it's too dangerous to send them out into the wilds without any protection," *Vaike replied and looked at Scattergood for confirmation. The leader of the Eight nodded his agreement.*

"I'll go fetch the carts, horses and supplies," *Colm said and disappeared down the mineshaft.*

"We'll have to load as many people into the carts as we can. A lot of them won't be able to walk to the edge of the forest, let alone back to the camp," *Resha said as she looked over the freed slaves.*

"I'll go find Merinda; we'll scout the area and see if there is any ground that is firm enough for laden carts to travel over," *Vaike said. He ruffled Natalia's hair, causing the young girl to giggle, as he turned and went back to the entrance of the mine.*

"I can't believe you found us. I prayed that you'd come. Every night, but it has been so long since we were brought here I was beginning to give up," *Jericho whispered to his brother.*

"We never gave up hope of finding you," *Scattergood smiled.*

"How did you find us?" *Jericho asked as he lay down on the floor of the mine.*

"The warriors of the Order helped us. They took us in when they found us wandering the wilds. Their spymaster kept searching for you. She is the one that heard of the slavers and sent us to you," *Scattergood explained.*

"Are you going to take everyone back to the camp?" *Jericho turned his head to look at the people that had been held prisoner with him.*

"Everyone who wants to come. We aren't going to force anyone to go who doesn't want to, but they will be safe there. Much safer than if they decided to try and survive out there on their own with no weapons or food," *Scattergood sighed.*

"I'll talk to them, explain what's going on. They'll be suspicious of anyone trying to take them anywhere in carts after what happened here," *Jericho said slowly.*

"Are you all right?" *Scattergood asked in a low voice.*

"I am now it's over," *Jericho said firmly as he rolled onto his side, struggled to his feet and went to talk to the other slaves.*

Kelmar sat in his quarters and thought. He had spent his entire life being raised to fulfil the role of Regent for the king. There were many reasons that a Regent was needed according to the law of Delma. Not only was he to act as a caretaker to the throne if the king was unfit to rule, but with the death of Prince Jayden, he was now the heir to the throne.

He had been schooled from an early age in the ways of court and diplomacy, conduct for the battlefield and how to fight duels, but he had not been trained for dealing with the situation that he now found himself faced with.

Kasna had been hauled away to the dungeons and he was expected to execute her. According to all his training in etiquette, the king had no right to sentence the princess of another kingdom to death, no matter what the charge – even if they were at war with them.

Kelmar had been sat in quiet shock for several days. He refused to leave his rooms and didn't speak a word to the servants that brought him food. Colonel Deena Mae had been put in charge of Kasna's incarceration, and the execution date had been set for three days' time.

As far as Kelmar could see, it was his fault that Kasna was to be executed and it was this that had caused him to retreat from the world.

In three days, he would have to stand before the king and queen of

Delma and execute the woman that he loved for the sake of his duty. He thought back to the time in he and Kasna had spent in the Spire, how close he had come to spilling her blood to save his country and end the war that raged. A knock at the door to his rooms caused him to stir from his reminiscing.

"I said I wasn't to be disturbed!" *Kelmar yelled. There was a pause and the handle on the door slowly turned. Kelmar narrowed his eyes and got to his feet. He drew his sword as he marched to his door, determined to dissuade the interloper with force if necessary. He grabbed hold of the door and threw it open.*

"Some might consider being greeted at the door with a drawn sword as a breach of etiquette," General Avner said with a careless smile.

"What are you doing here?" Kelmar asked. He was shocked by the presence of the general. As he recovered from the initial surprise, Kelmar began to feel his stomach sinking.

"I came to talk to you about Kasna," Avner said as he stepped past Kelmar into the room and the duke closed the door behind him.

"I am sorry, but I do not wish to discuss the princess," Kelmar said flatly, but Avner ignored him.

"I understand why you have reacted like this, you have sworn to do your duty, and when duty conflicts with love it is a difficult course to navigate. However, I would say this - your duty is to your country, not to an individual," Avner said as he sat down.

"How can you say such a thing?" Kelmar exploded at the general. Avner looked at the man and smiled with satisfaction.

"With great ease, there are many things that we are called on to do in the service of our nations. We are called upon to die, to kill, to sentence those we

consider innocent to death for the sake of a greater number. And the higher the office, the greater those burdens are. But when it comes to a ruler who has turned his back on his people and serves to only increase his own power, something must be done," Avner said in a low voice.

Kelmar opened and closed his mouth several times as he processed what Avner had said.

"You mean I should go against the orders of my king?" he said, finally.

"Of course, why whatever did you think I meant?" Avner asked with amusement.

"That I should carry out the execution of Kasna because it is my duty to carry out the orders of my king," Kelmar said slowly.

"Baruch has clearly lost his mind. Though his madness is not as deep as reports from Grashindorph suggests that Mercia's sanity has sunk to, he is not making decisions that would benefit his nation," Avner said seriously.

"I don't know what I can do to save her," Kelmar shrugged helplessly.

"All I ask of you is that when you stand over her to take her life that you have the strength to refuse. If you can do that, then there is hope," Avner said firmly.

A second knock on the door to his rooms interrupted Kelmar's reply.

"Yes?" Kelmar shouted. The door cracked open, and a messenger stepped into the room.

"I'm sorry, your grace, I bring a message from the king," *the messenger stammered.*

"Well, what is it?" *Kelmar snapped.*

"The execution of Princess Kasna Nosfa is hereby delayed. It shall now take place in twenty days," *the messenger recited hurriedly and then rushed from the room, closing the door firmly behind him. Kelmar creased his brow and turned to look at Avner.*

"Was that your doing?" Kelmar asked.

"It's possible. I must bid you a good day, I have letters to write and send that need to arrive promptly. The earlier I can send them, the less likely they will be intercepted by spies," Avner said as he rose and walked past the duke towards the door. "Oh, something for you to remember when you ascend to the throne; if you are going to erect a heretical altar under the palace where dignitaries of many nations walk the halls, it would be wise to have it guarded. Otherwise, you may find that it has been desecrated and rendered completely unusable for, say, a scheduled human sacrifice."

Merinda and Vaike found a path through the slush and trees that allowed the Eight to drive the carts, filled with the freed slaves, out of the forest. There were several times when the carts got stuck and had to be pushed out of the boggy ground, but by the time night was falling, they had reached the edge of the treeline where they had left their horses.

The food and water that Vaike and Colm had discovered in the tunnels was rationed and shared between the freed slaves and the children of Ashpa.

Before they had departed, Jericho had explained that all the slaves needed to get into the carts so they could be taken to the camp of the Order. There had been protests and arguments that had lasted for a few hours. Eventually, they had all agreed to board the carts. The promise of food, protection from the war, and care for those who were sick and wounded was enough to persuade those who longed for home that traveling back to Kasnata's camp would be best.

It took the party far longer than the Eight realised to march back to the camp outside of Delma. The snow was thawing, and they had to stick to the roads with the carts where they could.

General Misna and the Mother of Dawn were waiting at the edge of the camp with Payne when the Eight and their company finally reached it. The freed slaves were cold, tired and hungry.

"I see you found something in the slavers' camp," Misna said wryly as she watched the carts being driven towards the camp.

"They were trapped in some abandon mines by the Wentrus caused by the blood moon," Lucinda reported as she halted the cart she drove. There were five carts that Lucinda, Scattergood, Colm, Adino and Resha all drove. Their horses were tied to the back of their carts and laden with the supplies that they had found in the mines.

Merinda and Vaike rode either side of the carts to protect them from moorin and bandits.

"I trust that you didn't leave any of them alive," Payne frowned as he stepped forward and climbed into the closest cart to check on the freed slaves.

"All the slavers that were there are dead. We left as fast as we could, didn't want to wait around to see if there were more of them," Scattergood replied.

"Did you find your brother?" Misna asked.

"I did, this is my brother, Jericho," Scattergood said as he introduced him to the general.

"And this is Natalia. She's the girl Jericho went to find when we lost him," Merinda smiled as she helped the young girl out of her cart.

"*I am glad to see that you found what you were looking for,*" the general said as she looked over the frightened and drawn faces of the former slaves.

"*There are a lot of people who need to be healed, general; we need to set up a camp for these people as soon as possible,*" Payne barked from the back of one of the carts.

"*I will see to it at once,*" the Mother of Dawn said with a smile.

"*Payne, I will leave these people in your care, the Eight are required elsewhere,*" General Misna said. Payne grumbled something under his breath, but his voice was too low for Misna to hear what it was.

The general beckoned for the Eight to follow her. The seven warriors of Ashpa left the slaves to the Mother of Dawn and Payne and followed Misna through Kasnata's camp.

"*We've had news from Delma,*" Misna explained as they walked.

"*General Avner?*" Resha asked.

"*Yes, King Baruch has sentenced Princess Kasna to death. The news came to the camp just after you left. General Avner has managed to delay the execution by two weeks, but time is running out. Her majesty has agreed to a plan laid down by the Guardian of the Wilds. They are waiting for us in the War Tent with Methanlan and Abendigo,*" Misna replied.

"*We're going into the city?*" Adino asked.

"*You will find out when we reach the tent,*" Misna smiled and the party quickened their pace.

King Mercia Nosfa sat on the throne in his palace outside of the city

walls. His face was haggard and drawn. There were rumours flying around his court that the Baron of Fintry had been captured by the rebellion and that the king's mistress had fled.

Any question that the servants asked him were met with a tirade of nonsense that was backed by an unbridled rage. None of the nobles would dare approach or even speak to the king. The guards in the city were left to continue their reign of fear over the populace and as the guards became more violent, and the people suffered, the riots began.

The streets of Grashindorph ran red with blood, and the Gibborim began to stir.

Chapter 14

Rathe rose early every morning. He was sharing the quarters of the queen and their children, and the babies were often awake long before the general and the queen wanted to be.

The command of the army of Nosfa had been turned back over to Rathe, with Tola acting as his second. The hero of the war of the east was only too glad to have the general back in the camp and the responsibilities of command taken off his shoulders.

Every morning when the babies awoke, Kasnata and Rathe would rise. The queen would take care of the children before beginning her day of command and Rathe would depart to inspect the condition of the men of Nosfa.

During the night, Tola was given the task of dealing with whatever arose. He didn't sleep during the night and barely slept during the day, so Rathe thought it best to keep the man busy during the darker hours.

Every morning, when Rathe walked from his tent to the camp of the men of Nosfa, he felt a sense of peace settle in his chest, the same feeling he used to get when he would walk around the city of Afdanic.

When he had first been assigned to command the army of Nosfa for the king, he had never imagined that he would feel comfortable in the camp of warriors.

"Good morning, Pup," *Benaiah greeted him as the general walked past the forge. The doors to the forge were flung open and the forge master was hard at work.*

"Good morning, forge master, how are you this morning?" *Rathe asked, smiling at the usage of the name that Yoav had given him.*

"Well, the snow thawing is a good sign that Spregan is coming. Will be a welcome season after this extended Wentrus," *Benaiah replied as he worked the bellows on his forge.*

"As the forge master, I wouldn't think that the cold bothered you too much," *Rathe said*

"Aye, well it isn't an unpleasant place to work when it's cold. How are the berns?" *the forge master grunted.*

"They're safe and well. Glad to be back in the arms of their mother," *Rathe replied.*

"Well, that I can understand. Child is never happier than when it's with its mother. There's something I have for you. It's a gift from her majesty. She asked me to craft something for you, thought you needed a blade that was more fitting to your position. I finished it not long after you were recalled by the mad monarch. Think she'd be happy knowing you finally got it," *the giant made his way to the back of his forge and returned a few moments later with a beautifully crafted blade in his hands.*

"For me?" *Rathe asked as Benaiah offered him the blade.*

"It's called the Cas Carlan, seemed appropriate for a man like you, seems that you have the heart of the hunt. Not many would be able to escape death at the hands of the mad monarch, save his children from the last heir of Valia, and return to the woman he loves with more allies for our cause," *Benaiah smiled.*

"Thank you, it's perfect," *Rathe said as he clasped the hilt.*

"You're welcome, guess that means you're one of us now," *Benaiah said gruffly as he returned to work, leaving the general to gaze at his new sword.*

The twins were asleep in their cradle in the corner of the War Tent. Tola, Rathe, Shamgar, Misna, Quisla, Princess Kia, Shaul, Samara, Amalia, Marissa, Asahel, Helez, General Kia and Kasnata were all stood around the map table discussing plans for the assault on the city of Delma.

"The Eight are going into the city tonight with Cassandra and Methanlan to help General Avner bring out Princess Kasna. The Order of the Wolf, under the command of General Abendigo, are going to provide an escape route for them and a distraction, should they need to divert attention away from them fleeing," Kasnata explained as she leaned over the table.

"When are you planning to launch our assault against the city?" General Kia asked.

"In thirty days. When the snow has thawed, and Spregan has arrived in force. The fields will have dried out, making any assault much easier to conduct. Samara, recall all those that can be spared from the outposts that are being constructed," Kasnata replied.

"What is the feeling in the city?" Marissa asked.

"The Mother of Dawn reports that the mood is dark. Rationing is being ever more restricted. The poorest are being refused food and water. The orphans she brought with her to the camp were the first to be excluded from the rationing. As things get worse, more will starve," Kasnata said grimly.

"What of General Avner, has he been excluded from the rationing?" Shamgar asked.

"I would imagine he has; he was sent into the city with his own supplies,"

Misna replied.

"He makes no mention of his treatment in his reports," Kasnata sighed.

"What about Kelmar?" Tola asked, looking up at the queen with dark-ringed eyes.

"The duke is not our primary concern in the assault," Amalia said gently.

"Damn you all!" Tola yelled. "He murdered one of your own, brutally cut her to pieces before our eyes and none of you want vengeance for that?"

"There is more at work here than you know, Tola. Our hearts all grieve for the loss of Renta and Yoav, but this is war and each of us would gladly lay down our lives, just as they did. By continuing your vendetta against this man, you are not honouring her, only yourself," Quisla warned.

"Peace!" Kasnata demanded. The raised voice of Tola had woken the babies, and both were crying in the corner of the room. Rathe and Princess Kia left the table to quiet the children.

"My scouting parties continue to search for the entrance to the city that Kelmar used in order to take Kasna to the king. So far, they have found nothing, but as the snow continues to melt, we may be able to find what we are looking for," Misna said, changing the subject back to the city.

"Very good. We want only to take the palace and surround the city battlements with our warriors. The inhabitants should be so demoralised that the sight of our forces will be enough for them to surrender. Once we have captured the king and the queen, then we will have taken the city and brought an end to this pointless war." Kasnata said, shaking her head.

The flap to the War Tent opened and closed again.

"I'm sorry to interrupt, your majesty, but there is someone here to see you," Nasus said with a smile.

The warriors assembled around the table all shared a confused glance before following Kasnata outside.

"Greetings, your highness. We have ridden a long way to join you. We bring back one of your number and a host more to add to them," Kania said brightly from the back of her horse.

Warner climbed down from behind the leader of Tulna and bowed before the queen.

"I'm sorry I was away for so long," Warner mumbled.

"You are forgiven, go find the other members of the Eight, they will tell you what lies ahead, and have a surprise for you too," Kasnata smiled and watched the young warrior race off through the camp.

Nodarto was sitting next to Kania and behind them was a long line of cavalry all dressed in the different garb of the Free Cities of Celadmore.

"We are here to bring an end to the bloodshed. The war of the nine kingdoms must end, and we will help see that it is done," Nodarto grinned.

"My friends, you are most welcome here. Come, we must see about getting you settled," Kasnata said brightly.

Behind her, Asahel and Helez stepped away to talk in private.

"Once they have ended this siege, they will be turning to march on Grashindorph. If the Gibborim have not started the uprising against the king before then, there may be nothing left for the queen to liberate," Helez whispered urgently.

"True, but there is nothing we can do about it. We just have to hope that the others have done their part in all this," Asahel sighed.

Misna watched the two young men closely but saw no reason to disturb *their conversation. They would be sent out at first light to search for the entrance to the city. Unlike most of those that had been placed under her command, the two men had spent much of their lives using secret passages to enter and leave the city they lived in. If anyone could discover the secrets of Delma's walls, it was them.*

There was no moon as night fell; thick cloud covered the sky obscuring all light from the heavens. Methanlan led the way across the open land between the camp of the Order and the city of Delma. Cassandra and the Eight were beside him.

They had no need of any secret passage to get into the city. The Mother of Dawn had provided them with detailed instruction of the sewers beneath the city and where to find the grates that would allow the band to sneak through them.

Though their party of ten was small enough to use the sewers on a mission of stealth, it was not a sensible way for the whole army of the Order to assault the city.

The Order of the Wolf were prowling the night not far behind them, waiting to cause mischief if the infiltration party was discovered.

It didn't take long for the ten warriors to find the entrance to the sewers and slip silently into them. They left the grating off the sewer entrance; in case their exit was a hurried one.

Cassandra led the way through the sewers, the way underfoot was treacherous, but after two hours of navigating by the light that filtered down from the city above, they found the exit under the palace.

The Mother of Dawn had told them that it would come up in one of the storerooms close to where Kasna was being held.

"Took you long enough," *Avner grunted as Cassandra emerged from the exit.*

"Glad to see you understood the message," *Cassandra retorted.*

"We don't have much time; Kasna has been taken from her cell to the catacombs already. They will begin the ritual at any moment, and I don't know whether Kelmar is strong enough to defy the king or not," *Avner said urgently as the others all exited the sewers.*

Kasna struggled as best she could against the two soldiers that held her. She kicked and screamed, she tried to tear her arms from their grasp, but it was all to no avail.

They marched her from her cell down into the catacombs. Deena watched as the princess was taken down into the depths of the castle and wished there was something that she could do to help her.

Kasna didn't pay any attention to the path that the soldiers were taking; she simply dug her heels in so that she had to be dragged to the altar that waited for her.

The king and queen were waiting with Kelmar stood beside them. The duke looked at Kasna with sad eyes, but in his hand, he clutched a crooked dagger that looked similar to the one that he had been offered by the Spire.

"Please, Kelmar," *Kasna begged as the soldiers chained the princess to the altar.*

The worshippers of the Seven Stars had all gathered in the catacombs to watch. They were chanting in low voices as Kasna was chained.

"Tonight, is the night that the Seven Stars shall burn brightly once more!" *the queen cried as she stepped forward.*

"The blood of Arala shall be spilled and it shall be her undoing!" *the king cried beside his wife.*

Kelmar closed his eyes. He could feel the clawing at the back of his mind growing stronger, the desire that drove him to slaughter Renta, the desperate need to spill blood boiled in his own as he slowly stepped towards the princess.

Kasna wasn't struggling against the chains. Her face was fixed in an expression of defiance and disgust. She was chained so that when her throat was cut, the blood would pour over the altar that had been prepared.

Kelmar stopped behind the princess and slowly brought the dagger to rest against her throat. Kasna closed her eyes and waited for strike to come. She stretched out her neck to make it harder for the duke to cut, but the strike never came.

Instead, Kelmar dropped the dagger.

"I am not one of your pawns. I will not be the one to shed innocent blood for your schemes of power any longer," *Kelmar shouted.*

"Traitor!" *the king yelled.* "You shall share the same fate as your beloved then."

"Halt in the name of the king," *Deena demanded as she confronted the Eight, Cassandra and Methanlan.*

"Stand aside or die," Adino said abruptly.

"I cannot do that," Deena replied.

"Then we shall kill you and step over your corpse to free the princess," Methanlan said with a nasty smile.

"Peace, all of you," Avner instructed, stepping from the back of the party.

"General Avner, you know I can't let you do this," *Deena said quietly.*

"Go sound the alarm. Raise all from their beds because there are intruders in the city," *Avner instructed.*

"Well, do as the general says!" *Deena shouted at the guard that stood beside her. The terrified soldier sped off down the corridor and moments later the sound of warning bells broke out across the city.*

"The wolf pack will deal with distracting them, now we must focus on saving the princess, and the duke," Avner smiled.

"I'll come with you," Deena said after a moment's thought.

"You know what it will mean if you do," Avner said gently.

"I do, but it is a sacrifice I am willing to make," Deena said firmly.

"Very well, do you know the way to the chamber?" Avner asked.

"I do," Deena confirmed.

"Then lead the way," Avner instructed.

The infiltrator party followed the general and the colonel into the catacombs.

"I am not one of your pawns. I will not be the one to shed innocent blood for your schemes of power any longer," *Kelmar's voice echoed down the passageway.*

"Hurry!" Cassandra urged. The party broke into a run, their weapons drawn as they reached the central chamber and the altar.

"What is the meaning of this?" Baruch demanded.

"We are here on the business of Queen Kasnata of Nosfa and the Order. You have something that belongs to her, and she wants it back," Methanlan grinned as the worshippers tried to attack the warriors.

"Cut them down!" Cassandra shouted.

The warriors went to work carving a path through the faithful of the Seven Stars as Kelmar defended Kasna from any that would try and harm her.

The king and queen fled from the chamber, shouting for the guards.

"We need to be quick; there will be guards here at any moment," Deena yelled over the sounds of battle.

Cassandra raced to the altar. She pulled out a small vial of a coarse black powder and poured a small amount into the locks on the chains.

"This may hurt a bit, but save for finding the key, it's the only way." Cassandra apologised as she brought the flame of a lit candle into contact with the locks on the chains. There was the sound of bursting metal as the chains sprang open.

"Are you all right?" Kelmar asked as the princess collapsed to her knees.

"I am, that didn't hurt as much as I expected," she said with relief.

"You'll need to carry her; I doubt she can run after all that," Cassandra instructed the duke.

"Where are we going?" Kelmar asked, as he scooped the princess up in his arms and followed the infiltration party from the chamber. The worshippers of the Seven Stars all lay dead save for the king and queen.

Deena led the way back to the entrance of the catacombs and abruptly stopped.

"*Lay down your weapons and you will not be harmed,*" a voice instructed *from outside the catacombs.*

"*Well, it seems the guards are here,*" Scattergood sighed.

"*Give it a moment,*" Methanlan said as the warriors crouched in the darkness. Deena moved back to crouch beside Kelmar and Kasna.

"Are you all right?" *the colonel asked.*

"We're both fine," *Kelmar assured her.*

"Good," *Deena smiled with relief.*

"We must get Kasna out of here. Are you with me?" *Kelmar asked.*

"To the death," *the colonel said without hesitation.*

"Fire! The city is on fire!" *a shout came further in the palace.*

"*Fire?*" Deena frowned.

"*The Order of the Wolf,*" Methanlan grinned.

"*But there is no water in the city, how can they put out the fires?*" Deena asked as she rose to her feet and ran to the end of the catacombs. The guards had gone, leaving the palace completely unguarded.

"*They will have to throw sand and dirt on the flames to try to smother them. They'll need every available body.*" Cassandra said.

"I have to go help them," *Deena said with a look of panic on her face.*

"Very well, when the siege is ended, I will find you," *Kelmar smiled at his oldest friend.*

"You're leaving?" *Deena asked with a sad look her in eyes.*

"I have to, I defied the king, he sentenced me to death. I have to go," *Kelmar sighed.*

"Then, until the war is over, I will keep the people safe from the madness of the king," *Colonel Mae said firmly.*

"Good luck to you, Deena," *Avner smiled and hugged the young woman.*

"Thank you, Avner," *Deena saluted Kelmar, turned on her heel and ran to help control the fires.*

"Come, we need to be quick," Resha urged, and the party returned to the sewers. It didn't take long for them to reach the exit on the other side of the walls. The panic and noise in the city above, combined with Kelmar leading them, meant they were out of the city well before dawn.

"You did well, my boy," Avner said warmly.

"I betrayed my country for the sake of the woman I love," Kelmar said, shaking his head.

"You defied the orders of a man king that wanted to turn you into a slave of a seductress who would destroy all life on Celadmore," Cassandra snorted.

"This is no time to stand around chatting," Methanlan said dryly. "We need to get back to the camp. Her highness will want to see her daughter."

The Order of the Wolf had sent the wagons that the freed slaves had travelled in rolling into the city gates. They had been filled with rotting hay and oil that made them burn straight through the wooden gates.

When the alarm bells had sounded Abendigo had moved quickly. The city burned for hours. When the sun rose, the fires were still not extinguished. It took a full day and into half the night before they had manged to put the last of them out.

Men were sent to barricade the entrance to the city until new gates could be made. The damage to the buildings was terrible and one of the food stores had been wiped out. People cried for those that had died in the fires and those that did not mourn talked of surrender.

Deena walked back through the city towards the palace. She was tired and covered with soot. Her only thoughts were of slipping into a warm bath, though the lack of water in the city made it an impossible dream. She was approaching the steps to the front gates when she heard the clanking of metal coming from all directions. She stopped in her tracks as she looked up to see the palace guards moving towards her with their weapons drawn.

"Colonel Mae, on the orders of his majesty, King Baruch Delich, you are ordered to surrender your weapons and come with us," *the guards had the colonel surrounded on all sides. Deena's hand twitched slightly by her side, causing the soldiers to grip their sword tighter and edge closer to her.*

"On what charge am I being arrested?" *she asked in a calm and clear voice.*

"High treason," *the captain of the palace guard replied.*

"Is that all?" *Deena asked with a smile as she closed her eyes.*

"You allowed and are suspected of enabling the prisoner, Princess Kasna Nosfa, and the traitor, Duke Kelmar DeLacey, to escape from the city," *the captain explained.*

"I see," *Deena said sadly.* "I'm afraid I cannot surrender my weapons to you, captain. Nor will I accompany you and your men."

"I understand, sir," *the captain saluted Deena.*

"Don't worry, captain, you are just following orders," *Colonel Mae sighed.*

"Maybe so, sir, but I am sorry," *the captain said as he raised his sword.*

Deena's last thoughts were of the children in the poorer quarters of the city. She didn't feel any pain as the blades and arrows pierced her flesh.

Kelmar, the rest is up to you.

CHAPTER 15

With every day that passed Mia grew stronger. The capture of the baron seemed to help her recovery as she not only became better physically, but every day she recovered a little more emotionally. It made Haston's heart glad to see his daughter recovering, though he knew she would never be the same girl she had been before she had fallen into the hands of the king and his men.

Haston knew that he owed a debt of gratitude to Mathias for taking care of his daughter, so the Lord of Afdanic asked the assassin to walk with him, leaving Mia to watch Leinad's sword practice.

"Mathias, you've helped my daughter through this ordeal, I don't think that it is a debt that I can ever repay you for, but as it is, I give you leave to ask anything you wish of me. If it is within my power to grant it, then I will make it so," Haston said. Mathias smiled at the lord and thought for a moment or two.

"I have one thing that I would ask of you, my lord. When this revolution is over, I would like your permission to seek your daughter's hand in marriage," Mathias replied.

Haston stopped in his tracks and turned to look at the assassin. He weighed the young man heavily as he gazed at him. He was an assassin, a skilled fighter, but not a noble. Though nobility would not be the same once the revolution had taken place, the idea of society circles would still remain.

"I see. I gave my word that if it was in my power, I would grant it to you, so I cannot refuse my permission. However, I would like to know one thing – do you love my daughter?" Haston asked with a heavy heart.

"I do. I have loved her since I first met her," Mathias replied.

"And does she return your feelings?" Haston asked.

"I don't know. I believe she loved Joab, but her heart is healing as she grieves for his loss. Though she may not accept me now, I have hope that one day she will," Mathias said reverently.

"Very well, I hope you will be very happy together," Haston smiled and shook the assassin's hand. "When will you ask her?"

"When Lieutenant Thomas Regus lies dead," Mathias replied.

The Order of the Wolf created an honour guard as Cassandra, the Eight, Methanlan, General Avner, Kelmar and Kasna entered the camp of the Order.

Kelmar was still carrying the princess. His arms ached but he knew that she was in no condition to walk after her time in the dungeons of Delma.

Abendigo had sent word ahead that Kasna was in need of Payne's attention.

"I have the children that came out of that city to care for, the sick slaves that were freed and now a princess in need of attention. I should not be this busy unless there has been a battle of some kind," *the healer complained to himself as he stood in the reception tent.*

Kia was waiting with her mother, Payne, Shaul, Rathe, Asabel and Helez for her sister to arrive. The babies were in Amalia's care for the moment, Kasnata thought it was best to not overwhelm her daughter with the news of her new siblings until she was certain that Kasna had recovered from her time in Delma.

The Eight left Kelmar, Kasna, Cassandra, Methanlan and General

Avner to report to the queen whilst they went to check on the condition of the freed slaves. The Order of the Wolf had duties to attend to around the camp and scattered as soon as they reached the edge of it. Word spread through the camp that Kasna had been saved and that Kelmar had been captured.

General Avner led the party to the reception tent, Kelmar carrying Kasna behind him, with Cassandra and Methanlan in the rear.

"Your majesty, may I present the Duke Kelmar DeLacey, your daughter's saviour, and the Princess Kasna Nosfa," General Avner said as he stood before the queen.

"Nini!" Kia gasped as she saw that her sister was held in Kelmar's arms. "Let her go!" she shouted.

"Calm down, princess," Methanlan said as he stepped between Kelmar and Kia.

"You don't know what he's done!" Kia shouted as Shaul wrapped his arm around the princess' waist and gently pulled her back away from Methanlan and the duke.

"It's all right, Kit," Kasna soothed as Payne stepped forward to examine the princess.

Kasnata looked down at her other daughter and smiled,

"From what General Avner has reported, we have a great deal to thank you for, your grace," she said warmly.

"Please, don't, your highness, I have a great many things to atone for. Protecting your daughter is nothing by comparison," Kelmar said in a small voice. Here in the camp of the Order there was a feeling of peace and serenity that was akin to the feeling of calm that he felt in Kasna's presence, only much stronger.

In the presence of such tranquillity, the guilt he suppressed for all the actions he had taken when under the command of King Baruch washed over him and threatened to overwhelm him.

"Kelmar?" Kasna said as she looked up at the man she loved and saw tears in his eyes.

"I am sorry for the pursuit of your daughters, for kidnapping Princess Kasna, for murdering General Renta, for leading the attack against your camp –" the words came tumbling out of Kelmar's eyes as tears rolled down his cheeks.

"Peace, Kelmar, peace," Kasnata soothed. "You have returned my daughter to me whole. There is nothing more I could have asked of you than that."

Rathe looked at the man that held the princess and pitied him. He had given up his country for the woman he loved and stood against a monarch whose mind was unravelling, something that Rathe understood all too well.

"Where is he?" the entrance to the tent was flung open as Tola entered, his voice filled with rage. Rathe moved quickly to intercept the hero of the war of the east, but Tola struck Rathe firmly on the jaw, sending the general reeling backwards.

"Tola! Be still!" General Avner shouted as Tola laid eyes on the back of Kelmar and charged. His voice formed a curdling roar as he barrelled forwards. Kelmar closed his eyes and waited for Tola to strike.

"Please don't," Kasna begged. She threw her arms around Kelmar, covering his back as best she could with them. Tola faltered as he recognised the pain in Kasna's voice. He collapsed to his knees, his chest feeling as though it had been ripped apart.

"He murdered Renta," he sobbed.

"He saved my life," Kasna replied.

"That doesn't wipe away the blood he spilled," Tola countered.

"It doesn't have to. He's not the same man that chased us, that attacked us, that took Renta from us," Kasna said gently as she eased herself out of Kelmar's arms and made her way to Tola's side.

"Princess, you don't understand," Tola sobbed as he felt Kasna's arms around his shoulders.

"I do understand. If you take his life now, then you will do to me what he did to you," Kasna whispered.

Kasnata looked at Rathe, who nodded to her and moved to collect Tola from the floor and escort him out of the tent. Asahel and Helez went with him, clearing people out of the way as the general half-walked, half-carried Tola back to his quarters.

"Will he be all right?" Methanlan asked with concern.

"Only time will tell," Cassandra replied. "Your highness, please allow us to make our report, then we can leave you to spend time with your daughters."

"Very well, what news do you bring from Delma that I don't already know?" Kasnata asked.

The streets of Grasbindorph were no longer a safe place to walk. The city watch cut down all those that dared to set foot on it. Brutal fights broke out between the guards and the city inhabitants until the water running into the sewers was all stained red.

"It's getting worse up there." Haman shook his head as he sat with

Hermia.

"I know. I have sent Layla to the camp of the Order with a message for the queen," Hermia sighed.

"What do you think she will do?" Haman asked.

"I can only hope that she will turn her armies to the south and march to aid us as we take the city," Hermia sighed.

"You don't think we can take the city without her warriors?" Haman frowned.

"I think we will lose a great many lives if her army is not spotted approaching the city," Hermia replied.

"What if she doesn't come?" Haman asked.

"Then in the streets of Grashindorph, the dead will outnumber the living," Hermia said flatly.

"So, what do you make of the Duke Kelmar DeLacey?" Rathe asked. He and Kasnata were alone in their quarters. Kia had taken the babies to meet their other sister, who lay in the infirmary.

Misna had taken Kelmar to talk to him about the city and Avner had gone with the duke, to ensure that Misna's questions remained as just that.

"He's a man in a difficult position. He loves his country and would fight to defend it against invaders, but he clearly loves my daughter and knows that a lot of what King Baruch has asked of him wasn't -" Kasnata's voice trailed off as she sighed. "He was raised as the second-in-line to the throne. His life has been about duty and honour, and prior to this war he was regarded very highly throughout the nine kingdoms - far more so than Jayden ever was. To be confronted with all of this and to defy the king, he will be struggling to accept every action he takes."

"You like him then?" *Rathe smiled.*

"Well enough," *Kasnata returned his smile.* "Why do you ask?"

"He re– it doesn't matter, though I suppose Kasna will be happy that you like him," *Rathe replied as he lay down on the pile of furs that their bed consisted of.*

"My daughters are grown and thanks to this war and the madness of two men, I have missed it," *Kasnata said with deep sadness etched on her face.*

"All children grow-up too quickly," *Rathe countered.*

"My daughters were magically aged by intense training with the Abbott in an accelerated time stream, not a common occurrence as far as parenting goes," *Kasnata retorted dryly.*

"I take your point," *Rathe laughed as Kasnata lay down next to him and wrapped her arms around him.* "But I'd hate to be the man seeking to marry your daughters though."

"Why is that?" *Kasnata mumbled into his chest.*

"Queen of two kingdoms, warrior with a reputation for being fearsome, merciless and unbeatable in battle; slightly intimidating," *Rathe teased her.*

"It doesn't intimidate you," *Kasnata said looking up at Rathe.*

"No, but it did. I was terrified when I first met you, even more so after you saved my life," *Rathe replied and kissed her forehead.*

"I don't think Shaul or Kelmar are intimidated by me,*" Kasnata said thoughtfully.*

"Shaul?*"*

"Yes, clearly he's fallen for Kia,*" Kasnata said with a grin.*

"Not many men would dare to wrap their arm around the waist of a princess that also happens to outrank him as a general,*" Rathe agreed.*

"It's such a shame for them,*" Kasnata sighed.*

"Why? Falling in love at their age would have benefited us both,*" Rathe said with a frown creasing his brow.*

"Because we are on the verge of assaulting Delma, it is not an attack that will be without loss,*" Kasnata said sadly.*

"And you're worried that your daughters may lose their suitors before the battle is done,*" Rathe said, understanding his lover's sentiment.*

"It is not only my daughters I am worried for,*" Kasnata replied.*

"I have already lost you once; I do not plan on losing you again,*" Rathe said firmly.*

"What we plan and what comes to pass are not always the same thing,*" Kasnata warned. The two lapsed into silence and lay in each other's arms until they drifted into an uneasy sleep.*

Chapter 16

Asahel and Helez were sent out in the company of the Order of the Hound to search for any sign of secret entrances into the city of Delma. For the first ten days of their search, the ground was too sodden to see where anything was, but by the twentieth day, the ground had dried out and there was the feeling of spring in the air.

The wind had lost its chill, the sun warmed the ground and the plants that had been kept asleep by Wentrus were beginning to bloom.

During Misna's questioning of Kelmar she had tried to ascertain where the entrances to the city were, but the duke refused to reveal any secrets of his homeland to the general.

"I will tell you all you want to know about the king, the queen, the palace and who to reach the palace with a small number of warriors to end this war with as little bloodshed as possible, but I will not hand over the keys to the city," he had said.

So Misna had sent out Asahel and Helez to search. They went out every day to look at different areas around the city, searching for any weakness in the walls, any secret passages that would make it easier to take the city.

Kasnata had ordered Misna to make ready several parties that would assault the city through the sewers whilst the Order of the Hound, the Condor division and the Eagle division were to lead a direct assault against the gates that the Order of the Wolf had destroyed.

The gates had not been replaced; instead, the entrance to the city had been closed with whatever the soldiers could find. There was a mixture of rubble, broken beams, items of furniture and even statues had been pulled down to try and keep the forces of Kasnata out of the city.

Samara's warriors poured into the camp each day, bringing with them refugees that they had come across as they travelled. A second camp behind those of the Order and the men of Nosfa had grown. The Mother of Dawn oversaw the camp, refugees that were left outside the walls of the city came to it in hope of food and protection.

The freed slaves, for the most part, remained in the camp, helping to find food and other resources for the newly arrived refugees. Quisla had been concerned that the growing camp would have a detrimental effect on the two armies, but the opposite had proven to be true.

With the ground thawing, those that were farmers were turning the fields beyond back into farmland. Livestock that had been abandoned was discovered and driven to the camp. The children from Delma proved to be adept at foraging and were finding more than enough food to provide for the refugees.

There were whisperings amongst those in the refugee camp about the new settlements and fortresses that Kasnata had commissioned. After a few days of resting and gathering supplies in the refugee camp, some of the people sought permission to settle in these new places.

The reputation of the Order as barbarians was destroyed by the simple fact that they were the only ones providing aid to the refugees and the lack of deserters from the army of Nosfa.

The sight of the growing camp beyond the war camp caused a new current of dissatisfaction to surface within the city and every day soldiers fled the city to surrender to Kasnata's army.

It was the deserters that provided Asahel with an idea.

"We need to spread out in pairs around the city and watch for deserters appearing from nowhere," he explained to Helez and the Order of the Hound.

"You think that the deserters are using secret passages?" Avner asked.

"It is a possibility, it's more likely they are using the sewers to escape, but searching without any idea of where they could be is doing nothing to help us," Asahel said thoughtfully.

"Very well, as the lad says! Spread out in twos, stay low and wait," *Avner ordered.*

Asahel and Helez watched as the Order of the Hound disappeared in pairs and left Avner to wait where he was. They needed an assembly point to report back to if any deserter or secret passage was discovered, and the general was more than happy to act as that point.

The two men of the Gibborim watched the Order of the Hound spread themselves in a ring about the city, equally spaced and at least 1000 yards from the walls, well out of the range of any archer that might be lurking on the parapets.

"I would keep searching beyond their perimeter if I were you," Avner said to the two men.

"You think that an entrance might lie further out than that?" Helez asked.

"I think that assuming anything leaves us at a disadvantage we can ill afford," Avner replied as he settled himself down in the grass.

Helez nodded and the two men left the general to watch the city. They turned to the north of the city and looked for any signs of tracks. They searched for a few hours until they came across an overgrown track that had deep ruts that could only have been created by overladen carts being driven down them.

"It doesn't look anyone has used this path for decades," Asahel sighed and shook his head.

"No, but that doesn't mean we shouldn't follow it and see where it leads," Helez grinned.

They followed the path running parallel to the city walls until they reached what looked like an impassable wall of rock that was covered with grass and vines.

"A dead end. We should head back to the camp and see if anyone has discovered anything," Asahel said with disappointment.

"It'll be dark soon, there's now point trying to find our way back now. It's sheltered enough here; we can bed down for the night and start back at first light," Helez said and started to gather kindling for a fire.

Asahel smiled to himself and watched his friend work. He settled down and leant back against the rock face, only to find that he fell backwards through it.

"Helez!" he shouted.

"What is — well I'll be," Helez said with amazement as he looked over at his friend and saw only his legs sticking out from the rock, grass and vines.

He abandoned his attempts to build a fire and walked over to where Asahel's legs were. He drew his sword and hacked at the vines and grass to reveal a low entrance to a mine shaft.

"Not a dead end after all," Asahel said with a wry smile as Helez offered him his hand and pulled him back to his feet.

"We'll need torches to explore it," Helez said and returned to the pile of wood he'd gathered to fashion some. Asahel knelt down to examine the ground.

"Two people passed this way recently," Asahel called.

"How recently?" Helez asked.

"Since Wentrus started," Asahel replied. "There are traces of water that has been slow to thaw in the footprints."

"That's hardly recently," Helez retorted.

"Compared to when these mines were last used, it is recent," Asahel countered as he straightened up and accepted a torch from his friend.

"You think that this is how Kelmar got into the city?" Helez asked.

"It seems worth investigating. From what Misna said, they never saw the princess or the duke when they returned to the city," Asahel said and set off into the tunnels.

The two men followed the trail that had been left by the two that had passed this way before them. The tunnels wended across the landscape, were narrow in places, but finally they came to an end with a wooden ladder that led upwards to a trapdoor.

Asahel handed his torch to Helez and started to slowly climb the ladder. He wanted to be as quiet as possible, not knowing what lay on the other side of the trapdoor.

Helez retreated down the mineshaft so that the light from the torches wouldn't shine through the trapdoor and attract unwanted attention.

Asahel slowly lifted the wooden hatch and could make out the trappings of what looked like a basement in a public house. It was empty of patrons. None of the lanterns around the basement were lit.

"I need a torch," Asahel whispered back to Helez. He climbed quickly down the ladder and took his torch from Helez so he could examine the room. There were mugs of ale on the tables that seemed to have been abandoned for a few days.

Asabel crept into the basement to look around. He moved deftly between the tables as Helez climbed the ladder into the basement.

"What do you think?" Helez asked.

"Something bad happened. The fire!" Asabel said with a sudden strike of inspiration. The two men walked to the foot of the stairs that led upward and tried the door to the floor above.

It was unlocked.

Helez pushed it open carefully to be greeted by the sight of fire damage. There were bodies lying on the floor of the pub that had been burnt to a crisp. The building looked to be sound, but there was a hole in the roof where the fire had eaten away at the building and clear signs that no one would be coming back to the pub for a long time.

Asabel moved to the windows of the pub and glanced out into the street beyond. There was a lot of damage to the surrounding buildings and the area seemed to be abandoned for the most part.

"We need to go back and report to Avner and Misna," Helez said and led the way back out of the basement, Asabel careful to shut the doors behind them as they went.

Avner and the Order of the Hound had made camp at the assembly point. They had captured two deserters fleeing from the sewers, but neither knew anything of any secret entrances to the city.

Avner had decided to make camp and wait for Asabel and Helez to return. He wasn't worried about either of the men. They had spent their lives avoiding being captured and living under the madness of Mercia. They were men that knew how to survive.

"Who goes there?" one of the sentries called out.

"Helez and Asabel," the reply came out of the darkness.

"Ah, my boys, what did you find?" Avner asked with a broad grin as the sentry brought the two men into the light of the fires they had built.

"A way into the city and a place to hide the army," Helez grinned.

The raucous laughter in the camp lapsed into a stunned silence as the Order of the Hound all turned to look at the two men.

"Show me," Avner said.

Kelmar sat quietly in his tent. He was being treated as a guest by most of the Order, but he suspected that was for the sake of Princess Kasna rather than as a sign of respect.

He had done his best to answer the questions that General Misna had for him without betraying his country. He knew that he owed nothing to Baruch, but the lives of the civilians in the city were something that he needed to protect.

"Good morning, your grace," Rathe said as he entered Kelmar's tent.

"Good morning, general," Kelmar replied politely.

"I was wondering whether you would join me in a stroll through the camps this morning," Rathe said brightly. Kelmar looked at the general with suspicion. Since he had arrived from Delma, the general had seemingly avoided him at all costs.

"Why?" Kelmar frowned.

"Because I understand something of the position you are in, there is a beautiful spring day outside to be enjoyed and you could use the exercise," Rathe said with a shrug.

Kelmar rose to his feet and nodded his agreement. Rathe held open to the entrance to his tent and Kelmar ducked through it. The duke half expected to see a line of soldiers waiting to arrest him, but instead the camp of the Order was preparing for the assault on the city.

Benaiah's forge was working to repair armour and damage to blades. The swordmaster and swordmistress were hard at work training the warriors who wished to improve before the coming battle. The horsemistress and horesmaster were schooling the cavalry of both the Order and Nosfa. The bowmaster and bowmistress had taken the archers into the woods to practice with their bows where they would be sure that they wouldn't injure any innocent passer-by.

Rathe led the way through the camp of the Order. Warriors nodded to him as he passed, and others called out friendly greetings.

"You are well liked by the Order, it seems," Kelmar said as they walked.

"It wasn't always so, but my actions have shown the people of the Order that I am a friend to them, not an enemy," Rathe replied.

"Did they ever treat you as such?" Kelmar asked.

"From the moment I arrived to serve as the commander of the army of Nosfa for King Mercia Nosfa," Rathe laughed.

"And yet now you are the lover of the queen and have sired two children by her," Kelmar said coldly.

"I served a mad man who uses tools of fear to control people. He used Kasnata's children to control her. He used my sister to control me and my father. Can you claim that Baruch is any different?" Rathe asked.

"No," Kelmar said shortly.

"Then why do you continue to protect him?" Rathe asked.

"I am not protecting him," Kelmar replied.

"Then what is you are trying to do?" Rathe asked.

"I am trying to protect the people in the city," Kelmar scowled.

"The innocent that are so often the victims in these terrible conflicts?" Rathe asked with a sad look on his face.

"Yes," Kelmar said with a small amount of frustration.

"I can understand that motivation," Rathe said kindly as the two men reached the edge of the camp of the Order and entered the camp of the refugees.

"Good morning, your grace," the Mother of Dawn greeted Kelmar as she saw the two men walking between the tents.

"Mother of Dawn?" Kelmar frowned as he recognised the old woman.

"Of course, you wouldn't expect to find anyone else caring for the unfortunate, would you?" she asked with a smile.

"How can you be here?" Kelmar asked, not quite believing that she was standing before him.

"I brought the children out of the city. There was only death waiting for them in those walls," she replied sadly.

"Why come here?" Kelmar asked.

"Because Kasnata is not a cruel woman. She isn't interested in killing civilians. She was sent here by her husband to seize the city, but she fights now to end the evil within it. She has no desire to bring Delma into her empire," the Mother of Dawn explained as she beckoned for Kelmar to follow her.

"If you'll excuse me, I have troops to review," Rathe said with a smile. He bowed slightly and disappeared between the tents.

"He tricked me," Kelmar said, shaking his head.

"He didn't trick you; he knows what a crisis you are facing and brought you to where you can do the most good," the Mother of Dawn soothed.

"What good can I do here?" Kelmar asked.

"Here you can help those that have suffered because of Baruch. You don't have to march with the army into the city and sack your home. You can wait here and help those that flee the fighting. When the battle is done and Kasnata is victorious, you can take them back to their homes and set things back to how they should be," the Mother of Dawn said seriously.

"You think that after all this that I can take the throne of Delma?" Kelmar asked in disbelief.

"No, but then you were never supposed to sit upon it. Your destiny is going to lead you elsewhere, somewhere with that beautiful princess you fought so bravely to save," the Mother of Dawn flashed a brilliant smile at the duke.

"Then how can I restore the city?" Kelmar asked, shaking his head.

"When you return home, you will know what needs to be done," the Mother of Dawn said gently. "Now, come meet those that have escaped already."

"The deserters are not being imprisoned?" Kelmar frowned.

"Of course not, Kasnata has an army to lead, she has no time to guard prisoners that have been running for their lives. She brings them here. They are told to protect the refugees. If they choose to run from there, well there are consequences that have to be faced," the Mother of Dawn shrugged.

"What kind of consequences?" Kelmar asked with a slight edge of reticence.

"The kind that are too dire to contemplate," the Mother of Dawn said with an evil grin.

"It's easy to forget that you're a dangerous woman to cross," Kelmar sighed.

"It is the only reason I have lived for so long," the Mother of Dawn replied and steered Kelmar towards the centre of the camp.

CHAPTER 17

Shaul sat beside Kia on his horse. The two were out ahead of the lines of cavalry that belonged to the Eagle division. On either side of the cavalry, the Order of the Hound were painted for war and ready to run. Avner was stood at the head of his men, stripped to the waist and covered with war paint.

Beside Avner the war dogs of the Order all lay, awaiting the order to attack. Behind the Eagle division, the Condor division was mounted with their bows in hand, alongside the foot soldiers of the army of Nosfa.

Rathe and Samara were sat in front of their troops, all awaiting the order to advance. Kasnata hadn't appeared on the battlefield yet. The lines of the armies had been preparing during the night so that when the sun rose, those on the walls of Delma were confronted with the sight of the armies ready to attack.

During the night, the Raven division under the instruction of General Misna had made their way into the sewers of Delma and were spreading under the city, waiting for the moment to move.

Horns sounded from inside the camp of the Order as Kasnata rode forward through the lines of her army. The twins had been left in the care of Nasus and Haras with clear instruction to take the babies to Benadrocca if the battle should turn against them.

Kasna rode beside her mother, she had healed enough to ride and fight, though she would have preferred to have been part of the infiltration party in the sewers, her mother had explained that it was necessary to show Baruch that she was alive, well and riding into battle with her mother and sister.

The two rode forwards to cheers from the warriors and soldiers. As they passed Rathe, Samara, Avner and Kia fell into place around the queen. Rathe rode to Kasnata' right, Kasna to her left and Kia to the right of Rathe. Samara rode at Kia's side and Avner ran at Kasna's.

"May Arala be with us," Kasnata said with a sigh, before she drew her sword and raised it skyward. Horns sounded once more, signalling the start of the attack.

Kia raised her sword and led the line of cavalry forward. They started at a walk, the Order of the Hound beside them and the war dogs running between the horses in excitement.

500 yards from the walls of the city the line halted and the Condor division came running forward carrying cauldrons of hot coals. The cavalry pulled torches from the loops on their saddles that normally were used to rest their spears in. The torches were thrust into the cauldrons until they set alight.

The archers put arrows in their bows and ran forward, firing up at the walls as they did so. They were spread out in a broken line that would have been easy to sweep aside with Cavalry riding from Delma, but with the gates to the city destroyed, the archers would have retreated before cavalry could ride round from one of the other gates.

Kia raised a horn to her lips and blasted it three times. The cavalry lurched forward. The walked for 50 yards before breaking into a trot, when they were 400 yards from the walls, the horses began to canter.

The line of archers was broken to allow the cavalry to easily ride through the line without getting struck by the archers' arrows and without trampling the archers under hoof. As the cavalry advanced, so did the archers, firing arrows and running forward a few paces at a time.

As the horses came within 300 yards of the walls, they were in the killing *ground for the archers above, but few arrows could fly with the archers on the battlefield below firing their longbows in an unrelenting flurry. Runners from the army of Nosfa were providing the archers with a fresh supply of arrows.*

When the cavalry were 200 yards from the walls, they began to gallop. At 100 yards, they funnelled into a column instead of a line and moved with a practiced precision. They rode into the shelter of the walls, using the angle of the walls above to shelter them as the rode, two file past the makeshift blockade.

As they passed, they threw their torches into the breach, setting fire to the makeshift defence. As they threw their torches the cavalry retreated past the line of their archers.

The sound of horns from the right of the battlefield told the warriors of the Order and soldiers of Nosfa that the cavalry was approaching.

The forces of Nosfa had attempted a pincer movement, using two branches of cavalry to ride round from the north and south of the city to crush the archers and cavalry between them, but this had been what Kasnata intended them to do.

The army of the men of Nosfa were ordered forward and formed a protective square that the archers retreated into. As the cavalry of Delma rode against the square, spears skewered horses, shields were used to knock riders out of the saddles, and they were peppered with arrows from within the square.

The cavalry charge was broken on the walls of the square and forced away into the waiting jaws of the Order of the Hound and the retreat cavalry of the Eagle division.

Kasnata and Kasna were inside the square with Samara and Rathe, from where they sat, they could see the cavalry of Delma being torn apart.

Inside the city of Delma there was panic. The sight of fire burning in the city again was enough to bring despair to the people, but what was worse for morale, were the defenders that were fleeing from the walls and those that were now being marshalled by the burning gate ready for the forces of the Order riding through them.

"Sire! We must do something!" the court of Delma was gathered within the palace, each man and woman begging the king to save them and the city.

But Baruch was deaf to their pleas. He sat beside his wife and ignored every word that his nobles spoke. The army of Kasnata was coming and with it came the blood of the goddess that could still be harnessed for his own ends.

Kelmar sat in the camp of the refugees and winced at the sound of every horn. The sounds of battle carried clearly across the field. The Mother of Dawn was busy keeping those the camp calm.

Some of the deserters had tried to flee when the battle had begun, but those that tried found themselves facing the blade of Cassandra as she patrolled the edge of the camp with some of the warriors from the Free Cities.

The Mother of Dawn had been concerned that Baruch would attack the camp of refugees as a diversionary tactic, so some of the veteran warriors from the Free Cities had chosen to remain out of the fray to guard them.

Kelmar felt completely helpless as he sat and could only wait for the battle to be over.

Asahel and Helez crouched by the windows of the burnt out pub. From their view point they could see everything that was happening in the city outside and wait for the moment to attack.

Since they had discovered the entrance to the city, Asahel, Helez and the Order of the Hound had spent every day in the city, checking the burned-out buildings and clearing them.

Two nights before the battle, the Phoenix, Kestrel, Hawk and Vulture divisions had filtered into the mineshaft and taken up residence in the buildings. The night before the battle the Order of the Bear, the Order of the Wolf and the warriors from the Free Cities had joined them.

Asahel and Helez's eyes were fixed on the gates. The moment the flames took hold and panic started to spread they started to count to ten.

When they reached ten the army of the Free Cities and the army of the Order poured out of the burned buildings and surged onto the walls of the city. The people screamed and ran from the invading army. The warriors chose their targets carefully, those that raised arms against them fell where the stood, the rest of the population they left alone.

People retreated to their homes, into temples, they fled trying to escape from the ravages of war, but for the most part, they surrendered. The soldiers didn't. They fought hard, but their lives were cheap as far as the king was concerned. Their commanders were in disarray as neither Kelmar nor Deena were there to give orders, and the other generals of Delma were cowardly creatures that had no stomach for war.

In the palace of Delma, the nobles cried and wailed at the sounds of battle outside. An order was sent to have all troops recalled to the palace to protect the king, but the messenger didn't manage to leave the corridors of the palace before General Misna cut him down.

The Raven division had infiltrated the palace and removed most of the guards that protected it, without the king knowing they were even there. The only guards that remained were those that were assembled in the throne room with the nobles, the king, and the queen.

Before the blockade to the entrance to the city had finished burning, the city of Delma had fallen.

Chapter 18

"King Baruch Delich of Delma, you are to open these doors and surrender," Kasnata shouted as she hammered on the doors to the throne room.

"Impossible!" terrified whispers ran around the room as the nobles realised the city had been taken.

"I will never surrender to you!" Baruch shouted back.

"Break down the doors," Kasnata ordered. There were three sets of doors that led into the throne room. The warriors of the Order picked up statues from around the palace corridors and began to batter the doors with them.

The guards inside the room were veterans of many wars, but the sound of battering rams on three sides was enough to set their nerves of edge. They split into groups to defend the doors, though they knew they were throwing their lives for nothing, they couldn't surrender unless the king ordered it.

The doors to the throne room were flung open as the wood finally gave way, and warriors poured through the doors. Kasnata led the charge from the top of the hall, Kasna from the door to the left of the throne, and Kia from the right.

Confusion and chaos were unleashed in the confinements of the hall, and in the pandemonium, Baruch saw his chance. Adina sprang from the throne and opened a passageway behind the thrones, whilst Baruch seized Kasna's arm and dragged the girl through the mass of confusion.

Kasna tried to fight back against the king, but her sword was knocked from her hand, and she could do nothing but cry out of help amidst the din of fighting.

Kia wheeled around at the sound of her sister's voice, and she charged after the king and queen, followed closely by Shaul and Avner.

The passageway led down into the depths of the catacombs. Avner led the way downwards as quickly as they could take the stairs. There were no guards to be concerned with, but all three knew that the king and queen had to be stopped.

They followed the sound of Kasna screaming until they reached the sacrificial chamber that both Avner and Kasna had seen before.

In the centre of the room was the great portal and the altar that the king and queen intended to sacrifice Kasna on. The king and queen had stopped dead in their tracks halfway between the altar and the three that pursued them.

"A great man once told me 'If you are going to erect a heretical altar under the palace where dignitaries of many nations walk the halls, it would be wise to have it guarded. Otherwise, you may find that it has been desecrated and rendered completely unusable for a human sacrifice.' Clearly no one ever gave you that advice," Kelmar said as he stood in front of the altar with General Misna beside him. The altar had been overturned, covered in oil and set on fire.

"It makes no difference!" the queen cried and drew the sacrificial dagger from her waist, "the princess will die he—" the words died in the queen's mouth as Avner drove his sword through his daughter's chest. Adina's face was a mask of surprise; Avner's a grim expression as he ended her life.

"Release my sister or suffer the same," Kia snarled at the king.

"You wouldn't dare," Baruch laughed. His eyes widened as he felt pain shooting through his body as Kia slowly drove her sword through his back.

The king released his grip on Kasna's arm and collapsed to the ground, wheezing as he fell. Kia pulled her sword from his back and in a single stroke brought it down on his neck, severing his head from his body.

"And so passes King Baruch Delich, the mad king and last of his line,"

Kelmar sneered.

"Are you all right, Nini?" Kia asked.

"I'm fine, Kit.=," Kasna smiled as she looked down at the dead king and queen.

"Come, we should return to the throne room," Avner said sadly as he looked down at his daughter.

"My warriors will bring the bodies," Misna said gently to Avner, who nodded his thanks to the Raven General.

Kelmar led the way back through the catacombs to the throne room, where Kasnata was anxiously searching for her children.

"The king is dead," Kelmar shouted, announcing their arrival. The nobles that were assembled gasped and whispered amongst themselves. Some hailed Kelmar as the king, others as a traitor.

But the comments of the nobles mattered little, for Delma had been taken, the siege ended and now it could be rebuilt.

The armies of the Free Cities, the Order and the men of Nosfa retreated from the city of Delma to their camp beyond the walls. General Misna and her Raven division remained in the city to maintain order as things were set to rights within the walls.

The Mother of Dawn returned to the city to see what destruction had been wrought. In the days that followed the end of the war with Delma, the burned buildings were all pulled down and the wreckage removed from the city. The king and queen were buried, along with all the dead in the city.

Funerals were held thousands both within the city and in the armies of Kasnata. Pyres were built and the fires marked an end to the violence on the fields of Delma.

Farmers returned to their farms. The Order of the Bear, the Order of the Wolf and the Order of the Hound ran patrols across the land of Delma to ensure that any raiding parties, any bandits and any slavers were discouraged from violence against the recovering populace.

As Regent and heir to the throne, Kelmar was given the responsibility of restoring the city to order. Kasnata had spoken to the duke about whether he wanted the throne for himself, but Kelmar had refused it.

He had learned of Deena's death at the hands of the palace guard and mourned the loss of the colonel for several days. Kasna stayed with Kelmar in the city, helping the people however she could. Cassandra came with the Mother of Dawn and supported the work of both Kelmar and Kasna.

There was much to be done, but morale was improved when the water supply to the city was restored and the men of Nosfa were told that they could finally march back to their homes. Many of the men of Nosfa had already decided to leave Nosfa and to settle in the new fortresses, villages, towns and homesteads that Kasnata had built.

The members of the Condor unit returned to their duties in setting up the new colonies that spread over Celadmore, outposts to oversee the land and watch for new dangers surfacing.

In Delma, Kelmar found that a sense of normalcy had returned to the city when petitioners that came to audiences with the interim king brought petty disputes that no longer hinged on where people were to sleep, how food was to be distributed and reporting outbreaks of disease in the city. He waited for this sense of normalcy to return before he chose new rulers for the country.

He called for all the nobles in Delma to attend the palace for the naming of the new monarch of the nation. Hundreds of nobles came to the city, some from exile, others from outlying towns and cities, to attend the ceremony.

The piled into the throne room talking excitedly, though many became subdued when they saw General Misna and her warriors were guarding the palace.

Kasna was acting as Kelmar's herald. The princess waited until the throne room had filled with people before she rose to her feet and cried,

"Pray silence for his grace, Duke Kelmar DeLacey, Regent of Delma,"

Kelmar stood from the throne and took a few steps towards the assembled nobles.

"Marquess Lorne Underwood and Marchioness Amber Underwood, you have served Delma faithfully through many crises. You have not sought to advance your position to the detriment of others, but rather to serve those that you have dominion over. It is to you that I abdicate the rule of the nation of Delma," *Kelmar said as he took the crown from Kasna and placed in on the head of the marquess.*

"But, you can't, I mean, we are hardly-" *the marquess stammered.*

"The king is dead. Long live the king," *Kelmar shouted, and the cry was taken up by the rest of the assembled nobles.*

Misna carefully watched the proceedings, making a note of those that looked less than happy at the appointment of their new rulers. There would be problems enough for the country recovering from war without an internal power struggle for the throne.

As the army had retreated from the city, Kasnata had sent the Eight out as envoys to spread news of the death of the king and an end to the war. They rode with the news and instructions to return to Anamoore once they had completed their mission.

The armies of the Order were withdrawn from the camp outside the city of Delma in good order. The men of Nosfa returned home first, and then those of the Free Cities departed. The Kestrel and Phoenix divisions left for Anamoore, followed by the Vulture division. The Eagle division remained, under the command of Kia. Some of the warriors were detailed to escort Kasnata, Tola, Rathe and the royal children back to Anamoore, the rest were to remain to help with the restoration efforts in the city and to ensure that the refugee camp emptied.

Without the army there, the refugee camp was a target for bandits and scavengers that the city of Delma didn't need growing on their doorstep after all they had endured.

Forty days after the city had been taken, Kasnata bade her daughters goodbye and rode for Anamoore. Once her children were safe on the island, there was the city of Grashindorph to deal with.

"Do you think things will ever be normal here?" Kia asked as she and Kasna walked through the city.

"There is a rhythm of life returning, slow though it is in coming, but

yes, I think it will. I don't think that we are the best people to judge what is normal," Kasna giggled. Kia elbowed her sister.

"You know that I mean normal for them," Kia said as she slipped her arm into Kasna's.

"What do you think will happen next?" Kasna asked.

"What do you mean?" Kia frowned.

"I mean we aren't in Grashindorph anymore, but surely we can't just leave father as king. He's destroying the lives of people in the same way that Baruch did," Kasna said.

"I don't know, who is there that can be king? Leinad? He's still a boy," Kia argued.

"Ironic that this war has meant that you are now older than your older brother," Kasna said dryly.

"There are lots of things that are different because of this war," Kia said sadly.

"There's also the portal under the city, I can't imagine that it is safe for it to be left in such a condition," Kasna continued, not wanting to dwell on the sadder realties that the war had left behind.

"I think that Cassandra and the Mother of Dawn are doing something about it. They have been down in the catacombs for several days now," Kia said as she pursed her lips in thought.

"General! Messenger approaching," one of the warriors of the Eagle called out to Kia as she and Kasna walked onto the walls.

"A messenger? From where?" Kia asked.

"It's Layla," Asahel said. Asahel and Helez had remained behind in Delma to help restore the city as they couldn't return to the Gibborim.

"Who is Layla?" Kasna asked.

"The Shadow of Lady Hermia Nosfa, your grandmother and the leader of the Gibborim," Helez said.

"There's trouble in Grashindorph?" Kia asked.

"It would seem that way; Hermia wouldn't send Layla unless it was serious," Asahel confirmed.

"Find Misna and tell her to meet with us and the messenger at the gates," Kia sent a runner to find the Raven General.

"I'll find Kelmar and Shaul; they'll want to know what is happening," Kasna said and disappeared down the steps from the parapet into the city below.

CHAPTER 19

Kasna sent word to her mother and Kia, to ready their forces to leave the city of Delma.

"Your highness, I suggest that you and your forces remain here. The Eight and the Order of the Wolf, Hound and Bear are still on the mainland, as well as my own forces," *General Misna said as she took Kia aside.*

"We grew up under the madness of this man and you want us to stay here and wait for others to fight to end his reign of terror?" *Kia asked with surprise.*

"You were held captive by this man; he manipulated your mother because you were expendable to him. By riding to Grashindorph, you would simply be giving your father an advantage over your mother," *Misna said in an even tone.*

"This is our fight too," *Kia said earnestly.*

"No, it's not. Your place is here helping Delma to rebuild and ensuring that the peace is maintained. This is our fight. We have watched your father torture your mother for years; it is now our turn to visit some of that pain on him," *Misna said sternly.* "I have already sent word to the others to make for Grashindorph; we will meet your mother there."

Kasnata had only been on Anamoore for seven days when word came that there was trouble in Grashindorph.

"Rathe, we have to go back to the mainland," *the queen sighed.*

"What is it?" *Rathe asked with concern. He was enjoying spending time on the island; it was peaceful in the city and it felt like home to him after a few short hours.*

"There are riots in Grashindorph, the Gibborim has isolated the king, but the people are rioting and the violence in the streets is beyond what Hermia expected. She's asking me to march my army to the city to restore order," *Kasnata said as she handed Rathe the missive from Kia.*

"We need a faster way of sending messages than sending them with a rider and fleet horse," *Kasnata said with frustration.*

"Do you think you could have reacted faster to Hermia's request for aid?" *Rathe asked.*

"I might not have disbanded my armies, or returned here to Anamoore. I could have simply turned the combined armies to Grashindorph and brought an end to all of this," *Kasnata stamped her foot with frustration.*

"What do you suggest?" *Rathe said, laughing at the queen's show of temper.*

"Birds, kestrels, we keep them here for hunting, but they could carry messages," *Kasnata suggested.*

"And how would they know where to go?" *Rathe asked.*

"I can ask the high priestess to enchant some message vials. They can direct the bird," *Kasnata smiled.*

"So magic?" *Rathe asked.*

"Yes, magic. I will send a rider and a bird with news to Hermia that I am coming. If the bird reaches her first, then we know it works," *Kasnata left the room momentarily to send someone to fetch the high priestess.*

Rathe resisted commenting on how messenger birds would cut down on locating people when they wanted to talk.

"Do you want me to prepare the generals to leave?" *Rathe asked instead.*

"No, they can all stay here. There are enough of my army on the mainland already. Misna will have sent messengers to tell them to meet me at Grashindorph," *Kasnata assured him.*

"Then it is you and I that must depart. I don't think that Tola is in any condition to see Grashindorph in flames," *Rathe said candidly.*

Since returning to Anamoore, Tola's grief had only deepened and he had taken to wandering around the open fields, crying out for Renta.

"Do you think he will ever recover?" *Kasnata asked sadly.*

"I think he has allowed himself to become so consumed by grief that there is no way back from this. One day he'll go out and not return," *Rathe sighed.*

"Since it is only the two of us, we shall need something more powerful and quicker than anything we currently have," *Kasnata said changing the subject.*

"Excuse me?" *Rathe asked almost certain that he had misheard her.*

"The sky dragons," *Kasnata explained.*

"You have dragons that can be used in battle and have not used them yet?" *Rathe asked in disbelief.*

"There are only two of them currently in existence. They were hunted mercilessly by the other kingdoms before my parents brought about the peace. They were brought here to breed and rebuild their species in safety. They are powerful creatures, but they also are wild animals. They do not accept just anyone to ride them and to borrow their strength requires a sacrifice,*" Kasnata said slowly.*

"What kind of sacrifice?*" Rathe asked warily.*

"The sacrifice is not set. It depends on who asks and what favour is requested,*" Kasnata replied.*

"Are you certain that you wish to ask them for their help?*" Rathe asked with concern.*

"I am, no matter the price, to bring a final end to all of this, it will be worth it,*" Kasnata replied.*

Kasnata led Rathe out of the city and down a rarely used road. Outside of the two cities and the port, Anamoore was a wild place. There were farms in between the cities, but away from civilisation, there were forests that were filled with wildlife, both predator and prey alike. Due to the ready availability of prey, the predators rarely bothered the farms, especially as they were well protected.

The path the pair took led them into one of the forests towards the waterfalls. Kasnata had only been there once before in her life, when she had been a young girl and had snuck out of the palace.

Behind the waterfalls lay a cave in which the dragons lived. The entrance to the cave had two torches either side of it and was the major source of light in the cave. The cave was filled with gold, which reflected the light from the torches around the whole cavern.

The dragons were sat, waiting for them as they entered.

"Welcome, daughter of fire. It has been a long time since last we saw you,*" one of the dragons spoke and brought its great head down to the eye level of the queen.*

"It has indeed. The years have blessed you both,*" Kasnata replied.*

"They have. We have hatched four children. All have gone to find homes of their own. We are grateful to the house of your ancestors for the protection they have offered,*" the second dragon spoke but kept her head high.*

"What brings you to see us today?" the first dragon asked, eyeing Kasnata with suspicion.

"I come to beg your aid,*" Kasnata replied.*

"And what is it you offer in return for any aid we could offer?*" the second dragon asked with curiosity.*

"What is it that you would wish of me?*" Kasnata asked.*

"We already have enough gold for our nest, we have plenty to eat here in these woods. There is nothing that you can offer, save for the future,*" the first dragon said and what looked like a smile spread across his face.*

"The future?*" Kasnata frowned.*

"We see a great deal, across time and space. Your ancestors revered us for these abilities, but it has been many centuries since we have used our powers. With all that has taken place in the last few years, we decided to look into the future. There are a great many paths open, but few that lead to the destination that sees the final fall of Hyse and her followers. The price for our help is that future. When the Guardian of the Wilds comes to you, you shall have a choice to make. That choice must be to embrace the unknown to leave behind all that you both know. That is the price of our help. Can you accept these terms?" *the second dragon asked.*

Rathe looked at Kasnata and saw the confusion on her face. She glanced over at him, and he nodded his agreement.

"We agree," *Kasnata said as she turned her attention back to the dragons.*

"Then we shall aid you. Climb on our backs and we shall ferry you to whatever end. Know this though, our service to your people shall not end here. The children we have in whatever years remain to us, and their children shall be dedicated to your people and the service of the Order," *the second dragon said and pulled one of the scales from her foot to hand to the queen as a sign of their vow.*

The sight of a bird flying around the sewers of Grashindorph caused a stir amongst the Gibborim. Mia found it charming to watch it racing round in circles.

The sound of the cheers and cries brought Hermia, Haston and Haman out of their meeting to see what all the commotion was. On seeing Hermia the bird flew straight to her and landed on her shoulder.

"What on earth?" Hermia exclaimed.

"There is something attached to its leg," Haman said as he took the vial that was tied to the bird's leg off. Inside the vial was a folded piece of parchment.

Haman handed the parchment to Hermia as he examined the vial.

"Hermia, we are coming. Look to the sky and the earth. Kasnata," Hermia read the note aloud. "To send the bird back, replace the vial and tell it to return to Anamoore."

"How ingenious!" Haman said with delight.

"Kasnata is coming, she will be here soon. Our time is now," Hermia said firmly. The queen mother climbed onto a stack of boxes that lay close by and called out to the members of the Gibborim.

"Our time has finally arrived. Make ready, tonight we go to the surface and take back our home from a tyrant!" Hermia shouted. The people of the Gibborim cheered, though not everyone was assembled in the same chamber, the news spread quickly through the ranks of the rebellion until every member, down to the smallest child, were preparing for revolution.

"One day there will be a revolution without blood being spilt," Haman sighed as he looked out at the people of the Gibborim preparing to go to the surface.

"Revolution, by its very nature, is violent and bloody. There will never be a revolution without bloodshed. Those who hold the power in the old do not want to give way to those that would take it from them. There is no rationality left when revolution is required. People are willing to give up their lives for ideals in revolution; to change the darkness for light is worth dying for. To have revolution without bloodshed is to have no revolution at all," Haston replied, shaking his head.

As night fell in the city above, the rioting continued. The city had descended into nothing but violence and chaos. Most of those that had once lived in the city had fled or joined the Gibborim. There would be no innocent bystanders hurt in the violence that the overthrowing of the king involved.

Jephthah prepared by bringing all the children and those that were too old, too sick or too fragile to fight and telling them to wait until someone came to collect them. Mia was to wait with them.

"If I don't come back for you within three days, then flee to Afdanic with Lady Mia, you will be safe there and able to build new lives," the man mountain said firmly.

There was no reason to mollycoddle the children, they needed to understand the reality of what was about to happen and accept that not everyone would be alive at the end.

The Gibborim was split into three sections. One followed Haman to the north of the city, where they would attack and move to the south. Haston led another section. They were to attack from the east. When Kasnata arrived, she would attack from the south. Between the two sections in the city and the army coming from the south, those that opposed the revolution would be driven from the city into the desert.

The third section was a small party of elite warriors that followed Hermia and contained Jephthah, Mathias, and Prince Leinad. That section was to head to the palace outside the city and remove the king from his position with as little blood spilt as possible.

Goodbyes and good lucks were exchanged as the members of the Gibborim marched out in three directions. By 10 o'clock they were all in position. They waited until midnight when they heard a roar that shook the ground beneath their feet before they launched their attack.

Rathe couldn't believe how the city of Grashindorph looked from the air. There were fires burning, buildings had been destroyed and blood stained the streets. It looked like the city had been sacked by raiders.

The sky dragon on which he rode was a strange creature. It would have been more accurate to call it a sky serpent. It had two large wings, but the rest of the creature was nothing more than a giant snake. Yet it roared like the dragons of legend were said to.

The noise echoed out across the land below and the men that lined the walls of the city cried in panic and tried to fire arrows at the great beasts.

Kasnata was circling low; guiding her sky dragon through the streets of the city with her legs as in her hands she clutched the black staff the Abbott had given her.

As she flew between the buildings, she chanted the power of the staff drawing all the fire to her until it hung about her body and that of the serpent as burning armour, not harming the queen or the dragon.

Outside the city gates the Order of the Wolf, Hound and Bear all howled. The warriors emerging out of the dark like some mixture of wild beasts set to tear apart their quarry with their teeth.

The members of the Raven division scaled the walls of the city and opened the gates before any of the soldiers knew that they were there. The Eight had two more riders as they led the charge into the city, Asahel and Helez rode with them, the two men finally home to help their brothers free their homeland.

The wolves, hounds and bears ran behind them, the warriors still *howling as they ran.*

The sounds of battle from above, the screaming of the men as the colour of the fire around the queen changed from a burning orange to black. The queen vanished into the dark of the night and only the intense heat of the fire told the guard that she was close by.

The terror that the men of the guard had unleashed on the people of Grashindorph was nothing to the torment and anguish that the hellish display of the Order now visited upon them.

The guards ran from the heat of the fire, the ten stampeding horses and the rampaging wolves, hounds and bears. They threw down their weapons and fled with screams in their throat and waste on their trousers.

They ran without looking where they were going and the Raven division cut them down from the shadows. By the time the Gibborim sprang from the sewers, they city had been taken and all that remained was Mercia and his palace.

Jephthah heaved the grate off the sewers and climbed into the basement of the palace. He had already come into the basement during the day and made sure that the door was open to the floor above.

The man mountain reached down and helped the young prince climb out of the sewer. The others pulled themselves up after.

"Do you know the way to your father's bedroom?" Hermia asked the young prince.

"Yes, follow me. There will be lots of guards around so be careful,"

Leinad warned.

The prince led the way out of the cellar and up the narrow flight of stairs that led into the kitchens. The fires were still lit, but the servants had all gone to bed.

The small group slipped up the servants' stairs that led to the second floor of the palace where the bedrooms were. The corridor that ran around the second floor was lined with guards.

"Hermia, you and the prince wait here until we've dealt with the guards," Jephthah said gruffly as he drew his sword and led the rest of the party in a charge against the guards.

Haman and Haston led their members of the Gibborim through the streets of Grashindorph. The fighting was over and none in the Gibborim had needed to take up arms against their own people.

Layla was talking with Avner, Abendigo, Shamgar and Misna as they approached.

"Is it over then?" Haston asked.

"Not yet, not until Mercia is dealt with," Layla said firmly.

"Hermia took Mathias, Jephthah and Leinad to the palace outside the walls to deal with the king," Haman replied.

"Kasnata has gone there too with Rathe and the dragons," Misna said. "Asahel and Helez are waiting outside the city with the warriors. They're keeping watch in case anyone sent for reinforcements."

"There are no reinforcements that will come. All those loyal to Mercia *were in the city," Haman replied.*

"The more dangerous of them will have gone into hiding when the dragons were circling the city, before the attack began. It will take some time to find them all, but we will," Layla said with pursed lips.

"Then we should begin removing the bodies and burning them, no reason to allow disease to fester after all the city has suffered," Shamgar said, clapping his hands together with enthusiasm.

The sounds of the dragons roaring woke Mercia. He didn't lie in his bed and try to ignore the horrific sounds that were filling the night, but instead rushed to the windows to see what was happening.

"You were always a disappointment," Hermia said as she opened the door and stepped inside with Leinad.

"Ah, mother, it's been too long. How has life in the sewers been treating you?" Mercia sneered without turning away from the windows.

"Well, child, my people have flourished and yours have perished," Hermia said calmly.

"My people? I have no people, just sneering vassals that abandon me at the first sign of trouble and peasants that are nothing more than ants to be crushed," Mercia scoffed.

"You were never fit to bear the name of Nosfa, let alone inherit your father's throne," Hermia said bitterly.

"Not fit to bear the name of warmongers? To have a vapid woman as my mother? To have my father conspire to take my birthright from me? I took what

I was dealt and my name will endure because of all I have done," Mercia snarled.

The dragons drew closer to the palace as Mercia watched them. They flew in a straight line for the city towards where the king stood staring.

"You were given everything a good ruler needs in order to become great, and you tossed it aside without a second thought. You married a wise and brilliant woman, and then turned your ire on her and your children. You are nothing if not worthy of forgetting," Hermia snapped.

"Children? Half-bred whelps that should have been drown at birth," Mercia spat.

"Yet for all your trying, no other woman has ever born any children by you," Hermia grinned.

Mercia slowly turned away from the window to look at his mother with cold eyes. He didn't notice that Leinad was stood next to him grasping a wooden practise sword in his hands.

"What did you do?" he demanded in a low voice.

"Me? Nothing. I didn't marry the daughter of the blood. I didn't have her people curse me for breaking her heart and stealing her children," Hermia gave her son a nasty grin.

"They cursed me?" Mercia narrowed his eyes at his mother.

"Of course not, you stupid boy. But you rutted with a Valian, you brought a vile mistress into your bed who had no desire to bear your offspring," Hermia snapped.

"Neesa," Mercia whispered fondly at the mention of the last heir of Valia.

"The city of Grashindorph has rotted to nothing in your care. The

country has been left decimated by war. We are here to relieve both of the burden of you," Hermia said as she grew tired of talking to her son.

"Rotted to nothing? Your rot began it," the king retorted.

"What my rot begun, it is all at an end now, your time has come," Leinad said as he drove the practice sword he carried into the chest of his father.

Mercia's eyes widened as he recognised the child. The sound of glass breaking behind him barely registered as he felt agonising pain spreading through his body.

"Leinad, get away from him!" Kasnata shouted from outside the windows. The dragon she rode had shattered the windows with its tail.

Leinad look over and saw his mother on the back of the great beast as the door to the bedchamber was flung open by Jephthah.

"It is done then. We need to go," the man mountain said firmly.

"Mother? Mother!" Leinad cried as he realised what he had done.

"Tell everyone to come this way; I am sure the guards on the lower levels of the palace will be coming after all this noise," Hermia instructed. Jephthah ducked out into the corridor and brought the five members of the Gibborim to survive the altercation with the guards in the corridor.

"Can your dragons carry everyone?" Hermia asked Kasnata as she picked up Leinad and carried him to his mother.

"Three at most, we can make two trips," Kasnata said as she took Leinad from her and helped Hermia onto the back of the sky dragon.

"We didn't have time to send back your bird before we launched our attack on the city. I will be sure we send it once things have become a little more settled," Hermia apologised as she stood in the Hall of Kings next to Kasnata. The hall held a great many memories for both women.

"I am glad it arrived. There will be a messenger that rides looking for you in a day or so with the same message. I didn't know if the bird would make it," Kasnata replied with a slight smile.

"How are my other grandchildren?" Hermia asked.

"They are both well, and both in love." Kasnata laughed.

"They are much too young for that!" Hermia cried with horror.

"They are both much older than Leinad now. This ridiculous war has cost them both their childhoods," Kasnata said, shaking her head.

"There are many who have paid with more than their childhood. At least they all survive," Hermia said firmly.

"Are all the preparations complete?" Kasnata asked as she looked at the throne.

"They are. The ceremony will be held tomorrow," Hermia replied.

"Good. Did Layla succeed in destroying the palace outside the city?" Kasnata looked sideways at Hermia.

"She did. It is a pile of ash now and Mercia's remains with it," Hermia said with satisfaction.

"Excuse me for interrupting," Misna said as she approached the two women. "Your highness, there are two visitors here to see you," she said to Kasnata.

"I will see you at the ceremony tomorrow," Kasnata said and took her leave of Hermia. The queen followed the Raven General outside, where Kania and Nodarto waited.

"Greetings, dark angel, it has been too long," Kania bowed to Kasnata.

"That it has. What can I do for you both?" Kasnata asked as Misna disappeared into the shadows.

"We need to talk to you about the portal under Delma. Cassandra and the Mother of Dawn have told us all they know of it and all that transpired with the Seven Stars."

Chapter 20

With Mercia dead and the war with Delma finally at an end, the city of Grashindorph could be restored, as could the rest of the nation of Nosfa.

Leinad was crowned king, with his mother and grandmother standing beside him during the ceremony. Haston and Hermia were appointed as guardians to the boy, to help him grow in the grace that his father had failed to.

Asabel and Helez were pardoned by the new king. Helez was appointed to the position of Knight-Marshal of Grashindorph, and Asabel was named as the Shield of the King.

The Gibborim was finally able to disband after years of existing under the surface of the city, its people were free to return to their homes with their families.

As the city was slowly restored there was a feeling of joy and celebration that spread through the city. Haman was made the new Baron of Fintry and Lady Mia was named as the ruler of Afdanic.

When Mia left her father to return home after so long away, Mathias went with her. He had spent weeks searching the city for any sign of Lieutenant Thomas Regus but had found no sign of him.

Kasnata and Rathe returned to Anamoore, though there was a sorrow in her parting from those in Grashindorph that Hermia didn't quite understand. The queen had said nothing of what Kania and Nodarto had wanted to talk to her, but Hermia sensed that there was something that still had to be done.

The Order of the Bear stayed in Grashindorph to help Helez as he established order and built a new garrison in the city, though the rest of

Kasnata's forces left with their queen.

As news spread that Leinad was now king and that Mercia had been killed, a man named Jack came to the city looking to serve in the household of the new king.

Helez found that his new role suited him well. He spent the daylight hours walking around the city and understanding the problems that the people were facing, what the new garrison was doing and listening for rumours.

In the darker hours, he buried himself in paperwork as he found his thoughts became increasingly consumed with the Madame Ella.

After so much destruction in the city, he wasn't sure that her house of devilish delights would have survived, but he was sure that the madam would have found a way to keep her girls safe.

He walked around the city listening for news of her, but when several days had passed without any mention of her, he went to the inn on the square where the two had first met. The same bartender was stood behind the newly crafted counter.

"Knight Marshal, a pleasure to see you sir. What can I do for you?" the innkeeper asked.

"I am looking for Madame Ella," Helez said as he leaned on the bar.

"I'm not sure that looking for her will do any good, sir," the innkeeper said sadly.

"Why is that?" Helez asked as he cast his eye over the patrons in the inn.

"She's dead, sir."

Helez felt his stomach lurch. He turned round to stare at the bartender in disbelief.

"What happened to her? Was it the riots?" he demanded.

"No, sir. It was a while before the riots happened. Her whole house was set ablaze. All of the girls died in the house that night, and some of the most important men in the city too. There were rumours that it was down to the king, you know, trying to remove those that had outlived their usefulness, but I don't think the king had anything to do with it," the innkeeper said as he stuck out his bottom lip.

"Why is that?" Helez asked impatiently.

"Because Lieutenant Regus was seen outside the brothel that night and his whore was seen shouting to him to save her from the window. He just stood there and watched the place burn. He was found in an alley with his tongue cut out and his hands badly broken. Come to think of it, it all happened not long after the king's wedding was stopped by Lord Rathe," the innkeeper said as he tapped his chin.

Helez slammed his fists down on the bar in frustration.

"Where can I find Regus?" his eyes were wide with fury as he stared at the innkeeper.

"I don't know, sir. A lot of people have been looking for him, but no one's heard anything of him," the bartender said, sounding terrified.

Helez span away from the bar and strode out into the city. He made his way down to the docks and asked in the inns and public houses whether anyone had seen Lieutenant Regus.

No one had any news for the Knight Marshal, that was until Helez noticed that a child was following him. He ducked into a doorway and waited for the child to walk past and look around wildly for any sign of the Knight Marshal before he grabbed his shoulders.

"Why are you following me, boy?" Helez demanded.

"I was paid to," the boy stammered.

"By who?" Helez asked crossly.

"I don't know his name, sir, but I can take you to him."

Helez followed the boy until they reached the sight where Madame Ella's house had once stood.

"Here?" Helez growled.

"He's down in the cellar!" the boy yelped and Helez sent the child on his way. He climbed through the rubble of the house until he found the hatch to the cellar.

When he opened it, the stench of waste flared up into the air. He dropped down into the gloom and found a wretched figure sat in the grim and foul waste.

The figure recognised Helez instantly and jumped to his feet.

"Lieutenant Regus, I've been looking for you," Helez said nastily. He didn't give Regus the opportunity to move. In three swift steps Helez had grabbed the lieutenant by the hair and forced his head into the wall of the cellar, breaking his nose.

"We should never have let you live," Helez whispered into Regus' ear as he held his face into the wall. "But don't worry, it's a mistake I intend to correct."

Helez took his time dealing out punishment to Regus. The lieutenant could only make mewing noises at best, but Helez knew he was begging him to stop.

The Knight Marshal ignored him.

After four hours of brutality, Regus' body was broken, tears flowed from his eyes and the rage had left Helez's heart. He stared down at the pitiful form of the man that had caused such destruction. Helez didn't say another word to him, but knelt down and stabbed Regus in the chest three times.

He left the body in the cellar for the rats and climbed back to the city above.

"There were reports that there were odd noises coming from around here," Asahel said as Helez climbed out of the rubble.

"What kind of reports?" Helez asked grumpily.

"The kind that the king asks me to investigate when you are nowhere to be found. What happened?" Asahel asked as he looked at the mixture of blood and filth on Helez's armour.

"Regus burned down Madame Ella's with everyone inside," Helez shrugged.

"He was in the cellar?" Asahel asked.

"His body still is," Helez replied.

"We should have killed him the first time around," Asahel said, shaking his head.

"I know; it's not a mistake I intend to repeat again," Helez said with a clenched jaw.

CHAPTER 21

2433GL 91st Wentrus

It had been almost a year since the city of Delma had been freed of the influence of the Seven Stars and the war with Nosfa had been brought to an end. Kelmar, Kasna, Shaul, Kia and the Eagle division had remained in the city, awaiting the order to withdraw to be sent by Kasnata.

The city was established, and it was clear that they no longer needed the military presence in the city, yet no order came from Kasnata.

Cassandra and the Mother of Dawn had taken up residence beneath the palace of Delma, which had made the new king and queen feel slightly uncomfortable, but Kelmar made sure that he eased their minds on a daily basis.

Kia had taken to walking the walls in the hope that a message would arrive.

"General!" the call came from the lookout.

"What is it?" Kia asked as she strode over to where the lookout stood on the wall.

"Riders approaching," the lookout replied.

"Can you see who they are?" Kia asked.

"It's Queen Kasnata and the generals," the lookout said slowly.

"Nini!" Kia yelled as she turned away from the wall and raced down to the gardens where Kasna was lying.

"What is it?" Kasna asked lazily.

"Mother's here!"

Kasnata had brought all her generals, Rathe, Haston, Hermia, Mia, Mathias, and Leinad, with her. King Underwood had been delighted to welcome them to the city, and a banquet was held in their honour.

Kasnata saw it is a positive sign of things to come.

"The Abbott's arrived," *Misna whispered in Kasnata's ear as the shuffling monk appeared in the corner of the room.*

"Take him to Cassandra. We'll be done shortly," *Kasnata whispered in reply.*

"Your highness, can I have a moment of your time?" *Shaul asked nervously as Misna departed.*

"What is it?" *Kasnata asked, indicating that he should sit down beside her.*

"I am here to ask for your daughter's hand in marriage," *Shaul blurted out. He stared at the table and waited for the queen to respond.*

"I see. I will not answer you now. There is something else that requires my attention, but I will give you my answer before the night is over," *Kasnata promised. Shaul nodded to the queen and stood up abruptly.*

Kasna and Kelmar were missing from the feast; they were in the catacombs below.

"Do you think this is really necessary?" *Kelmar asked as he stood watching the princess work. She had a book open on the floor and was casting incantations.*

"I do," *Kasna said firmly.*

Kasnata had taken the duke and princess to one side and explained what was going to happen that night and the reasons for it. The two had listened carefully to what the queen had to say, when she had finished, Kasna had disappeared to the library and returned with armfuls of books.

She had told Kelmar she needed his help and the two had been working in the catacombs ever since.

"This is the last one. I promise," Kasna said.

"You said that five incantations ago," Kelmar said wearily.

"I mean it this time, there. I'm done," Kasna seemed satisfied with her work.

The two returned the books to the library and then entered the banqueting hall. Most of those attending were drunk and didn't notice the two arrive.

They sat down and began to eat until Misna appeared behind them.

"It's time," she whispered and led the two down to where the portal stood.

Kasnata was stood in front of the portal with Avner next to her. The general had a jar of ashes in his hand and a vial of blood. He was stood in front of the portal chanting.

"What is he doing?" Kelmar whispered to Misna.

"Sealing the evil that was allowed to creep in here," Misna replied.

"With the ashes of those that summoned it and the blood of those that would have shed the blood of others, be bound here in the name of Arala," Avner said. He poured the ashes and the blood into a bowl. There was a loud crack, and the smell of honey filled the air.

The ashes and blood had become precious gems that now sat in the bowl.

Avner walked across the chamber to where the Abbott stood and handed him the bowl.

"The Spoils of Avner," the Abbott grinned as he looked down at the gemstones. "I will see that they are hidden properly so their power cannot be abused."

"There is only one more thing that must be done. The portal must be closed. It can only be closed by a ritual performed on both sides. We have already performed the ritual on this side, now we must go through and perform it on the other," Kasnata said firmly.

Kia looked at her mother with horror as she spoke.

"No!" she cried.

"I name Princess Kia Nosfa as my successor to the throne of the Order. She will lead and guide you, even in the darkest of times," Kasnata said as she looked at her daughter with tears in her eyes.

"We shall love and protect her," Samara said.

"Our lives we will lay down for her," Marissa said.

"There will be no other that we will gladly serve," Quisla said.

"By the blood and light of the goddess, we swear," General Kia said.

"Your generals have sworn loyalty to you, and I leave you an empire to rule and a peace to maintain," Kasnata said as she placed her hands on her daughter's shoulders.

"What of the others?" Kia asked.

"We are going with the queen and General Bird," Misna said.

"Rathe?" Haston asked as he turned to his son.

"My place is with the woman I love and my children," Rathe told his father and offered his hand to him.

"You have made me prouder than any man that has lived has any right to be," Haston said as he ignored his son's hand and embraced him.

"Goodbye brother, thank you," Mia said as she tried not to cry. Rathe laughed at his sister's efforts, causing the lady to breakdown into floods of tears.

Haston let go of his son so that Rathe could bundle his sister into his arms.

"Take care of her," Rathe said, looking at Mathias.

"Of course, she's finally agreed to marry me; it will be the sole goal of what remains of my life," Mathias assured Rathe. The two men shook hands as Mia ran to her father for comfort.

"Shaul, you have acted as a Shield to my daughter, you have served my family well and are a credit to our people. I will gladly see you married to the pride of my heart. In marrying my daughter, you will no longer be her Shield. Rulers no longer need a shield; they need a sword. Defend her, fight for her. Find a Shadow that will guard and protect her, be her Sword,"

Kasna hugged her sister tightly. Kia bit her lip to hold back the tears that threatened to spill from her eyes.

"We'll never see each other again, Kit," Kasna sobbed.

"It's okay, Nini," Kia said. "We'll meet again in Halsanda."

Kasnata watched her daughters embrace and felt a pang at having to leave Kia and Leinad behind.

"It's not the same, Kit," Kasna said pulling back to hold her sister by the shoulders. "We won't ever ride into battle together. We won't get to grow old telling stories of stupid things we did in our youth and lived through. We won't _"

"We won't get to grow old together," Kia said sadly. "We won't get to raise our children together. Nini, you saved me so many times. I don't know how I will do all this without you."

"Kit, you could always do things without me. Look at everything you did whilst I was in Delma. You did more than I ever could have done in your place. You will be a queen to make our ancestors proud; I just wish I could have stayed to see it."

"You don't have to go!" Kia cried.

"I do," Kasna said firmly. "Your place is here, with our people, looking after our brother. My place is off in the unknown. There is finally peace, there is no place for us here any more, but you, you were born to make our legacy to this land greater than any before you."

"But what if I need you?" Kia demanded.

"You won't. You have Mia," Kasna let go of her sister.

"She's not a replacement for you!" Kia said as she grabbed for her sister's hand.

"She doesn't have to be. Just remember that I love you, Kit. I always will."

"Are you ready?" the Abbott asked gently as he approached Kansa and Kia.

"I am," Kasna said firmly. She gently slipped her hands away from her sister and allowed the Abbott to steer her over to where the others waited.

"No! Nini, don't go," Kia tried to reach her sister, but Shaul stepped forward and wrapped his arms around the princess. She collapsed into his arms and cried.

"Goodbye, Kit. Don't let me down, okay?" Kasna smiled as she cried and took Kelmar's hand. The two stepped through the portal and were gone.

Kasnata looked over at her daughter and her son.

"Be brave, little one," she smiled down at Kia. "You have a whole world of work ahead of you. I know you will be a better queen than I was." she kissed Kia's forehead.

"Please, mother, please don't go," Kia begged.

"It is the way of the world. We must go to places we do not wish to and leave behind those that we wish we could take with us. No matter where I am, my little one, I will always hold you in my heart and be so proud that you are my daughter. Take care of her, Shaul."

"Yes, your majesty."

"Leinad, what a fine man you will be," Kasnata said, turning to her son.

"Mother, I don't like this," he said, looking up at her with frightened eyes.

"Neither do I, my child. But you will be brave, won't you? You will listen to your grandmother and to your sister?" Kasnata asked as she knelt down in front of her son. He pouted and nodded his head firmly. "That's my boy." Kasnata smiled. Leinad threw himself forward, wrapping his arms around his mother's neck.

"I love you," he said before letting go and stepping back.

"I love you too," the dark angel smiled and kissed his forehead. She nodded to the others that were assembled, there was nothing else to say to those that she had fought beside and bled beside. They understood what had to be done and would follow Kia's rule as they had followed Kasnata's. The queen turned towards the portal where Rathe stood holding the twins.

"Your majesty, the staff," the Abbott said, holding out his hand. "It will

be of no use to you. Let it stay here, with your children." he said firmly. Kasnata frowned and removed the black staff from her back and handed it to the Abbott. He nodded his thanks and stepped away from the portal. Kasnata sighed and looked at Rathe. The two passed through the portal and there was a great explosion.

"It is done," the Abbott sighed. "So, what will you tell of this to those that you lead? How will your mother be remembered?" he asked as he walked towards Kia and handed her the staff.

"What do you mean?"

"Should all that follow you know about the portal and this sacrifice? Or are there better stories to tell them?"

Kia was silent as she thought.

"They can't know the truth of this. No one outside of this room can."

"Then what do you want them to be told?"

"That Queen Kasnata, queen of two kingdoms and torn by her love for her people, her children and for General Rathe Bird killed King Mercia Nosfa VI and then drowned herself and her lover out of guilt," Kia said firmly. The Abbott smiled.

"Very well, what about your sister?"

"Fearing for the life of the Duke Kelmar DeLacey in the wake of the war, the two disappeared into the Gauntlet with the children of Kasnata and Rathe," Kia dried her eyes and regained her composure.

"It shall be recorded as you say, your majesty. All those here, you will not speak a word of what has really happened here. You will tell those that ask what Queen Kia Nosfa has said and nothing more. The queen is dead," the Abbott said, turning to face those that were assembled.

"Long live the queen."

The Guardians of Light Saga is only just beginning! Come back to the land of Celadmore to find out what happens next for the royal line.

A princess made Queen. A dark threat hiding in the shadows. As she strives to heal the land in the wake of war, can she face this new dark threat or will she die trying?

Queen of Rising Hope is book 4 in Guardians of Light Saga.

Want to stay up to date with all the latest news from the Guardians of Light and all my other series, then you can sign up to my newsletter here.

Want to help a reader out? Review are crucial when it comes to helping readers choose their next book and you can help them by leaving just a few sentences about this book as a review. It doesn't have to be anything fancy, just what you liked about the book and who you think might like to read it. Leave a review for *Empress of New Beginnings* here.

If you don't have time to leave a review or don't feel confident writing one, recommending a book to your family, friends and coworkers can help them choose their next book, so feel free to spread the word.

About the Author

I was born in Macclesfield, Cheshire, UK, and raised in the nearby town of Wilmslow. From an early age, I discovered I had a flair and passion for writing.

I began writing at the age of 7 and was first published in 2010. I currently live in Christchurch, New Zealand and write under many pen names, including Mia Herald Hill.

I am an avid horsewoman and gamer, with a passion for singing, dancing, the theatre, and my garden.

Social media links: https://linktr.ee/thecswoolley

ACKNOWLEDGEMENTS

Writing can be an extremely lonely profession at times, but thankfully I never have to go through any of the pressures alone. My friends and family have been a wellspring of support that I could not have coped these past few years, and the terrible few months without.

Writing is not something I stumbled into either, my mother, Helen, took me, and my sisters, to the library every weekend when we were young to get different books, and I always maxed out the number of books I could get. Not only did she encourage me to read, but to write as well. To say I have been writing stories and poetry since I was 7 is not an exaggeration and the development of my writing career is due in no small part to her.

My mother-in-law, Lesley, has also been a source of unflinching and unwavering support, something I could not do without.

To Hollie, Frankel, and Mags, you guys are an amazing source of support and I love you all. I have known you all for so many years, you have seen me through good times and bad and have given me the drive to carry on, even in the darkest of times. Through the highs, and lows, you have been there and your friendship has always given me courage and strength.

To Holly, Dan, and Nick, who have both known me far longer than anyone else. You know my thoughts before I know them, when I am about to be incredibly stupid and when I should trust my instincts. You have driven me to search within myself for the strength I have lost over the past few years and rediscover the woman that you all love so dearly.

Dear Steve, you are a sounding board of great wisdom that is unparalleled in my life. You listen better than anyone I know and you weigh any response you give me with the greatest of care. You have been such a blessing to me and I hope that I have been an equal one to you, though I highly doubt it!

Chez, you are so dear to me and I have so enjoyed all of our experiments, plot talks, and sharing the journey of being authors together. To cheer each other on and provide understanding and an ear when others don't understand this struggle that we willingly undertake is something worth far more than any accolade or riches.

Vicki, my partner in crime, my wonderful reality check, and sounding board. You made my life in New Zealand what it is, without you it would not or could not be as amazing as it is, and I am so blessed to have you in my life.

To Ellie, you have been such a wonderful addition to my life that I hardly know where to begin or what to thank you for, but know how precious you are to me, and I will love you forever.

Courtney, you are such an incredible woman of fire and fun that I hardly know what my life was before I met you. For all the adventures to come, I know that you will make them all the more memorable by simply being you!

Karl, I have no idea how I survived before we met. Of all the people I have known and probably will ever know, you are my favourite human. The most awesome driving buddy, a constant source of support, knowledge, and helpful suggestion, my life was so much poorer before we met, and is the all the better with you in it. You've made so many things possible and helped me in more ways than I can count. I know that there is nothing I cannot do, nothing I cannot achieve, especially when I have to try and explain to you why I can't do something. You push me when I need it most, challenge me to do better, and every day show me that I never have to settle for good enough.

And finally, to you, dear reader, without you there would be no books, no series, no career. I want to thank you for all the time that you spend reading my work, reviewing it, sharing it with your friends and family. Without you there would be nothing. Thank you from the bottom of my heart.

Until we meet again in my next book, thank you and adieu.